The Accident

A Novel

Curt Finch

Curt Finch (signature)

ISBN: 1489543139
ISBN-13: 9781489543134

Acknowledgments

A number of people were of tremendous help in getting this novel published. I thank my friends, family members, and co-workers who read early drafts and offered helpful feedback. I appreciate the work of Dorla Pake who assisted with editing. My wife, Debbie, deserves a special acknowledgment as she served as both my primary editor and as a source for creative guidance.

I am indebted to the writings of Pierre Teilhard De Chardin for inspiration and subject matter. I am also indebted to Harry Emerson Fosdick whose book, *On Being a Real Person*, guided my thoughts in writing about prayer.

Also written by the author: *The Accusation*

chapter One

WHERE DID SHE go that night? So many questions weigh upon me, but this one dominates my every waking thought. How do you go on if you can't resolve in your mind an issue this critical to closure? I have several theories and assumptions, speculations based on a paucity of clues. I need to know why she was on that highway at that time, where she'd been, where she was going or coming from. Why do I have to live with more questions than answers? I can identify with Teilhard when he wrote, "As much as anyone, I imagine, I walk in the shadows of faith."

***

The small rural church sits at an intersection of three two-lane highways. It's a simple, single story structure nestled on a corner lot surrounded by tall pine trees. The white frame building is a minimal icon of unpretentious faith. This meeting of roads is part of a popular route many often choose as a shortcut to Highway 17 which leads to the northeastern section of the state. The roads are narrow and the curves numerous on this informal bypass of New Bern.

Like other people in eastern North Carolina, I have passed this way on frequent trips to Greenville—often to the sprawling medical center which serves this part of the state. On occasions I have also used this course as a means of traveling north to the Outer Banks. It's not an inviting way at night, however, as the many twists and turns demand careful attention and wary eyes.

They found her small SUV upright in the churchyard, a few feet away from the pine tree it impacted. The highway patrol assumed she did not slow down for the stop sign across the main road, veered to the left, and slammed into the large tree at a speed of about forty miles an hour. Her seat belt kept her in the vehicle; the air bags deployed, but her head hit the side window causing her to black out.

A middle-aged man approached the intersection from the east and spotted her Honda as his truck came to the stop sign at the church; he pulled into the parking lot and ran to the wreck, then called 911. Her CRV had come to rest probably less than five minutes before he arrived. It took the highway patrol only ten minutes to reach the scene. Several people had gathered before the officer arrived; they pried open the door and carefully checked the unconscious driver. One of the people who stopped was a nurse coming home from a shift at the Carolina East Medical Center. She joined the others hovering over the injured woman and checked her pulse, confirming she was still alive but this was likely a severe head injury. The rescue squad arrived, and the team placed the accident victim into the ambulance.

They estimated the time of the collision to be around 12:05 a.m. The phone rang at 12:38 in my home on the island. The highway patrolman asked if I was related to Katherine Brewer. I said, "She's my wife."

I will forever remember his exact words to follow, "Mr. Brewer, there has been an accident. We found your wife's driver's license in the car."

After collecting my thoughts, I said, "Is she seriously injured?"

The voice on the other end was hesitant. "She hit her head, and the medics say she may have suffered a brain trauma. Mr. Brewer, I'm sorry; she was unconscious when they found her. She's on her way to the emergency room at the hospital in New Bern."

It took me a few seconds to process the news. A minute earlier I was awaiting her return. The waiting is transformed to the wait is over—she's headed to the hospital, unconscious.

"Is someone there with you?" the officer asked.

I looked around the living room, out the window to the street, and then down the hall to the bedrooms. "Just my children; they're asleep."

"Are you going to be okay, Mr. Brewer?" He asked.

Am I okay? Such a simple question with so many complicated responses to be sorted out.

After a moment I said, "Yes, I'll be fine."

"Will you be able to come to the hospital?"

That's a more demanding question. It requires, however, a simple yes or no answer.

"Yes, of course. I'll be there as soon as I can."

Brain trauma. I sat for a couple of minutes at the kitchen table repeating the words over again in my head. I removed my wallet and looked at her picture, my favorite one of Katherine. It was taken on the front porch of our house two years ago. Her smile is so wide it dominates the photo. Her auburn hair is long and curled. In the print she's wearing the dark green sweater I gave her. I realized then that I didn't even know how she was dressed when she left the house.

Luke and Grace were asleep in their rooms, Luke having turned in around ten after giving up waiting for his mom. I'd spent most of the seven plus hours before the call on the couch in the living room wondering where Katherine was, occasionally getting up to look out the window to the street in front of our patio home. I don't remember how many times I called her cell phone that evening and reached her message. At eleven I dialed the local police but hung up after one ring, afraid to admit I didn't know where my wife was.

I'd arrived home at 5:30 that night. Dinner was on the table, the children both seated at their regular spots for family mealtimes. Brunswick stew and grilled cheese sandwiches were neatly placed on three sides of the round, kitchen table. There was no plate or bowl at Katherine's place. I washed my hands for supper in the hall bath. I heard the front door open and close; she got into her Honda and drove away. She said nothing to the children or to me. I watched from the front porch as the tail lights disappeared around the corner.

Those were agonizing hours from the time she left until the time of the call informing me of the accident. In that fretful period

I considered many possibilities of where she might be. To be honest, I was too embarrassed to call any of our friends. How could I tell them she walked out the door without a word and has not come home? Everyone we know well is a member of the church. A pastor does not call people in the congregation and report you and your wife argued the night before; now she's gone. I did consider calling her parents to see if they'd heard from her. I made the call to them later but for a different reason.

The imagination's a tricky counselor; it can offer assurance or instill panic. In those hours I vacillated from dread scenarios and worse case possibilities to having hopeful visions of her taking a needed night off for herself. The positive prospects diminished as the hours mounted.

I refused to accept the worst of the options even though such thoughts were hovering like a violent storm threatening to extend its funnel down to uproot our house, our family. When the call came, the swirling cloud did indeed cross over our modest home.

At 12:47 a.m. I called Susan, the person closest to my wife and children. After several rings my church associate answered. "Susan, I need your help. Could you come over to our house and stay here with the kids? Katherine's had an accident. I have to go to the hospital."

"What happened?"

"It's serious. I'll tell you more when you get here."

Within fifteen minutes Susan stood at my front door in sweat pants and a wrinkled shirt covered by an open wind breaker, her short dark hair more ruffled than usual. The night air was mild for mid March, but she was shaking, more from emotion than weather, I assumed. There on our porch I shared the awful news that Katherine had been taken to the hospital, unconscious. Susan bent over, hands on her knees, and took several deep breaths. I put my hand on the top of her head. The bracket light by the door illuminated the scene, the shock, the awareness that this was to be a long night. When she stood up the moist wideness of her eyes revealed the depth of her anguish. I hugged her in an effort to console and to keep her from seeing my despair.

Five minutes later, in our living room, Susan struggled to hold back her fear but showed a resolve to assume her duty. She insisted I go ahead to the hospital, telling me she would call our chairman of deacons. My children were still asleep, in good hands.

I made the forty-five minute drive to New Bern and the hospital in a daze. I don't remember my exact state of mind but do recall not being able to swallow, emotion coating and closing my throat like a strep germ. The long stretch from the bridge up Highway 58 was dark and desolate as usual in the evening; that late at night it seemed foreboding. Two deer stood beside the highway as I slowed to determine what they might do. As I passed by, they froze at attention as though they sensed my situation and wanted to allow me to continue my journey undisturbed. The streets in the village of Maysville were deserted, and the sign in front of the Baptist church proclaimed, "God is with you as you negotiate the journey of life."

It looked as if all of the traffic lights coming into New Bern changed to red as I approached them. It was as though a barrier to my advance had been erected. The shopping mall parking lot was empty. On many occasions our family stopped there to shop at the Belk's store. In recent years the mall has lost tenants and some of its luster, testifying to the power of entropy or recession.

I pulled into one of the parking spaces reserved for clergy at the hospital as I'd done on many other occasions. This is the hospital where my daughter was born. There was no need to stop for directions as I knew well the place where Katherine would be. The tile floors had been polished and appeared to be brown ice as I made the walk to the emergency room.

The hospital chaplain was looking for me as I turned the corner next to the waiting room. "Are you Mr. Brewer?"

"Yes."

He looked too young, late twenties. His name tag indicated he was a Board Certified Chaplain. He was soft-spoken, serious, and wore a starched white coat. I could tell his next words were well-practiced, "I'm here to help you in any way I can. My name is Greg Manning."

"Thank you," I said. His eagerness to greet me was disconcerting. It did not bode well, I considered, that he had been dispatched to intercept me. "I have come to see my wife. Do you know where she is?"

"She's down the hall. Let me get the doctor."

Another cause for unease—the choreography a signal for alarm.

Soon, a short, balding man in green scrubs appeared and invited me to sit on a couch in the waiting area. I declined the offer to sit. "Mr. Brewer, I am Dr. Howell, the emergency room physician on call this evening." He frowned when he spoke, his glasses riding down his nose.

"They told me Katherine was unconscious when put in the ambulance." I said. The doctor nodded. The chaplain stood to the side, hands in his pockets.

"We suspected your wife suffered from a brain hemorrhage when she arrived," Dr. Howell said. "We called for a surgeon as soon as we determined the extent of her injuries." He hesitated briefly and then continued, "I am so sorry; she passed away a few minutes after she arrived here. We did all we could do."

It took a moment for me to convert "passed away" to "she's dead." I refused to consider this possibility on the drive up, even though it sought several times to force itself upon me. I looked away from the doctor and became aware that several others at the nurse's station were looking in our direction. I realized I was the object of sympathetic attention.

I excused myself and walked over to the window. The view was of heating and cooling equipment on the flat rooftop to my right. Steam spilled from a large vent and drifted past my sight line. A wall of windows across the way revealed dozens of hospital rooms. I wondered about the personal stories beyond each pane. How many of them were critical? How many worried family members were pacing the floors awaiting reports on the status of their patient? In just a matter of minutes I had passed from worry to the final juncture of medical care—death. I was not ready to accept this. Ready or not, my world had just been transformed.

In the window I caught the reflection of the young chaplain standing behind me. I turned to face him; he looked away at first. He then put his hand on my shoulder. "Would you like for us to have a prayer?" he asked. I didn't answer him, but he proceeded on, taking my silence as agreement. His prayer was brief, generic, and typical for the situation. Looking back now I recall the statement of Martin Luther, "The fewer the words the better prayer."

I felt sorry for him, that he had to perform this awkward duty. Training in counseling is never enough in times such as this. I found myself considering what I would say if I were in his shoes. I counted the occasions when I had sat with families at a hospital when a loved one had just died. Five came to mind, two from accidents.

The young minister handed me his card and said, "Please, let me know if I can do anything for you."

The doctor approached me, adjusted his glasses, and said, "Mr. Brewer, you can see her when you're ready."

For some reason I felt the need to be calm and collected on the outside, to refrain from showing any excess of emotion. The doctor and chaplain must have thought me a cold person in that I didn't cry or even demonstrate any indication of sorrow when first told the horrible news. Inside, I tried to sort out the meaning of what her death will do to me, my children. My children are at home, still asleep, I assumed. I pictured a rush of memories, images of times together. Then the images all disappeared as though a curtain had been drawn.

A nurse approached and apologetically asked me what funeral home I preferred. How does one prefer a funeral home? She had a kind face. "Mr. Brewer, I'll give you some time to think about it."

I pictured a green canopy with white letters. It was a name I had seen often in my ministry the last few years. I told the nurse my choice; she thanked me and wrote it down.

Katherine was in a small, sterile room, placed on a typical hospital bed. Only her head was visible, the rest of her under the white sheet which covered her lifeless body. I thought that after a death they usually pulled the covers over the head, not so in this case. The four steps to her side seemed like a dozen yards. I saw only one minor laceration on her forehead; several blood spots were on her cheeks and chin. A dark bruise was under her left eye. The bump on her head did not appear to be so large as to take her life. It took me a minute or more to gather the courage to pull back the sheet further. I stood beside the bed and stared at her swollen and bruised neck. Eyes closed, she appeared to be anesthetized and ready for surgery. I remember wishing that she would be transported to an operating room where the damages would be repaired, the death reversed.

Her wedding ring was not on her finger, a faint pale band of skin visible. I gently picked up her hand and images of our wedding day flashed in my mind. She was so vibrant that day, so beautiful. Lying there on the hospital bed she was still lovely but inert. I pulled up a chair beside the bed, touched her hair, and put my index finger on her cool lips. She often put her finger there to pause my conversations; occasionally I would remove her's and replace it with mine to signal it was time for both of us to be quiet. It was so hushed in the cubicle, so still, so peaceful, and so bleak.

"Where did you go, Katherine?" I whispered. I needed for her to answer. I needed to hear a response. I sat there for at least fifteen minutes in silence as the hum of hospital activity reminded me of the world outside of my private desolation.

It was not too long ago that I lay on a bed in this very same row of cubicles. Katherine sat beside me and held my hand as I waited for the shot to take its effect and relieve my pain. She'd driven me here as I writhed and moaned in the seat beside her, the kidney stone lodged in such a way as to make any position I tried unbearable.

"I can't stand to see you suffer," Katherine said that evening as she winced with every pained expression I exhibited. "I wish I could take your place."

I think she meant it. Katherine was always sympathetic to my hurts, physical and emotional. She could not have been faking her concern. She could not have always harbored resentment towards me—not that evening for sure. She was there to support me that night, and I welcomed her care.

"Katherine, I know you can't hear me, but I would give anything if I could be here supporting you through your injuries if you had survived the accident. You were always stronger than me."

Outside of the pulled curtain, I heard people talking. A voice was telling someone, "Her husband's in there. Let's give him a few more minutes."

A few minutes. Fifteen years of living together—now a few minutes to get used to her being gone forever. One loose, auburn hair lay on the white sheet. I held it up, examined it, rolled it between my fingers—and then placed it in my shirt pocket. A few minutes to tell your wife you can't imagine life without her.

I wanted to cry. I couldn't. But tears are only an external manifestation of grief. Inside, pain was flooding my entire body, spreading through me like dye injected into my veins. For several minutes I sat there coaxing myself to pull out of the dive before I collided with the bottom of my despair. I stood up and moved away from Katherine after my composure returned.

I recall the doctor telling me an autopsy was not required, but I might request one if I wished. He said they will do a blood toxicology test. I thought at the time this will not be necessary as Katherine never was a drinker, and she didn't use drugs.

Two men from the funeral home were waiting for me in the hall, there to take Katherine from the room. They wore dark suits, not the common attire for the wee hours of the morning. What a dreadful duty they had, these undertakers. It dawned on me I didn't know the origin of that word as it applied to their profession. In the middle of the night they were there to carry out a grim task—to remove a body.

After verifying the person on the bed was indeed my wife, and signing a few forms, a nurse advised me to go home. I agreed after considering that my children had been left in the care of others and my most pressing need was to be with them now.

Again, I slipped behind the steering wheel of my car and headed back to the beach retracing my lonely journey; this time the image of Katherine's quiet repose dominated my thoughts. I don't remember any part of the trip other than that one picture in my mind. I did muster up the courage to call her parents as I left the hospital. Claude and Diane Rosier live in Raleigh. Claude's last words were, "We'll be there in three hours."

I decided to call my house. Jim Albright, our chairman of deacons, answered. I told him she was dead.

"What can we do?" Jim asked as I entered my home forty minutes later.

"I don't know," I responded as he hugged me. "Where are Grace and Luke?" I asked.

"They're both in bed, still asleep. Susan and my Joan are in the den," Jim answered.

Susan looked up as I entered the room. It was evident the news of Katherine's death and the long night had drained her of energy for she seemed unable to get up from the couch. A box of tissues sat beside her, the one in her hand well used.

Joan put her arms around my neck and whispered, "We love you, Paul."

Susan has spent much time with Luke and Grace in the past three years since she joined our church staff. Jim's wife, Joan, is one of those people who exude warmth. I remember being very relieved they were the ones watching over my children the past few hours.

Thankfully, both Luke and Grace had slept the entire time I was away. They woke up around six, and it was my somber task to tell them their mother was gone. Luke is perceptive. He knew from my demeanor as I began to talk with them it was bad. At first he appeared outwardly emotionless; the tears came later. Grace did not accept the truth. She kept saying, "I want my mommy." For a good few minutes I held her and patted her back. Luke sat with Susan as they both cried.

Claude and Diane were there when the children awoke and both sought to console their grandchildren. They had arrived around five-thirty while Luke and Grace were still asleep. Diane immediately went to work wiping down kitchen counters as though her grief could be expunged with physical energy. Once, she excused herself and stepped outside on the patio; Claude followed her, and through the French doors I watched as they held each other. Katherine was their only child.

My house was the setting of several stages on which grief was the central character in each act. The supporting cast was striving to manage a script which was not yet written.

Around nine-thirty I fell asleep. Two hours later I awoke to the realization my world had changed. Alone in the bedroom a rush of emotion overtook me, and for the first time I cried. It was almost noon, twelve hours since the accident. I tried to imagine how it would be possible to manage the next twelve hours and the many to follow.

chapter two

BEHIND ME NOW are over four hundred people gathered for the funeral of my wife. I sense their attention, their curiosity, their sympathetic interest in my plight. The words of kindness have been overwhelming, many seeking to support their pastor of five years now. My private thoughts are privileged information, however, my counsel reserved for myself this day. I don't look to others for support as much as I seek to find my inner strength.

Three blocks south of our church the ocean waves are crashing upon the beach with their relentless frequency. Grief hits me in waves, breaks upon me with surprising regularity, and engulfs my spirit. At one moment I'm standing on firmly packed sand then a sizable surge of intense emotion smashes into me, and the sand begins to wash away; my foothold erodes, threatening my stability. I try to focus on a reasoned thought, such as how this is affecting those around me, in order to build a breakwater to divert the flood of feeling. This effort is of minimal success in abating the persistent force of sentiment which washes over me with the same tenacity as the incoming tide on the beach.

The small, soft hand of my daughter is resting limp in my left hand; the pressure of my son's narrow shoulder is indenting my right arm. Both of them are clinging to me, trusting in my strength and confidence. It's their loss too. I want to answer their questions, heal their sorrow but feel so inadequate to meet their needs now. They're my primary concern, but my questions about the night of the accident compete for my focus.

The minister, a friend of the family, is reading scripture, the twenty-third Psalm. "The Lord is my shepherd, I shall not want." How many times have I read this passage at funeral services? The familiar Psalm fades into the background as my mind returns to my preoccupation with questions of what happened to my wife. At dinnertime Katherine walked out the door and did not return, not alive anyway.

On our last evening together she told me she hated me. I try to remember every detail of the conversation. I reconstruct a portion of it in my mind.

"You know nothing as to what I feel," she said to me.

"If I don't it's because you've changed," I said.

"For several years now you've not cared much about what I want. "You're so dedicated to the church and all of your other interests that you're oblivious to what's important to me and the children."

"That's not fair. I care about my family. My kids mean everything to me; you and they are the center of my life."

"You are the center of your life. We're just handy attachments."

"And you're the all-giving mother, I suppose, the selfless servant?" As soon as I said it I wished I could strike it from the record, delete the veiled sarcasm.

"I take care of them every day; you don't have a clue as to what that involves. You come home and expect us to hear about your day. What about our day, my pressures? How can you be so self-centered? I hate you!"

It was our last exchange of words. The next morning she was silent and aloof, refusing my overtures to talk. That evening she slipped out the door moments after I arrived home. The next time I saw her was on a hospital bed, unable to hear my pleading for another chance to show my love.

The casket is light blue with silver trim, shiny under the array of flood lights reflecting off the metallic surface. Numerous flower arrangements crowd the front of the church, each tagged with the names of those who need a way to offer condolences. I tried last night to take note of the contributors but found the effort futile in my state of mind. She would love the roses and appreciate the colors and aromas of this temporary garden. She would record the names on the cards and make mental and written memos of the style and type in order to respond to the senders. Katherine was always good with details and able to recall the most insignificant of the particulars.

At the viewing last evening my daughter placed one small hand on the smooth surface of the open coffin and deliberately stroked her mother's hair with the other hand as her brother held her up. I could not determine what thoughts held sway in her seven-year old mind as she was suspended only a foot away from this resemblance of her mother. Like her mom, my little Grace is not one to divulge her secret thoughts. Katherine's parents, Claude and Diane, stood behind their granddaughter and took in this tender scene. No one made a move to interfere in this innocent moment of last rites.

For a few minutes late last night in my bedroom at home my sorrow took control of my mind and body; my stomach trembled, my legs ached, and my tears were unstoppable. The energy depletion was so intense I collapsed on the bed in utter fatigue. I suppose the concentration of gut wrenching despair lowered my emotional reservoir and has allowed me to keep it together today.

The pianist is now playing "Rock of Ages", requested by my mother-in-law. I steal a furtive glance down the row to see what effect the mournful hymn is having on this woman who invested so much energy into her daughter who has been the center of her life for years. I remember the call I made just a few nights ago to tell her that her only child was dead. "No, this can't be" were her only words.

The morning sun penetrates the stained glass windows over the baptistery. Yellow, blue, and red beams of light illuminate the floor, bathe the pulpit, and create a fresco of indeterminate images on the side wall. The bright sacred window art testifies to the hope our faith brings, witnesses to the power of divine help. The broken reflections confirm, however, the confusion in my heart.

Susan Martin, our associate pastor, has asked if she might honor Katherine by sharing some thoughts.

Katherine was my friend. Neither she nor I had a sister growing up. We became sisters, confidants, these last three years. Katherine had enormous curiosity; she craved knowledge, and

held a vivid imagination. **When she was ten years old she went to the Baptist Church but secretly pretended to be a Roman Catholic. Impressed by the Chartres Cathedral she visited in France with her French grandparents, she would imagine her louvered, bedroom closet door was a confessional booth. The make-believe priest on the other side of the door would hear her admissions of misdemeanors. "Bless me, Father, for I have sinned" she would whisper. The only problem was she was so well-behaved she could not come up with enough naughtiness to share with the cleric in the closet.**

The congregation laughs. The levity breaks the somber mood.

Katherine was the most compassionate person I've ever met. She had an innate gift of listening to the life stories of others. She was warm and nonjudgmental with those who sought the assistance of the church for food and clothing. Katherine was a gift from God to me, to us. We will miss her so much.

Susan is not able to continue. The room is filled with sentiment as if some poignant air has seeped in through the ventilation system.

The service is closed with a prayer. **The peace of God, which passes all understanding, shall guard your hearts and your thoughts in Christ Jesus.**

Claude, Diane, and I stand at the front door as the slow procession of well-wishers passes by at a deliberate pace, each person speaking words of consolation. Her parents are composed, remarkably poised. I extend my hand, nod my head, engage with my eyes, form words with my tongue, but my mind is not present, still in a room of despondency somewhere else.

***

The internment will not to be until tomorrow. Everyone has left the church now. I sit in my office and my mind is flooded anew with questions. The one I try hard to suppress is the probing possibility that Katherine may have intentionally headed for the tree that night. I struggle to dismiss it, to relegate it to a place where such thoughts are padlocked away.

It was a few months ago when Cindy Johnson came to this office to seek my guidance as her pastor. The high school senior is the daughter of one of our most active families in the church. She surprised me by her reason for coming to see me.

"I considered suicide the other day," she began.

"Could you tell me why?"

"Because everything in my life sucks."

"Why do you say that?"

"Because it does."

"Would you share with me what you mean by everything?" I asked her.

"Sure. My parents are on my case about my grades. My boyfriend broke up with me. Most of my classmates think I'm weird, and my face is covered with zits."

"Those are reasons to be upset. Do you think they are reasons to take your life?"

"I'm still alive."

After my best attempts to guide Cindy I suggested she talk with a psychologist friend of mine who is trained in helping young people through their problems. She agreed to do this. I followed up and found she was making good progress.

When I got home that evening after meeting with Cindy I told Katherine about my session. Often I shared with her my counseling experiences, trusting her confidentiality. I could tell she was very concerned for the troubled girl. "It's never easy to understand what goes on in another person's mind," Katherine said.

One of the tools my counselor friend employs is what he calls the RFL or Reason for Living Inventory. He asks people who share the negatives in their lives to then to make a list of the positives. Sometimes he prompts them to include: I still have much I want to do—I do care for those close to me—there are others who depend on me—I am curious about the future.

I know Katherine had been struggling with her negatives. I'm sure her positives far outweighed them, however. Her death had to be an accident; any other speculation is ridiculous.

***

Spring is almost here. The tourists are returning; the air is getting warmer. Soon fishermen will again stand in the surf and cast their lines into the ocean. The pier will be crowded, and the highways will be flush with vehicles. The bike paths will welcome mothers jogging with strollers. Runners will pace themselves across the bridge, and boats will fill the sounds, rivers, and inlets.

It will not be spring for me. It will be a second winter, a period of chill and darkness in my soul. I cannot avoid the pain of the absence I feel nor expect it to go away soon.

chapter three

"Do you believe humans will ever reach the Omega point?"

These were the first words Katherine ever said to me. We were both students at Campbell University, a small Baptist college in Buies Creek, North Carolina. It was the fall semester; she'd transferred from Meredith College in Raleigh where she had completed her sophomore year.

The course was philosophy of religion. Katherine was a philosophy major; I majored in religion. It was the second week in the class. Like almost every single guy in the room, I'd spent the first few classes watching this attractive, auburn haired girl as she made her way to her seat. On this day, she sat beside me, opened up her notebook, settled her purse on the floor, and turned to me to pose the question.

It must have taken me a half-minute to get over the shock of first her speaking to me and then the exact nature of what she'd said. She turned her head and looked over her right shoulder anticipating my answer. When I turned her way my face was two feet from hers. I remember thinking much was riding on my response. Here was an opening to get to know this exceptional looking girl, but was this a serious question or was she making fun of the matter at hand? I decided to treat her inquiry as serious but try to be engaging as well.

"I think Teilhard had a great deal of confidence in humanity," I said. "I'm not sure he would think we have advanced very far since the nineteen fifties when he passed away."

"So you're skeptical of the concept of a noosphere?" Her inflection gave no clue as to her solemnity.

Here I sat, still with my perplexing dilemma. Could this captivating girl be serious in asking a guy she didn't know his opinion regarding the noosphere? I thought I detected a slight smile emerging when she pronounced the strange sounding word. I didn't want to blow the opportunity by making fun of the subject or by giving away my nerdy interest in the concept. The day before, we had been introduced to the works of the French priest/philosopher, Pierre Teilhard de Chardin. The truth—I was intrigued by what the professor had said and went to the library to read more that evening. I took in Teilhard's theory of the Omega point where perfect unity will exist, and was fascinated by the concept of a noosphere, a kind of collective consciousness.

"I suppose such a revolutionary idea takes some getting used to," I said.

"Good answer, Paul," Katherine said.

She knew my name. Of course, I had made a point to learn hers; you do not but wonder about a girl with a French name like Rosiere.

"So, you're interested in Teilhard?" I hoped she would answer me without another question.

"Yes, I think his optimism is refreshing. I found a quote last night which makes me hopeful. He wrote, 'Driven by the forces of love, the fragments of the world seek each other so that the world may come to being.'"

The "forces of love"—it sounded so wonderful coming from her wide, full lips. I turned away and looked down at my desk for a moment. With a thoughtful rub of my chin, I countered with a Teilhard quote of my own, "The most satisfying thing in life is to have been able to give a large part of one's self to others."

"So, you did your homework. Nice quote. Paul, would you like to meet after class and share notes on Teilhard?"

I'm sure I blubbered a "yes" as my response.

We spent an hour sharing our love of philosophy that day and sat beside each other in the class from then on. It was the beginning of our years together as philosophical soul mates. After meeting

Katherine, I became convinced Teilhard was right when he wrote, "The future is more beautiful than all the pasts."

**

After the funeral service, we're back at our home. Our home—a strange thought; this is no longer our home, not mine and Katherine's. It's now the place where I live with Luke and Grace. How am I to maintain the feeling of home without her?

Diane's busy in the kitchen organizing the abundance of food which has been donated by church members. She's spent many hours in this kitchen with her daughter in visits over the years. Keeping busy is her way of coping. Claude's on the porch with Luke playing with our brown Lab. Grace sits on the oversized chair, her mother's favorite, hands in her lap, eyes locked on the array of family photographs on the built-in bookshelves. Susan is by the door greeting the well wishers who have chosen to stop by. She's incredible with names and carries on the duty as if she was at her door at church after a Sunday service.

There are over three dozen people in the areas which comprise our great room, dining corner, and kitchen. I remember well the hours Katherine spent choosing paint colors for this section and stressing over the blend of brown and gold walls with white moldings. She had an exceptional eye for which tones complimented each other. This was just one of her many talents. She was not as comfortable as a hostess, however, as her mother is. Diane's so self-assured and gifted in the social graces. Katherine was so different from her—both confident, but daughter more reserved, mother so outgoing.

My mother sits beside my daughter now who snuggles close to her. Grace has always loved her Nana Brewer. My mom is content to care for her granddaughter, letting others do the hosting. Her recent heart problems have slowed her. There was a time when she'd never have allowed anyone to wait on her.

I'm not sure who needs my attention more, my seven-year old Grace or her older brother. Luke's certainly more outgoing, and yet he looked to his mom for stability. My daughter has always been quiet and able to be by herself for long periods of time without seeking her mother's notice. I've seen Katherine and Grace sit for an hour in the same room without either of them speaking a word. They called it "hushed time" and seemed to cherish the wordless proximity. Luke does not go a minute without talking and never lost the ear of his mother, even when she was tired. How am I to fill the space she's left and offer my children the support my wife gave them?

Claude finds me in the garage. I've come to take the trash out and linger for a few minutes to collect myself.

"Did my daughter ever tell you anything of the village we visited in Provence when she was ten years old?" Claude asks.

"She told me that she went to France that summer for the first time, but I don't remember any specifics about a village. All I know is the trip made a great impression on her and caused to her love all things French."

"The name was Ansouis. It was a typical little parish with an old castle dating back to the tenth century, not far from where I grew up. What was memorable about the day was Katherine's interest in talking with a few of the senior villagers. My child was so curious about their personal histories and always wanted to converse with those who lived well into their old age. I'd hoped she would live to be old and experience the joy of looking back over many decades of accumulated wisdom."

There are no tears in Claude's eyes, but his voice betrays the emotion behind his carefully chosen words. His French accent has been diluted through forty years of linguistic amalgamation with North Carolina dialects. He's a small man, but his rigid posture gives him a stature greater than his actual height.

"Katherine was interested in everyone's story," I say. "There are so many people whom she befriended. She had a passion for those economically disadvantaged."

"I think my daughter was special in many ways. There's a great cavity in our family with her gone. Paul, I appreciate your allowing her mother and me to stay so close to her these last few years."

"She always loved having you and Diane around. I did too."

Claude takes a few steps toward the door into the kitchen. He stops and turns back facing me. His head is bent down and his right hand holds the fingers on his left. Several deep breaths follow, and then he looks up and around the white, sheet rock garage. Shovels and rakes hang from brackets— hand tools fit precisely on their assigned pegs—plastic bins hold a labeled array of nails, screws, and bolts. I know he approves of the orderliness because he helped organize the space after we moved in. We both stand in stock-still silence trying to suppress the emotion which is our tie, two men feeling anguish, each unable to find a way to express it. Then my self-disciplined father-in-law steps towards me and embraces me with a tenderness which surprises. I hold him. The hollow garage has become a place where we seek to offer a measure of support and receive such as well. After a couple of minutes we both return to the great room. He sits beside Grace and my mom.

Our house is a twenty-four hundred square foot patio home in a gated community near the church. My brother Matt sits out on the patio taking in the afternoon sun on this warm coastal day. Matt's wife, Angela, is helping my mother-in-law in the kitchen. Matt and Angela have both tried to find ways to comfort me, and I appreciate their efforts. The truth is I'm not ready for comfort yet.

Clark Teale, one of our new deacons, takes me aside. "Paul, the deacons are going to fill in as needed in caring for the congregation these next few weeks. I know this is not a time to talk church, so that's all I will say."

"Thanks, Clark," I reply. "I appreciate how considerate the church leaders have been these last few days."

"Most every person in the church has offered to help. You would not believe the volunteers who have come forth to take on certain aspects of ministry. I think the biggest job we'll have is finding a way to make everyone feel useful. Not that your work isn't demanding—just that there are more offers of assistance than there are specific assignments."

It does make a pastor feel good to know the church family is so willing to pitch in. I know Clark well; he's a very capable leader. He's a recent retiree who moved to the island four years ago. He's earned the respect of the congregation. This is the nature of our church and our community; many talented people move here to retire and seek ways to live active and productive lives. It's a relief to know the church is in good hands.

"Pastor, your house is not what I imagined." Thelma Covington is one of the many widows in our congregation. "These patio homes are mighty small."

Thelma sings in our choir and her flamboyant style of dress is one reason some in the church have pushed for choir robes. Robes don't seem to fit, however, with the laid-back style of the coast. I can't wait each Sunday to see what the silver-haired shag queen and Jimmy Buffett lover will wear. Thelma's a member of the Parrot-Head Club here on the island and is very Key West in her fashion choices.

She lives on the oceanfront in what was a two million dollar home before the recession hit. Our coastal community has experienced a severe loss in home values in the last five years. A major topic of conversation on our island is the "what if I had bought or sold property back then" discussion. It's a conversation held by a drove of could-have-been-millionaires who missed out on the housing boom. Thelma's experience is the opposite story. I've been told she and her husband bought their house years ago, and it tripled in value until the recession brought it back a notch.

"The house suits us well, Thelma," I say. "Of course, if you want to trade even I will give it some thought."

"My dogs would get claustrophobia in one of these little cottages, and what a shame it is to live so close to the beach and not be able to see the ocean every day."

I smile at this eccentric gal who lives with her three large Irish Setters in her mansion by the sea. She loves to dance and is quite a party-goer for someone her age.

"Oh, we get over to the beach enough to appreciate where we live," I say.

"Well, from now on you just bring your children over to my place when you want to go swimming. You can park in my driveway, use my outdoor shower, and don't hesitate to knock on the door for some lemonade if I'm home. I would offer you a rum cola, but it's not likely you would accept."

"Thank you, Thelma. Luke, Grace, and I may just take you up on the parking matter."

"Paul, Katherine was a real treasure. You know she and I were related. Her mother and I are first cousins." Thelma turns sideways and says, "Look at this profile and then look at Diane over there. Do you see the resemblance?"

"Yes, I can see it." She's told me this before. It's a stretch, but they do have common features, the long pointed noses for example. Both she and Diane share robust figures; the women in their clan all have some shade of red hair. The clothes disguise any other resemblance as Diane is far more modest in dress than Thelma.

"Diane married well; Claude's a good man," Thelma says. "Her father was a mechanic, a decent man too. My mother married a bum. He was my father, but he was a no good rascal, a mountain redneck who left us when I was two. That's one reason I made sure I found a nice Yankee with money. My Ralph was in textiles, you know. The poor man always wanted to live at the beach. We weren't here a year before he passed away."

"I'm sorry I never got to meet him," I say.

"The good people always pass before their time."

I can count a dozen couples who moved to the coast after retirement, and either the husband or wife passed soon after coming here.

What a strange tradition this is—the after the funeral gathering where family and friends eat and talk. I look around the house and take note of the activity and the enclaves of people trying to overcome the despondency with enough inane chatter to blot out the reality of the loss for a moment or two. I remember reading that suffering is not something to avoid but to overcome. In all of the conversations today, the ones most helpful are those which acknowledge we have lost someone we cared for and need to find the will to accept that passing. All people must endure times of pain and loss.

Katherine is not here. I know this is a ridiculous thought, but it comes to me that my wife's not in the house. This is, was, her house more than it was mine; it's full of people, but not one of them is her. They stand in her kitchen, sit on her favorite couch, hug her children, and speak her name. She should be seeing to their needs, conversing with them, smiling at their jokes, sympathizing with their concerns. She will no longer love, laugh, and play here.

chapter four

KATHERINE'S TO BE interred at the Historic Oakwood Cemetery in Raleigh. The graveside service is today; the funeral at the church was yesterday. She told me on several occasions she didn't want to be cremated but wanted to be buried in the plots my parents bought years ago. Katherine has always been afraid of fire. Claude once told me that when she was six a cinder from an exploding log in the fireplace landed on her leg. The experience traumatized her. He traces her fear back to that event. Whatever the reason, she's always been adamant about her unwillingness to consider cremation.

Luke rides with me on the three hour drive up to Raleigh; Grace is in the car with Katherine's parents. Luke's amazed that his mother's grave will be at Oakwood. He went online last night and googled the cemetery. In the car he tells me what he found.

"Dad, did you know that many famous people are buried at Oakwood?"

"I remember that Josephus Daniels is there. He was a leading newspaper editor in Raleigh and once secretary of the Navy."

Luke says, "Would you believe N.C. State basketball coach Jim Valvano?" Luke's a big fan of Wolfpack basketball.

"No, I wasn't aware his grave is there," I say.

"I found that the cemetery's really old. It dates back to 1867, given by some guy named Henry Mordecai for Civil War soldiers. The really neat thing is that in 1871 they brought the bodies of a hundred and three Confederate soldiers who died at the battle of Gettysburg and reburied them in Raleigh, at Oakwood."

Luke's interest in the Civil War is insatiable. He says he wants to teach history when he's grown. Our family went to Gettysburg when Luke was ten.

He was so excited when we toured the battlefield. He wanted to stand where Robert E. Lee stood on that last day during Pickett's charge, and where Lincoln delivered the Gettysburg Address. Katherine took a video of him wearing a stovepipe hat and reciting the first lines of the address, a few feet away from where the president stood to read his famous speech. She's watched that video many times.

As we enter Oakwood under the stone arch, Luke says, "Man, this place really looks ancient."

I'm pleased that his mind is on something else today other than just his mother's death. He did sleep for part of the trip which allowed me to think of what we will do after we get back home and try to settle into life without Katherine.

We weave through the cemetery grounds on the narrow streets, passing the rows of graves of the Confederate dead, until we reach section C way in the back near the mausoleum. A number of cars have arrived before us, including several dozen which have come up from the beach. Claude, Diane, and Grace arrive within five minutes. Within fifteen minutes over two hundred and fifty people are here.

My father's marker is two spaces away from the open grave awaiting the casket still on the hearse, a spot for me in between. There's a place for my mother on the other side of Dad. On many other occasions I've positioned myself on this hallowed piece of land and said goodbye to one family member or another. My grandparents are buried here, two aunts, and my sister; now my wife will be added to the long row.

Katherine and I held hands here just three years ago at the graveside service for my dad who died of lung cancer. She loved my dad, and her tears that day were many. Dad always liked being around Katherine and loved to tease her. I would never have imagined that day I would stand here looking into the grave of my wife this soon. There should be a prescribed sequence for departures from this life, an orderliness that has some rationale tied to age and life experience.

In this row of graves there is no sense to be made of the timing, the progression.

The green canopy has room for twelve chairs. I sit on the front row with Luke, Grace, Claude, Diane, and my mother. My brother and sister-in-law are on the second row along with two of Katherine's aunts and an uncle. It's a cloudy March day but no rain. The graveside service is brief as we've requested; two Psalms and a prayer are the spoken words; then a fellow member of Diane's choir plays a version of "Softly and Tenderly" on a guitar. The minister speaks final words and then proceeds to shake the hand of each family member and offers brief condolences as he moves down the line. This is a formality which has been the custom for many years. It's clergy etiquette, cemetery protocol.

Diane begins to cry and say repeatedly, "my little girl, my precious daughter." Her husband puts his arm around her shoulder, and little Grace goes over to her grandmother and takes her hand. Without a word this mum child helps Diane up as Claude seeks to lead his wife from the tent. Luke is silent, not typical for my son; I can tell he's using every ounce of self discipline to refrain from tears.

After everyone else has made their way from the grave, I stand by the casket, holding down my rising emotions, and say in a whisper, "goodbye, best friend." The words of Tennyson make their way to the front of my mind, "God's finger touched him, and he slept."

The well-wishers linger and speak their words of consolation. It's my duty to move among the people who have come and offer my appreciation for their thoughtfulness. It's the ritual of the cemetery, the procession of the afterwards. At times the congestion of bodies and hugs hems me in to the point of initiating a rush of claustrophobia. I've never had a panic attack; I wonder if my first one is imminent. I feel the need to move around, to circulate, and be free of the crowd. One of the keys to good health is good circulation, physical and emotional health.

In a few minutes almost everyone has left the cemetery, and my family waits over by the cars. I pause alone in the open space surrounded by a sea of tombstones. Two men in work overalls stand over by the fence; I assume they're the grave closers, shovels at parade rest position. Their services will conclude the funeral process, the physical aspects at least. The mental course will not be over anytime soon.

"Would you like to take a few more minutes?" the assistant funeral director says.

I know I must move to my car. They have their work to do. It's just that I can't find the will to budge. Samuel Johnson once wrote that we must "wait for grief to be digested." How long will that take? The young associate remains silent, waiting for my response. Arms folded, he looks away in order to not be obtrusive, I assume. It would be insensitive of me to keep him and the two men with shovels here any longer.

"No, I'm ready." I say. That's not the truth. My grief will have to be processed elsewhere. The grave closers wait for me to get in the car before they proceed on with their somber task.

***

I've never spent three hours in the car with my two children without my wife being there also. As we leave Raleigh on interstate forty, both Grace and Luke are quiet, Luke beside me in the front, Grace in the back seat behind her brother. In my mirror I can see the top of my daughter's head, the bangs of her red hair almost reaching her eyes. She's staring out the window as we pass through the open country of Johnston County. Luke rests his head on the passenger window, his eyes closed. His long legs and lean torso stretch out like an extension pole open to its full length.

The resurfaced highway is smooth, and the traffic moves at speeds in excess of seventy miles per hour for the most part. Many drivers pass going eighty or above in their determined pursuit of the fast lane. The art of driving on the interstate is to find that in-between position where one can navigate the traffic without losing one's chosen momentum. This is a parable of my desired life—the need to maintain my forward motion, a measure of steadiness, consistency.

Not long ago I ran across a poem by Natasha Trethewey called "Graveyard Blues." This poetic description of the after burial experience is stark. One section has stuck with me:

The road going home was pocked with holes,
That home-going road's always full of holes;
Though we slow down, time's wheel still rolls.

The metaphor impresses upon me the challenging journey ahead for our family. What holes will appear in the next few days and weeks to cause our way to be bumpy in the process of dealing with our grief? How do I help my children deal with their sorrow? I've read that each child grieves in their own way and the best clues come from the children themselves. How will these two deal with their loss? How did I deal with my childhood loss?

Luke and Grace knew something was wrong with their mother in the weeks before her death. We've not talked about what they saw and experienced. Now there's the finality of her demise. What coming nuances of their behaviors am I to anticipate? What fine distinctions of their past conduct did Katherine detect? How do I help my son and daughter travel this new road?

"Actually," Grace says softly from the backseat, "I don't understand why all of those people were there when Mommy was buried. Did they all know her?"

My daughter uses the word "actually" quite often. Katherine used to say she was intent on getting the facts straight.

Luke, his head still resting on the window, says, "It's what people do to pay their respects."

"What does that mean?" Grace asks.

"It means people want to show they are sorry for us," Luke says.

Grace is silent for a minute and then says, "Why should they feel sorry? It was not their fault that Mommy died."

Luke doesn't seem to have a response for that one. It's my turn to try to answer my daughter's questions. "Grace, there are a lot of people who want to help when someone they know dies. They want to let us know that they care about us."

Again Grace is mum, her head turned toward the window. We ride for a few miles without another word spoken. Sadness is our companion, silence our connection. The interstate cuts through farms and housing developments where people are working and resting, oblivious to our journey of loss. A van comes up beside us with two adults in the front seat and three children in the back, bikes on racks, luggage carrier on top. Most likely it's a family headed to the beach on vacation.

Grace again speaks, "Was I supposed to cry at the cemetery?"

Luke sits up and looks at me as though he wonders the same thing. I can't help but remember the words of Henri Nouwen I quoted in a recent sermon, "Pain touches us in our uniqueness and our most intimate individuality."

I sit up straight and adjust the rear-view mirror so as to see Grace's full face. She looks into the mirror so that it becomes our conduit for visual communication. "Grace, everybody experiences grief in a different way. There's nothing you're supposed to do. If you want to cry you can, or you can be sad without crying. When someone we love dies strange new feelings come to us."

Luke looks over at me with moist eyes. "Will we ever stop feeling so bad?"

A slower truck ahead causes me to touch the brake pedal and disengage the cruise control. I check my side mirror and slip over into the left lane. Luke's still looking at me after I reset the desired speed back to seventy-five. A billboard promotes a Smithfield Barbeque at the next exit.

"Son, every day we'll replace a little of our sadness with some joy until a time will come when we're better. We'll always miss your mom, but we'll learn to go on without her."

"When?" Luke asks.

"I'm not sure."

Both Luke and Grace return their concentration to the passing landscape. I suspect their real attention is on an inner landscape of sorrow. Mine sure is. Our small family's on a new journey. There's no way to predict when and where we will arrive at a place where we will find some peace.

In the small town of Beulaville a patrolman stops traffic for a funeral procession. We're the first car stopped at the intersection. Both of my children sit up and watch as the hearse passes in front of us followed by two black sedans in which family members are being transported from the Presbyterian Church a block away, likely to the cemetery. A young girl looks out the window of the second Cadillac, face pressed against the glass. She raises her hand and gives a slight wave to Luke who has his elbows on the dash of our vehicle. Luke waves back. I suppose he feels a bond with the child in the procession and thus acknowledges her gesture of friendship.

chapter five

THE PINE STANDS straight and tall with only a slight indentation. In my hand I hold a piece of the bark knocked off by the impact of the accident, I assume. One can't hold a grudge against a tree, accuse a tree, or reprimand a tree. It has prevailed against wind, disease, and now human assault. The pine is innocent, blameless, and above suspicion. The fault lies elsewhere.

I try to envision the moment of the impact and what Katherine must have thought if she realized the gravity of her situation. I can't bear the consideration of her horrific final seconds and the brief pain she likely endured before everything went away. My hope is the medics and doctors are correct in their assessment that she was rendered unconscious immediately.

As I stand alone in the churchyard, and dozens of cars pass in all directions, the notion occurs to me that somewhere there must be someone who saw her that evening before the wreck. How can I uncover the trail of her mysterious journey that night? A blue Dodge Ram slows and the truck driver waves as if he knows me. It's likely most people who live nearby know this is the site of a traffic fatality.

"Can I help you?" The older man stands a few feet behind me. "Are you examining the site of the wreck?"

"Yes," I answer as the small man in a plaid shirt and khaki pants draws closer.

"Are you her husband?"

"Yes. How did you know?"

"I can see the grief on your face. I've seen the look a few times."

"Do you live around here?"

"I'm the pastor of this church. I understand you're a pastor down at the beach." He moves closer to shake my hand. "My name's John Williams."

"Reverend Williams, I'm Paul Brewer. My wife was named Katherine."

"Yes, I've seen her picture in the paper. We've had other accidents at these intersections, not a death. I came over that night as they were taking her to the hospital. Our church family is praying for you."

There is something about this pastor's demeanor which reveals wisdom and kindness. John appears to be about seventy years old. "Thank you for the prayers," I say.

"Do you want to talk about it? I know that sometimes we ministers don't have anyone to go to with our grief. I lost my wife four years ago to cancer. A pastor friend was there to help me through it."

I'm not accustomed to sharing personal matters with strangers, but this clergyman has a way about him that is so reassuring. "I'm sorry to hear about your wife. I'm trying to work through my loss as best I can."

John folds his arms across his chest. "It's only been a week. I'm sure you've told many people in your ministry how time will lessen the pain. I imagine you've also counseled that it's not automatic, this healing. Sometimes the hurt goes on until it runs its full course."

"Yes, I've said those things. I hope I've been right."

"You have. I imagine you've heard the old adage which says, 'The dictionary is the only place where success comes before work.'"

"I haven't heard that before. I like it."

A car passes and the driver taps the horn. John waves.

"In my experience recovery from the loss of one close to you requires a great deal of effort," John says.

I'm not sure why I tell him of my not knowing where she went that evening and why she had gone. I don't tell him about all of our problems. We stand for fifteen minutes in the shaded churchyard while he listens to my story.

"My wife's death was much different from your wife's accident," he says. "We lived through a year of cancer treatments. Your loss was so sudden. The long agony is worse for the one dying, but it gives the spouse time to prepare. Your wife's sudden demise gave you no time to adjust to losing her. Your questions about her behavior that evening makes it even harder, I assume. I remember reading a while back the words of the poet, Rainer Maria Rilke. She wrote, 'I beg you…be patient toward all that is unsolved in your heart and to try to love the questions themselves…'"

"You have me again on that one, Reverend. I'm not familiar with it, but I see the wisdom."

"When you're a widower you have a good bit of time to read."

"Have you been at this church long?" I ask.

"Actually, I'm just an interim here for a few months. The regular pastor has heart problems, so they asked me to fill in. He's taking a leave of absence."

"I'm sure you're just what the church needs."

"I'm what they have. There's a difference between what one wants and what one gets. The trick is to accept the difference and learn to work out the space in between."

"I'll keep that in mind."

"Paul, our church family feels a deep hurt for you and your family. I suppose it is the fact that her death occurred on our property; this has become personal for us. There is a connection which is hard to explain. It's like we lost one of our members."

"Thank your congregation for me, John."

On the drive back I can't help but thank God for Reverend John Williams. I always wonder if serendipitous occurrences are not God sent. The wise senior minister was very helpful. I don't think I can ever love the questions. I need answers.

***

Katherine was fluent in French. I have a weak handle on Greek and Spanish. She and her father would often converse in his native language. It was their special bond. Sometimes she would insert French words into our conversations just to confuse me. The subject at the dinner table a few months ago was a healthy diet.

I argued my case. "I don't see the problem with white bread. I grew up on Wonder bread. It didn't hurt me."

"Quelle bêtise," Katherine said.

"What does that mean?" I said.

"I think it was a put-down," Luke said.

"Was it? I have a right to my opinion, you know."

"Dad," Grace said, "Mom is the food expert."

"C'est bien cela." Katherine winked at Grace.

I got up from the table and came back with a French-English dictionary. "Okay, I found bêtise. It means stupid. We're not supposed to use that word in our house according to your rules, Katherine of Aragon."

"Mom's not from Aragon," Luke said.

"She thinks she is."

"Ne vous disputez pas"

"I got that," I said. I'm not disputing you. I was just saying that I would like to have white bread once in a while."

"A votre guise."

"Thank you," I said.

What did she say?" Grace asked.

I winked at Grace. "She said, 'father knows best.'"

Luke and Grace both looked towards their mom. Katherine shook her head sideways.

One French word I know well—"zut." It means "darn it." It is my only expletive in any language. A clergy person needs at least some mild form of profanity. I have never cursed God, but I say "zut" quite often.

Katherine was never profane. She was often profound. Her favorite French expression was. "En connaissance de cause." It means, "with full knowledge of the facts." She never argued unless she had done her homework.

My great frustration is that I must proceed with my life without full knowledge of the facts. Zut.

chapter six

THE RAIN WAS so heavy the wipers were fighting a losing battle. My father's head was locked facing forward, his full concentration looking down the road ahead. Mom's voice was calm but her fear still evident as she warned us to remain still and quiet. We each knew this was no time to defy her caution. Karen was on the left, behind Dad, Matt in the middle, and I on the right behind our mother. It was the week after my tenth birthday and Karen, seven, still held the stuffed bear she called Andy. Five year old Matt was restless in his car seat.

Once a year we took a family vacation, this year to our nation's capitol. We filled the four days there with sightseeing. Karen was fascinated by the Smithsonian, especially the Air and Space Museum. My dad kept calling her Amelia Earhart. Matt was mostly bored but did perk up when we rode to the top of the Washington Monument and looked out over the vast city. I found every part of the tour exciting and was surprised when my dad got down on his knees and was silent for a minute at the Vietnam Memorial. Mom was the consummate tour guide and the guardian of the schedules.

Highway 95 through Richmond was crowded on the busy holiday weekend as all three lanes south were filled with vehicles. Dad said he preferred to go through the city instead of take the bypass, more interesting he told mom. We had just passed signs which directed travelers to the Edgar Allan Poe Museum, Shockoe Bottom, and Dock Street. I remember a white U-Haul truck had kept its pace with us in the lane outside my window for minutes, the same kind of truck dad had rented a few months earlier when we moved into our new house. I'll never forget that truck; its orange and black logo is forever imbedded in my recollection of that day.

We had just crossed the James River on the Richmond-Petersburg Turnpike. I had peered below to the water, curious to see what was visible down below in the river bed. In the distance were factories and storage tanks, smoke stacks reaching higher than the elevated road-bed. Tractor-trailer trucks would often obstruct my view and form a moving wall of metal.

My Mom shouted, "Charles, watch out!"

I looked around her seat out the windshield to see a mass of vehicles all with their brake lights flashing. My dad pumped his brakes, but the pavement was wet from the heavy downpour. Keeping his attention on the road, he called out, "Hold on, heads down!"

I didn't obey him and still looked out my side window. There were many cars now attempting to stop. Our Chevy Malibu was slowing but sliding at an angle to the left. Karen was also looking out her window. All I could see was a jumble of cars and trucks gliding across the blacktop like a weaving conga line of dancing machines.

The first impact was when our front left bumper caught the edge of a service van in the next lane. I remember thinking that our speed was not very fast so this might not be that bad. Dad again spoke in a raised voice, "It's gonna be okay, just everybody stay down low."

I looked over at Karen and could see that she was holding her bear tight as to protect him. Matt was crying now. Mom reached through the arm rest opening and held his right foot. Horns were blaring, and the rain came relentlessly against my window.

My father was doing everything in his power to straighten the car. Our Malibu and the white van now formed a v; the front of our car sliding up to the side door of the other vehicle. Ahead there were many other cars and trucks sitting at angles all over the highway. Out my right side window I could see down the road where a black pickup had crashed into the guardrail; my mother was still holding Matt's foot. Karen had closed her eyes. We were sliding down the inclined roadway at a crawl locked into a strange choreography with the white van.

My father then yelled, "Stop!" He was looking over his left shoulder up the lane beside us. I recall turning my head the same direction as his which put me looking out Karen's window.

I saw what my father saw; the U-Haul was sliding toward us almost perpendicular to its lane. The rear of the large cargo area was headed straight for the side of our car. The orange and black logo kept growing so that it now filled the entire window opposite of me. Within a few seconds I felt the brutal impact as it smashed into our Chevy with a violent force which threw me into the back of my mother's seat and against my window. The sound was muffled by the rain, but the crunch was shrill like sheet metal being ripped away in a violent wind storm.

There was movement inside our car; from my vantage point it seemed like my family was exchanging seats in a slow motion shuffle of faces and torsos. The force of the collision lifted our car in the air, tilted it on the side out my window, and then sat it back down on the wheels to slide sideways, the U-Haul leaning on us like a huge box reaching from the pavement up and over us.

Out my side window a white car appeared, the driver's face looking straight at me. He was a young man who wore a baseball cap of some kind, his eyes wide and mouth open. Our faces were a foot or two apart as the truck pushed us up against his car. For a few seconds we stared at each other, and then everything was still.

chapter seven

I HAD A dream last night. I was in a courtroom with many other people, familiar faces but most not recognizable. The judge was my father—this I remember for sure. The prosecutor was my theology professor from seminary. I was on the witness stand, sworn in on the Bible by Reverend Williams. Much of it is clear to me even now.

Dr. Fraser, the seminary professor, asked me, "Paul, where were you on the night of March twelve between the hours of six and midnight?"

"I was at home," I responded.

"Where was your wife?"

"I don't know."

"You have no idea where she was?"

"He has answered that question," my dad says from the bench.

"Yes, your honor," Dr. Fraser says. "Paul, when did you last see Kate?"

"Her name was Katherine. I last saw her that morning."

"You didn't see her at dinner?"

"Yes, I forgot. I did see her briefly at dinner."

The prosecutor/professor then approaches where I'm seated. "Mr. Brewer, did you kill your wife?"

I look at him, then to the judge and plead, "I don't know."

There's a clamor in the courtroom, people shouting, and the judge pounding his gavel. I woke up in a sweat.

There's no doubt that I feel a measure of guilt for what happened to Katherine. She would not have been on that road that evening if I had done things differently. I can't prove that, but my inner self feels it to be so. I think it was playwright Arthur Miller who said, "Maybe all one can do is hope to end up with the right regrets."

My father was a strict disciplinarian when I was young. I can figure out why he is the judge in the dream. Dr. Fraser was my toughest teacher; I've not forgotten his notes in the margin when my papers were not up to his standard. Dreams often can be deciphered with a little insight. From psychology classes I learned that many of us punish ourselves for our earlier failures. We become our own parents and scold ourselves for our feelings of unworthiness.

The truth is I can't find it in me to blame Katherine. That evening when she drove away I alternated between worry and anger. The anger because I could not believe she was that inconsiderate—to go off like that without telling me where she was going. The worry came, of course, because I could not gauge her state of mind and feared she might do something rash. I imagined the scene when she came home. In one scenario I would fuss at her for giving me such an apprehensive night waiting for her. In the alternate scenario I would hold her and tell her how concerned I had been and was happy she was home. Quite possibly both would have been my choice. There was no opportunity for either.

***

I find a book that belonged to Katherine. I have not seen it before. It is in her bedside drawer, the one in which she kept her nighttime reading. The title of the book is, *Why I Don't Pray Anymore.* I find myself drawn in by this unusual personal account:

> I grew up in the church, Presbyterian. I used to pray, sometimes in public, often in private. Please don't misunderstand me; I am a religious person. My praying stopped after I lost my husband to leukemia. During his three years of illness I asked God every day to help find a cure for him. Evidently, God did not provide for Joseph in his budget for healing miracles. That was his decision. He has the right to decide who gets what and when. It's

just that he lost my confidence in prayer by the choice to not save Joseph. Before his death I calculated that my prayer requests were working for me about thirty percent of the time, a ratio I was willing to accept since I figured in a world of millions of people, God could not possibly grant all appeals.

My husband suffered so much for so long; he deserved relief from his pain. It seemed to me to be a valid situation for divine intervention. I understand that we humans do not have the full knowledge of God, that we see through a glass darkly during our days here on earth. Therefore, I refuse to ask for anything any longer from God. If I am so ignorant of how things work in the heavenly plan, why should I petition? Oh, I know that there are other types of prayers besides intercessory ones. I could praise God in prayer, thank him in prayer, or seek him in prayer. My assumption is, however, that God gets plenty of praise. Sure, there are things to be thankful for, but when the one thing most important to you is taken away—you know. And, why should I continue to seek God? If he wants me in his fold, then the ball is in his court. Bitter, yes, irreligious, no. I very much believe there is a God. I just don't think he deserves my prayers at this point.

I put the book down and ask myself if I could ever come to the point in my relationship with God where I could not pray. Why did Katherine have this book? Why did she not show it to me? I read on:

Human happiness is dependent on certain things working out well for us. If those key elements of our lives do not fall into place with some measure of frequency then we despair. Natural handicaps, lack of any measure of prosperity, social inequities, psychological disorders, catastrophes in the natural world, and of course—premature loss of a loved one. All of these are reason to despair. Anyone of these can cause a person to lose confidence in God.

The truth is that we have little influence in the world in which we live. I am the product of ancestors whom I never knew, shaped by events in the past of which I had no input, and at the mercy of fates beyond my control. I can only respond. People respond in different ways to the difficulties they face. Some take their own lives while others adjust their hopes and seem to cope well. Someone once said of Lord Byron: "He brooded over the blemish as sensitive minds will brood until they magnify a wart into a wen. His lameness certainly helped make him skeptical, cynical, and savage."

I am not as cynical as Byron, but in my God given freedom to respond to life as I choose—I choose not to talk with God any longer. I choose to cope with my loss by filling my life with work, family responsibilities, and projects of my choosing. God and I will coexist. I will respectfully do my thing and allow God to do his. If we bump into each other, then so be it. I will not get in his way, will not talk bad about him, and will not discourage others from an intimate relationship. It is only that I will no longer ask for his help.

I am well aware that I run the risk of avoiding any personal responsibility for my actions because I feel powerless. I am sure that many people will see my denial of the proficiency of prayer as a means of casting any personal failures on God's lack of reaction to my communications with him. I do not see that I have succumbed to fatalism with its grim view of human freedom, however. I do not deny that God is at work, nor do I often fault God for his way of working. I am sure he has a plan and that his plan is at work, even in my life. It is my belief that God does not allow for my plans to influence his plans.

I find the long days difficult to endure now that my husband is gone. At least in those terrible days of his illness there was a purpose—caring for him. My anxiety over his pending death is now replaced by anxiety over my pending life. I became afraid that I would not be able to cope with his loss. The truth is that fear is needed. It keeps us ready. The key is learning to be afraid of the things that do threaten us but not be paranoid.

Any person who has read much in the scriptures or in psychology can tell you that how one handles trouble is what matters. So I now spend my days calling forth the inner resources needed to handle my loss. Granted they are God-given, these inner resources, but I don't need prayer in order to ask God to give me what he has already provided.

I am well aware that our faith teaches that we are to be submissive to God. I respect God's power, and know that we humans have an inherent need to devote ourselves to a power greater than our own personhood. I have been taught my whole life to pray like Jesus did in the garden, "not my will, but Thine, be done." But it was God's will, or at least his allowance, that my husband suffer and die. However that fit into the divine plan, it did not fit mine. Therefore, I refuse to submit myself to God's will any longer through prayer.

I see people give themselves away to all sorts of allegiances. For some it is a church, for others a club, even for many to a charismatic leader. They acquiesce to the will of the group or the head because of this powerful need to belong. When we become devoted to groups or to other individuals we excuse ourselves from making the difficult decisions of life; we gain security, but we escape from the complexities of solving our problems by ourselves. I am not willing to be submissive now. I've traveled that road and found it to be unsatisfactory.

If you wish, you can accuse me of selfish individualism. You may indict me for my vanity, pride, or egotism. The way I see it, my need now is to work out my deliverance from grief on my own accord. My husband died in a horrible way. I watched helplessly as he suffered and passed. I asked God many times to spare him the agony. If he still wants my allegiance he will have to provide some answers for this tragedy. So far, he has not appeared to defend himself.

It is impossible for me to escape my low moods completely. To rebel against them, ignore them, and discount them would be absurd. For the three years of my husband's illness I would often ask God to lift me from my depression. The answer I heard through my inner connection with God was you can lift yourself out of your emotional cellar. Never once did I hear a still small voice instruct me to find professional help. So, I stuck it out with God. The result was I became stronger, but I also continued my periodic visits to this negative place.

I know enough about psychology to realize that some people identify with depression to the point of making it who they are. I have enough sense to understand that a healthy person builds his or her identity not just with the down times only but with the up times as well. To become sullen when life is abusive is natural, but mentally healthy people meet the negative circumstances with their own resolve to come through them. Where is God in all of this? It is He who places this resolve inside of us. So, what is the need for prayer? Should we not simply call forth the inner strength which God has already made available?

Therefore, I call upon the power of my will to go on after my loss.

I summon my innate resources to overcome the depression which seeks to keep me down. I do not need to be reminded that the cost of summoning such willpower can be stoicism and hardness. But such resolve to not let depressing situations defeat us can also help us see that good can come from the encounter with the cruelties of life. Again, what is my need to now seek God's assistance when I have already learned what Booker T. Washington called, "The advantages of disadvantages"? I have now come through the dark valley still coping to some degree. What else can God do for me?

The hospital chaplain came by almost every day my husband was there. This female minister was very caring. She once told me that faith is inherent; I told her I knew that. It is true that no person can unbelieve. Oh, we can kill within us a positive faith and replace it with a negative faith. We can lose hope and become proponents of despair. Either way we believe in something. I believe that the creator of the universe has a design for this world. I just don't believe that this creator is willing to let me have any part in modifying his design.

It is likely that many others have found their prayers answered. I know what the Old Testament Psalmist said, "I waited patiently for the Lord and he inclined unto me and heard my cry." The operative word here is "eventually." It is implied in the Psalm. Why does it always have to be the eventual, ultimate, final, concluding act of God that saves? What about the in-between, the ongoing?

I am a person of faith. I trust God. I believe God places within each one of us the means to survive the loss of those close to us. I just don't pray anymore, at least for now.

The author of *Why I Don't Pray Anymore* tells a story different from mine, but many of the feelings she writes about are not so dissimilar. I would imagine that many of the members of my congregation would not appreciate her outlook on life and faith. Her frankness makes me feel uncomfortable. At the same time, she touches some nerves which provoke thought. I can't help but wonder if Katherine read this book. Did she stop praying?

One evening about a year ago, I found Katherine in Grace's room on her knees after Grace had fallen asleep. I could not help overhearing her prayer.

"Thank you, God, for giving me this child. I hope she grows up to like me and trust me. Help me to instill in her positive feelings about herself. I'm not sure I'm up to this job, Lord, but I will try."

I came back in a few minutes to find her sitting beside our daughter's bed. I'm pretty sure she was crying.

I am a professional pray-er. It's a part of my job to share prayers in public that will guide others in their prayer life. The challenge of praying in public is the realization that other people are listening, and we sense the presence of those other ears, minds, life situations, and hopes. There is always the possibility in worship that some of the participants in the service are finding it difficult themselves to pray. True prayer comes from the heart, and there are times when our hearts are so burdened that any communication is impossible, even with God.

Katherine loved to quote Gandhi on prayer. He said, "Prayer is a confession of one's own unworthiness and weakness."

chapter eight

THIS AFTERNOON I venture out into the community for the first time. In a small town like ours it's nearly impossible for me to go anywhere without running into some of our church members. The Foodlion is my destination, and there's no disguise which will hide my identity. With a box of Rice Krispies in my hand, I stop as Judy Battle pauses in front of me, her two year old, curly haired daughter in the shopping cart.

"Reverend Brewer, how're you doing?"

"I'm okay, and you?" What an awkward interaction. Judy came to me for counseling a few months ago, marital problems.

"Things are better at home. I was so upset to hear about your wife. I've been praying for you and your family."

"Thank you, Judy."

"Whatever the circumstances we all have to eat don't we?" she asks.

"Certainly do." We're at a stalemate, the pause uncomfortable.

"You take care now," Judy says as she rolls her child and cart away.

How strange it is when people come to your office and share with you the most intimate of details about their lives but greet you with staid formality when encountered in public.

Susan is checking out at the self serve counter. I haven't seen her in a couple of days. It was three years this week when she joined our church staff. As I approach, Susan puts her items down and hugs me. The embrace lasts a few seconds; the feel of her consoling warmth remains as we part. There's no person who knew Katherine better than Susan, outside our family. In many ways she's been a part of our family.

"Can I come by and see Luke and Grace later today?" Susan asks.

"That would be great," I say. "They could use some Susan time."

"It was just three weeks ago that Katherine and I made our couponing run here. We almost cleaned the place out of toothpaste."

"I never did understand how you two saved so much money. There were things you knew about her I didn't."

"Not much," Susan says. Her eyes begin to tear up. "I'll come by your house later."

"Great."

About a year ago there was a couple in our church who began spreading the rumor that Susan might be a lesbian. They even approached one of our deacons as to what to do about it. When I heard of this, I immediately sought to head it off before it got out of hand. When I told Katherine, she was livid, and before I knew it she called the couple's home and made an appointment for us to visit. I asked her to let me handle it, but she demanded that we go together. It was the first time in our marriage she acted so boldly in a church matter.

Susan at the time was twenty-eight and single. She's not dated anyone since coming to our church that I know of; she's outgoing around others but keeps her private life very close. Susan's a natural in relating to people in the church with care and concern, earning their respect and usually their affection. As far as I knew the church family appreciated her ministry at the time, and no one had ever come to me with concerns about her. It does not take much, however, to undermine the work of a minister.

The visit to the home of the Greens was not one I was eager to make. Don and Lynette were fairly new to our congregation at the time, and I didn't know them well. They're in their mid fifties and have two college aged children. Don is a sharp dresser, buttoned down and starched. His wife is Martha Stewart stylish and prim. Their house is sound front, only a mile from ours. They welcomed us in and offered us coffee. Katherine declined, saying we could not stay long. That proved to be very prophetic.

Their living room is like a showcase from a coastal furnishings magazine. The chairs and couches are all white wicker with cushions covered in yellow and blue fabric sporting sailboats of several designs. All of the accessories are coastal, from lighthouse lamps to a boat shaped coffee table.

The home is also filled with pictures of their two children, a son and a daughter. It's evident they are proud of them.

"I've seen your children a couple of times at church. Chad and Beth, right?" I asked.

Lynette picked up a photo of the two. "Yes, Chad's a senior at State and Beth's down at UNC Wilmington, a sophomore."

"Nice looking son and daughter. You must be proud."

Katherine was silent, letting me carry the load of the small talk. I knew she was restless to get to the reason for our visit.

"Our kids have done well in school," Don said. "I won't mind when they graduate and go to work. College's not cheap."

"Yes, we're saving now. I'm counting on Pell grants, hopefully scholarships of some sorts," I said.

"Our Chad is at State on a swimming scholarship." Lynette said. "All of those years watching him at swim meets have paid off."

"Folks, let me get to the main reason for our visit tonight," I said. "I'm concerned about what you told Jim Albright the other day. You have been saying some things about Susan Martin. She's a valued member of our staff."

"I was hoping we would have a chance to discuss this with you," Don said. "We're just not comfortable with someone on our church staff with one of those lifestyles."

Lynette added, "We have known young women like her who have these tendencies."

"I'm not sure I follow," I said. "What tendencies are you talking about?"

"You know," Lynette said. "She wears her hair real short, is not married at her age, and doesn't seem to have any close male friends."

"We had a bad situation in our former church," Don said. "The pastor left his wife and announced he was gay. It was such a shock. So, I guess we're more wary of such as that now."

Katherine jumped in before I had a chance to respond. "I think you should know that Susan is a good friend of mine. She's also one of the most capable ministers I've ever met. It's important that we allow her to practice her calling without any undue intrusions into her private life. If you have any specific complaints about her work my husband will welcome you to his office to discuss them. I would personally appreciate if you could take the opportunity to get to know her and see for yourself how gifted she is in the Lord's work. I'm sure you would want the same consideration for your children if someone was making allegations about their lifestyles."

I was floored. For at least thirty seconds no one spoke. Finally, Lynette said, "I guess we should get to know her better."

Don sat forward in his chair and looked at both of us. "Our former pastor seemed to be good at his job and called by the Lord to minister. Sometimes people are adept at keeping it a secret. I'm not one for the don't ask, don't tell rule."

Lynette adds, "We just need to be careful and not appear to condone such as this in the church."

I could feel the energy of my wife warning me to not back pedal. "Don and Lynette, I would appreciate it if you would not continue with this kind of talk about Susan," I said. "Please come by my office if there are some specific matters you wish to discuss further. Katherine and I need to go home and see that our children have finished their school work. I hope we have the chance to talk more in the future."

Don stood, "Perhaps we can."

Lynette Green was visibly relieved that we were leaving; her husband, I sensed, would have liked to say more on the subject. Katherine and I stood up without any further discussion. Don accompanied us to the door and wished us good night. On the way home there was nothing to be said in the car. Katherine Brewer had spoken her peace, and I was proud of her. After our visit, the Greens backed off of their criticisms of Susan, and the subject did not surface again as far as we knew. Neither Don nor Lynette chose to talk with me further about this. As a matter of fact they have avoided me when they can, and are not all that active in the church.

***

Sergeant Tolliver of the Highway Patrol is on the phone. He's the officer who investigated Katherine's accident and called me the night she died.

"I apologize for the delay in getting your wife's belongings from the car to you. It takes a few days to finish all of the paperwork," the patrolman says.

"I understand." I say.

"Reverend Brewer, I know you have questions about your wife's wreck and I will keep you informed of anything we learn. We're treating this as a routine traffic accident and will wrap it up soon."

Routine traffic accident. How can the death of a person ever be routine? I understand what he means, however. I conduct funerals all the time which are a common part of my ministerial practice. They're not common for the people who love the deceased.

"Thank you, Sergeant," I say. "I would appreciate having any information you may run across which helps me know more of what happened."

"There were some things we found in the car which may interest you. There was a piece of paper on the console with the number 3452 on it. Perhaps you know what that represents. We also found in the floorboard a receipt from the Bojangles in New Bern for an iced tea dated the night of the wreck."

Katherine went to New Bern that night? Why? "Is there a time on the receipt?" I ask.

"It was printed at 5:53 p.m."

"Are you sure about the time?"

"Yes, I have it right here in front of me. One other thing—her car had over three quarters of a tank of gas. We didn't find a gas receipt, however. Did your wife typically use cash or a credit card to purchase fuel?"

"She always charged it and never printed a receipt."

"You may want to check with your charge card company as to when and where she last bought gas."

I thank the officer and tell him I will come and retrieve her personal items when they have completed their report. There must be some mistake with the Bojangles ticket. Katherine left our house around 5:35 the night of the accident. She could not have made it to New Bern by 5:53 as it's a forty minute drive to the outskirts of that city from our house. I suppose the time clock on the Bojangles computer could have been off. The thing is—the ticket means she went there that evening.

I go online to check the charges to our credit card. I don't know why I didn't think of this before. There was charge at a Handy Mart in Vanceboro, North Carolina, on that date, no time shown. We don't know anyone in Vanceboro. Katherine what were you doing going that way?

I'm not very experienced in detective work, but it dawned on me after some time that the Bojangles ticket in the car may have not belonged to Katherine. Did she meet someone at that restaurant who was waiting for her to arrive? I have no idea how to find out if this supposition is correct.

chapter nine

IT WAS A morning this past December when the call came. It was Katherine who answered the phone. I heard her say, "Oh no!"

Phil Maynard was calling from the hospital in Morehead City. His wife, Jillian, was in the emergency room. It was serious.

Without hesitation Katherine said, "I'm going to the Maynard house. Their boys are there with a neighbor."

The woman at the desk in the Carteret General Hospital emergency room said nothing after I told her I was Jillian Maynard's pastor. She pointed to her right to the double doors. It was not my first time visiting someone in this ward.

Phil was standing in the corridor with one hand resting on the wall. When he saw me coming, he moved towards me and shook my hand; his grip was firm and he held on for a long time. I put my other hand on his shoulder and could tell he was fighting to hold in his emotions.

His family has been in our church four years. Phil's a Marine captain and had just returned from deployment a month earlier. During his time away Jillian was a real trooper in taking the full responsibility for the home. Katherine visited with her several times during this period, and the two of them became close. She kept their boys for Jillian to have some time off one day.

"She has what they call an anomalous right coronary artery," Phil said. "They say the blood flow is cut off and she may not make it."

Jillian, at the time, was thirty-one years old, a busy mother of two little sons.

"What happened?" I asked.

Phil moved a few steps away and motioned for me to follow him. We stepped outside under the canopy entrance to the emergency room. For December it was a warm morning, in the fifties. An EMT van was just pulling away.

"She was in the kitchen fixing breakfast," Phil said. "I had the boys with me in the family room when I heard a crash. She was on the floor between the island and the sink. Her body was shaking, eyes closed with pain, and she couldn't speak. I bent down to check and see if she had hit her head. There was a small gash over her brow. I knew the cut was not the real problem."

Captain Maynard is a helicopter pilot. He flies the Cobra which requires quick responses in critical situations. It took him only a minute to assess her condition and call 911.

"Pastor, she complained last night of chest pain and took some aspirin. The doctor just told me that even if she'd been brought in last night they might not have detected the real problem."

A nurse stepped through the door and told Phil he could see her now. I waited in the hall. In a couple of minutes they took Jillian to surgery, and the two of us sat in the surgery waiting room for the next two hours. Phil spent much of the time looking out the window; twice he called to check on the boys. Jillian Maynard died at 11:45 a.m. Phil had to wait thirty minutes before he could see her. He paced the floor, cried, and asked me to pray. The brave Marine had faced the possibility of his death many times in combat; he never considered this loss before.

A while back in preparation for a sermon I looked up the word "tragedy" in a thesaurus and found the word "heartbreak" as one of the options. As I stood with Phil that day when the doctor came in and announced that Jillian did not make it, I could almost feel the tremors of a heart broken.

I don't believe that God predetermined that Jillian Maynard would have a heart anomaly at thirty-one years of age, or that my Katherine would die in a car accident at thirty-six years of age. I still cling to the belief that God cares for each one of us. I must admit that I sometimes wonder if God is looking away when our lives are upended. What I don't understand is why so many people must endure heartbreak.

On that December day after Phil was told of his wife's passing, I went by their house in the afternoon. Katherine was still there. I will never forget the scene as I entered their living room. Katherine was seated on the floor, cross-legged with three year old Michael in her lap. Five year old Gregory was beside her as they were playing with little green soldiers and toy helicopters. The boys had not yet been told their mother was not coming home.

Katherine was crying as the children moved the little figures around on the carpet. Her chin rested on top of Michael's brown hair; he could not see her tears. She looked up at me when I entered the room with a pleading expression. My wife was hurting for the children. Her telling mouth was quivering: the long thin fingers of her right hand holding a tiny American flag from the play set. On the way from the hospital I remember thinking of the pressure a pastor faces to find ways to help in a tragic situation. What I realized upon entering the Maynard home was that Katherine was also on the front lines of critical support.

As I trace back Katherine's depression, I stop on that day and wonder if something lingered from the time she spent with those children. Elizabeth Kubler-Ross in her seminal study, *On Death and Dying*, described what she called the fourth stage of dealing with death which is depression. It was as if Katherine that day took on the sadness of the Maynard family. It was as if she was entertaining the sorrow Jillian might have felt in knowing she would not see her children again. As Kubler-Ross says, "The patient is in the process of losing everything and everybody he loves." We never had an extended discussion of that day, but I could tell the experience changed her. As I look back, I wonder if she did not in some way internalize the loss and fail to get over it.

chapter ten

<hr>

BOGUE BANKS IS a twenty-five mile long island on the North Carolina coast. At one end is Fort Macon State Park; at the other end is the township of Emerald Isle. In between are the towns of Atlantic Beach, Pine Knoll Shores, Indian Beach, and Salter Path. This coastal strand is only a few blocks wide at some points. Two bridges access the island, one at Atlantic Beach, the other at Emerald Isle. One main highway runs the length of this strip of sand. Development on the Emerald Isle end of the island began in the late 1950's—Atlantic Beach and Salter Path, much earlier. The island runs east and west, unusual for those on the Atlantic coast. Live oak, cedar, yaupon, and holly trees shade the dunes, some pines as well.

Katherine was excited about moving here. She always loved the beach and enjoyed swimming and kayaking as I do. Luke was seven when we moved here, Grace almost two. One afternoon, soon after we settled in our home, we took the kids out on the sound for a family adventure. I took Luke with me on my red two-seat kayak; Katherine had Grace in her yellow one-seater, the little one on the floor between her legs. The water was calm and the breeze on the sound more sedate than normal.

We decided to paddle under the Cameron Langston Bridge which to Luke was a great thrill. The high rise span was well above us as we made our way down the channel, cars rattling the metal joints as they passed over our heads. Looking out for motorized boats and their rocking wakes, we paddled for some thirty minutes. On the other side of the bridge we pulled our colorful kayaks up on a small private beach, onto one of the many diminutive islands which dot the marshlands. Grace splashed in the water while Luke looked for shells. Terns made passes over the scrub trees behind us, and the pelicans demonstrated their aerial acrobatics diving for fish.

Katherine that day was full of energy and enthusiasm for life. "You know," she said, "This is a special place. I could get used to days like this. The children, the water, the sun; everything is so peaceful out here."

"And, we did not bring our cell phones," I add.

"Oh, if you're needed by a church member they will send the Coast Guard to find you," Katherine said.

I could see Luke trying to sneak up on a white egret wading at the end of our private getaway, without success. Grace sat at the water's edge, kicking her feet as schools of minnows darted in and out of the tide pools. The minnows thrive in the shallows and become food for the larger fish and birds. Some species of creatures spend their entire lives in the salt marshes such as: oysters, clams, and crabs. Spartina grass flourishes in this salty environment, adapting to the saline concentration through a strange osmosis. The sun barely reaches the roots of the grass and the tidal currents keep the growth free of debris. Much of the sound's natural fare has a peculiar means of surviving. Adaptation is the optimal word.

"Paul, do you ever regret entering the ministry?" Katherine asked. "I mean are there times when you wish you would have taught in college or done something else? Do you ever imagine a life different from ours now?"

This was something she had not asked before. I answered her, "I like what I do, feel it's a worthwhile vocation. You know that. There are days, weeks, when it's way too challenging. Why are you bringing this up now?"

"It's just that on a day like this, a time away like this, I wonder about what life would be like if we had chosen other paths. Life is made up of days; each day is supposed to be a microcosm of an entire life, and we are supposed to use each day to work on our lives, improve them. But out here away from all of the external pressures, I question what we are meant to be and do."

Grace was now collecting shells, former clam abodes the most abundant ones after the bi-valves have vacated their homes. She held in her hand a Periwinkle shell with ridges molded by the tides, and a couple of moon snail casings with holes drilled by predators. A marsh heron gulped air, inflated its neck sack, and thumped a mating song on the far end of our secluded getaway. Two small mud crabs captured the attention of the exploring child as she watched them scurry for cover.

Luke was tossing out crumbs from a cookie for the laughing gulls which had landed nearby. A stray heron tried to get in on the feast. Every detail of that day is still fresh in my memory.

"Do you regret your choices?" I asked.

"Sometimes," Katherine said. "We all do sometimes. You know that we are different people on different days. Remember when we discovered that we both love Walt Whitman's work. He wrote, 'I contain a multitude'. I think we are indeed many selves."

I recall that day now and wonder if my wife was trying to tell me she was not sure if she could continue being the person everyone expected her to be. I don't think she was always unhappy. I know there was a part of her which enjoyed her life but must wonder if another part of Katherine always wanted out of the roles expected of her. Indeed we are all a plurality of persons, but we also struggle for wholeness. Katherine's struggle was likely there all along. I was an idiot to have missed the signs.

***

It's Sunday morning, and I'm at home. Jim Albright and Brad Thompson, representing the deacons of our church, came by after Katherine's funeral and told me to take as long as I needed before coming back to work.

"You have to take some time off, to give yourself and your children a period of adjustment," Brad said. "Chaplain Foster will preach next Sunday. After that we will work things out."

"Susan will handle the hospital visits," Jim added. "We're fortunate to have such a capable minister as her on the staff. We know she was close to Katherine, so we will not ask her to preach this soon."

I thanked my two visitors and was surprised by what Brad said next. "Paul, a few weeks ago you led us in Bible study one Wednesday evening. We were studying Luke, chapter eight. There was one verse you emphasized that night. I remember it well: 'For there is nothing hidden that will not be disclosed and nothing concealed that will not be known or brought out in the open.' I know that you have a lot of questions about your wife's death. I believe what you said at the conclusion of that study, 'God will open us up to the truth in time.'"

I thanked Brad for this reminder. The truth—what is the truth? Did my wife hate me? Did my wife fall asleep at the wheel that evening? Why was she so unhappy as a pastor's wife, as my wife? Am I in some way responsible for her despair, her death?

I remember one day in Philosophy 201 at Campbell when we studied the "Correspondence Theory" of truth and the "Coherence Theory" of truth. The first one says that what we do or say is true if it corresponds to the facts. The second one says that a belief is true if it is part of a coherent system of beliefs. Both were circular arguments to me. Katherine understood the nuances of both propositions and tried to explain them to her denser classmate. I don't need theories today; I need facts.

Today's my second Sunday off. Luke's in the den watching television, Grace in her room playing with her dolls. I've decided to go through Katherine's clothes and give away what I can. I'm not one to put things off, even something this cheerless. Her side of the walk-in closet is filled with the dresses and pants she wore. The size twelve, black, sleeveless dress was a favorite of mine, worn by her on special occasions. Her bath robe is here, the one she was wearing that last evening when we argued before bedtime. Each item I remove provokes memories of times together. I lay all of her hanging items on the bed with care. Tomorrow I will take them to "the Hem" in Swansboro where someone may be able to use them. The now half empty walk-in closet is a bare symbol of her demise as I look at its missing symmetry, my side occupied, and her side vacant. The once crowded space has become a catacomb of discarded memories. There are so many signs of her missing presence in our house; the one-sided closet perhaps now the starkest.

Katherine was not obsessed with jewelry, but she loved to wear the pearl necklace her parents gave her and the birthstone ring I gave her on an anniversary, third I think. The dark wood jewelry box has two layers, the top displaying her rings and earrings, the bottom her necklaces and bracelets. Many of the items here she bought for herself, others gifts from me. Birthdays, anniversaries, and Christmases, are all now memories to be closed in a box and never again to be brought out to be worn by her as reminders of special times. This box I will keep for Grace.

Her white distressed dresser has six drawers, the top two filled with undergarments. The next level contains her folded tops and blouses. The purple cowl neck sweater is at the bottom of the middle set of drawers on the right. I gave it to her Christmas before last and am not sure I've ever seen her wear it. I knew purple was not her color of choice, but I liked the look and hoped she would appreciate something different.

In the bottom drawers I find the heavier sweaters, the blacks and greens she favored. Her auburn hair has always enhanced the contrasts of the black tops. I remove the neatly folded garments and feel an extra weight in the last wool sweater I place on the bed. I'm surprised to find tucked into the fold what appears to be a journal, light blue with an elastic cord around the outside. This is not the journal I've seen her write in at the kitchen table; that one I examined a couple of days after the accident; it holds many anecdotes about our children.

Sitting on the edge of the bed I remove the band and open the lined notebook. The entry on the first page astounds me:

January 6

Today I found Kyle on Facebook . I can't believe how easy it was. There are five photos, all of him outdoors with other people around. He's tall and thin, his hair a sandy brown, down to his shoulders like I remember. With my right forefinger I touched the monitor screen and traced each photo. In one picture he's wearing jeans and a white shirt, a drink of some sort in his right hand. He's as handsome as I thought he would still be, his smile broad and engaging like I recall.

He has sixty-four friends, sixty-five now. He readily accepted my request which surprised me. I thought he might not want to have anything to do with me considering our past. We exchanged email addresses, and I asked him to update me on his life. He commented on my Facebook pictures and said I look very good. We have both changed some but not that much. His sense of humor has not been lost, but I can detect a maturity in outlook which I was not expecting. I've never believed that people change significantly over their lives but could be wrong in this instance.

I hold the journal in my hands pondering what it means. A quick turning of the pages tells me there are many entries covering what appears to be two months or more. The last date on the top of the pages is the day before the accident. Closing out everything else, I spend the next hour immersed in the writings of my deceased wife. Who is Kyle?

chapter eleven

TODAY'S THE FIRST day back at school for Luke and Grace. When we pull up in front of White Oak Elementary, Grace sits still as the teacher's assistant opens the side door to let her out. We both wait as Grace looks straight ahead into the back of the front passenger seat as if she must decide if she will indeed go to school today. Finally, my stoic seven year old gets out of the car.

"I hope you have a great day, Princess Grace," I say.

This is the same send off I offer to her every school morning. Her normal response is to give me a wink of the eye and a royal wave. Today she does not turn around but slowly walks to the school entrance. With each deliberate step she appears to be making a decision as whether or not to take the next one. I pray she can make it through the day and am prepared to pick her up early if need be.

Luke insisted on riding the bus to Broad Creek Middle School. He's not said much since losing his mother, turning down any offers on my part for a father-son discussion. There was one brief time when he opened up a little.

"Dad, are we going to stay in this house now?" Luke asked me yesterday afternoon.

"Why do you ask that?" I responded.

"It's just that we might be better off in a new place."

"Do you want to move?"

"I think it might be easier. A fresh start would be good."

"Do you mean living in another town, you going to another school, my leaving the church here?"

"No, I like my school and the church. I just mean another house. I keep thinking of mom in the kitchen or being at the door when I get off the bus."

"We'll think about it and discuss it after some time has passed," I said.

"Yeah, we should not make any major decisions so soon, I guess. I heard Grandpa Claude say that."

My son has prompted me to give thought as to what would be best for my children and me at this point. We all have so many adjustments to make. Wherever we live, there will always be emptiness. I know this well from my childhood years. It's just that the math provides a harsh alteration, from four to three. It changes the formulas for everything, one parent to two children instead of the two on two ratio of our former everyday existence. Counsel is missing a second perspective; attendance at functions is singular, not double. The comfortable camaraderie of coupledom is now replaced by the loneliness of onedom.

***

Charles Lukas Brewer was born at Rex Hospital in Raleigh on a Tuesday morning at 9:38. Katherine was in labor for about three hours, an epidural keeping the experience from being any more difficult for her than it was. Much of the time I was in the delivery room supporting her, if you can call near fainting real support.

In the waiting room were Claude and Diane Rosiere as well as Charles and Margaret Brewer, all eager prospective grandparents awaiting the first grandchild. During the long morning wait, I would pop out to update them on the status. Claude spent the time reading magazines, Dad pacing and taking cigarette breaks. Diane and Mom both took turns coming back to the labor room giving Katherine pep talks.

"In the old days a father had to wait out here until someone came out to tell him the baby was born," my dad told me. My father shared this with me a couple of times that morning. "Before you were born I didn't see your mother for twelve hours. I ran out of cigarettes, and when I got back from the service station with more

Camels, one of the other men said they had come in looking for me. Your mother was very upset when she found out I was not there at the critical time."

Claude joined in the expectant father tales. "When Katherine was born, I sat in a room with two other men. One never sat down and paced the entire time. The other man cried off and on for five hours until they announced he had a daughter. He stopped his crying and proceeded to hand out cigars."

My mother and Diane did not share birthing stories. The two women were cordial to each other, but the differences in their personalities were evident when they tried to engage in conversation. Diane is so outgoing and my mother so reserved.

I was nervous for many reasons. I was anxious about what my wife was going through, jumpy over how the two sets of grandparents were getting along, and tense over the possibilities of there being something wrong with the baby. Katherine was philosophical about it all—pronouncing names like Plato and Socrates as her choice for expletives when the pain was sharpest. I suppose these fellows had caused her enough problems in the past that they were natural choices for invectives then.

A day later mother and child came home to the well equipped nursery in our apartment. That first evening of our family of three was one of the high points of my life. Luke was healthy and adorable. Katherine was radiant and filled with enthusiasm even though she was physically drained.

"Paul, I love my baby, and I love my husband," she told me that evening after the grandparents had gone home. I remember her words well; she repeated them many times over the next few days. Her mother came over and spent a number of hours caring for Luke while Katherine rested.

On a Saturday morning about three weeks after Luke was born, Katherine called to me as I was getting ready to go over to the church.

"Paul, there's something wrong with Luke's color."

We both looked at the little fellow as he slept in his crib. His skin did appear to have a blue tint. He was feeding okay, but his breathing seemed to be a little labored. He didn't have a fever, the best we could tell. As young parents we were both alarmed and tried to be calm hoping that we might be making something out of nothing. Katherine called her parents. In an hour Claude and Diane came over, and Claude advised we take the baby to the hospital.

Within an hour after we arrived back at Rex Hospital, the pediatric intern on call came in and told us they needed to keep Luke for observation. By that afternoon the little guy was bluer. A specialist was called in and tests were ordered. The result was the diagnosis that our Luke had what they called, "mitral stenosis." The mitral valve in his heart was not opening so as to let enough blood flow. They kept him overnight in order to try some medications. Katherine and I both remained at the hospital throughout the evening.

The next day a doctor explained that this is likely a congenital defect. He told us the mitral valve, or bicuspid valve, controls blood flow between the atria and ventricles of the heart. There are two flaps in this valve and it's likely that one of them was not fully opening. The good news was—the medication should solve the problem, if not, surgery later would. I asked a number of questions, Katherine was silent, tense.

A few days later Luke came home again. I went back to work; Katherine refused to leave the nursery over ten minutes at a time the first couple of days. She was filled with fear. For a week she ate and slept in the room with her son. Luke's color came back in a few days, and the follow-up visit to the pediatrician resulted in a positive prognosis. Katherine relaxed her vigilance.

Katherine, since that period, has always been skittish over Luke's health. She refused to let him try out for sports until he turned nine when he begged to be allowed to play baseball, the game he most loves. Finally, his mother gave in, but she nervously has watched for any signs of health problems. Over the years, she has often held his face in her hands and performed her own color check to see if his skin tones were normal. Luke called it his mother's "blue test".

***

Last year Luke was baptized at our church on a Sunday morning. The baptistery pool was filled on Saturday and heating element was turned on to bring the water up to "lukewarm." We thought the term funny. On that Sunday morning I tested the temperature when I arrived at the church; to my dismay the water was cold. I called our custodian and we checked out the heating unit. It wasn't working. One of the men in the church brought his propane burner to heat up buckets, and we emptied the church's hot water tank, replacing cool water with hot water in the pool. Still we did not make much headway in bringing the water temp up in the large tub in the short time we had.

There were three candidates for baptism besides my son, two young girls and one male adult. At the ten o'clock service the four of them were to walk down the steps wearing their long robes, wade into the pool, and be immersed, as is our practice. I would wait for them to move to me through the waters and lean them back so their heads would go beneath the surface. My wading boots under my white robe would protect me some from the chilly water, but my four about to be dunked future church members were in for a mild shock.

The two girls were first, and the congregation heard their audible expressions of alarm as the semi-frigid water penetrated their thin robes. Coming up out of the water they hastily made their exit up the steps to awaiting towels and dry clothes. Don Woodruff, our thirty year old former Methodist, was my third candidate. He took it like a man and left with a smile on his face, pleased to have been received into this part of the body of Christ, even with the unheated pool.

Luke was the last to enter the baptistery. He shivered as he waded towards me. I placed my right hand behind his head, had him grasp my left arm, and placed the handkerchief over his nose. Before I lowered him into the water, I said, "Charles Lukas Brewer, upon your profession of faith in Jesus Christ as your Lord and Savior, I baptize you in the name of the Father, the Son, and the Holy Spirit, Amen." Then I submerged him. Coming up, Luke looked at me and smiled. I was so proud of my son. After he dried off and changed clothes his mother gave him a big hug, and then saw his still blue lips from the cool water. She later told me that for a fleeting moment she recalled the blue baby in our home nursery those years ago.

This morning I fixed Luke a sandwich to take to school.

"Dad, we're having fish for lunch today at Broad Creek. I hate it when we have that on the menu. It makes me sick to smell it. Can I take my lunch?"

"Sure," I said. "What do you like?"

"Mom usually made peanut butter and jelly."

I realized that I had never made his school lunch before. Katherine was the one who assumed that responsibility. My son has likes and dislikes; I don't know them all. I don't know what I don't know.

chapter twelve

SERGEANT TOLLIVER IS friendly and helpful; his gray uniform is crisp like dry cleaning just taken from the platic wrapping. The black leather belt and holster are so shiny they shoot reflections from the fluorescents across the room. The officer is a large man with a pleasant smile. In some ways he reminds me of Sheriff Andy from Mayberry.

On the table in a small space behind the main office are all of the things they found in Katherine's Honda. There's her black purse, the cell phone, her shoes, her GPS which was not used that night, and the contents of the glove compartment. These have been placed in a large plastic bag with the one word label, "Brewer" written on a label. At least there could be some annotation such as: "These items once belonged to Katherine Brewer, a human being who unfortunately died in a car accident."

The patrolman seems to pick up on my feelings. "Reverend Brewer, I'm sorry we could not release these earlier, but in an accident that is not witnessed we have procedures we must go by. I know this is not easy for you."

"I understand the wait," I say.

"I'm afraid I've been involved in too many situations like this; I will never get comfortable with this part of the job. Law enforcement has many difficult aspects; this is as tough as they come."

"You said earlier that you think she may have gone to sleep at the wheel," I ask. "What makes you think that?"

"The time of night, of course. Also the path the car took. We know it travelled across the road at a thirty degree angle before it jumped the ditch. Quite often people fall asleep and the car veers at a slant like that."

"And you're sure she ran the stop sign?"

"From the angle in which she crossed the ditch, she must have come from that direction, and from the force of impact she must have maintained momentum, slowing some but not braking. My guess is she woke up upon crossing the other highway and tried to correct at the last second, too busy steering to hit the brakes."

"Thank you, sergeant, for being so thorough."

"You still don't know why she was there that late at night?"

"No."

The Bojangles ticket is among her belongings. Holding it in my hand my questions about whom she met that evening resurface, if indeed she did meet someone. Could it have been Kyle?

I thank the officer and ask him if I can see the car. He gives me directions to the garage over across the river. The garage owner is named Cliff, a ruddy faced man in his fifties. His office is cluttered with all sorts of scattered paperwork; no surface is free of dust, oil stains, and cigarette ashes. There are several vehicles in the many bays out back, all in some state of disrepair. I spot our Honda in the very back room.

"Last Friday this other fellow came by to see the car," Cliff tells me. "He said he was the father of the woman in the accident. This guy stayed for an hour or more and went over the car like a cop might. I guess he's your father-in-law then?"

"Yes, his name's Claude Rosiere."

"He asked me a bunch of questions like what I thought the speed at impact must've been. I told him I agreed with the highway patrol report that it might've been around forty. He said he had read the report but just wanted my opinion. I told him that if the collision had been anywhere other than on this corner of the bumper it would not have been fatal at that speed. I've handled a number of vehicles involved in fatalities. Most of them were high speed accidents. The thing is—this one was not as messed up as most."

Cliff points to the passenger side of the vehicle which is undamaged. "Go ahead and take all the time you want. The engine block is pretty messed up. It's totaled in my opinion."

I'm not surprised that Claude came to look at the car. He's meticulous in his detail collecting in everything he does. I guess he wants more answers, just as I do.

The front end of the car on the driver's side is mashed up; the windshield is shattered, indented about eighteen inches over the dash. Sergeant Tolliver told me that the point of impact was instrumental in the full force of the collision concentrating on the driver; the driver, of course, being Katherine.

We took many family trips in this SUV. The blue Honda is two years old but has almost thirty thousand miles on it. Opening the door to the front passenger side, I slip into the seat which is still in its normal position. I try to imagine what Katherine was thinking that night. The supposition by the highway patrol that she dozed off at the wheel is still hard for me to believe; it was not like her. It was midnight, however, and the country road likely had little traffic. Still, it's difficult to imagine my wife not stopping for the sign at the intersection. She was always such a careful driver—never had an accident in her life which was her fault.

The air bag has been removed. I've read that airbags contain sodium oxide, and it takes fifty milliseconds for one to deploy in a front end crash. The concave, left side of the windshield is pushed over the steering wheel, glass still strewn over the seat. I wonder if the air bag was any help or did it contribute to her death. I've also learned that some people each year are killed through early air bag deployment.

The seat on the driver's side has been forced back into a reclining position. This is where Katherine spent the last moments of her conscious life. I don't want to get out of the car, want to stay here beside her, hoping for some answers. I suppose I expect that by sitting here some vision will manifest itself to me; the mangled vehicle will provide clues to its last journey through some mechanical revelation. The only images which appear, however, are those from my imagination.

Out of habit I check the Honda thoroughly to see if the authorities missed anything. The many times I've traded cars this is my standard routine—look under the seats, between the seats, in the stowaway compartments. There's nothing to be found as the patrol has done a thorough job. I agree with Cliff—the car's obviously totaled.

On the way home I pull out items from her purse making a cursory inventory while negotiating the long straight stretch of highway 58 from Maysville to the bridge. Katherine always scolded me for doing things like this while driving. She would warn me that I was going to have a wreck someday while not concentrating on the road. I'm the one prone to mistakes—she was the careful one, always quoting Ephesians, "See then that you walk circumspectly, not as fools but as wise." I've never known what it means to walk circumspectly, warily, cautiously. She was always the vigilant one.

I pull a slip of paper from her purse with only a number on it—3452. I try to imagine what this refers to, a partial phone number or perhaps a house number. Her driver's license is loose in her purse, a habit she had of not returning it to her wallet. It's a good picture of her, and her wide smile causes me to think of the way she would respond when we took family photos while on vacation.

Our last vacation was to New York city in the fall. Luke was interested in looking over the city from the Empire State Building, and taking the harbor cruise to the Statue of Liberty. Grace wanted to see the Metropolitan Museum where she heard they had mummies. Katherine's desire was to see a Broadway play, specifically The Phantom of the Opera. My priorities were Yankee Stadium and Riverside Church. It was my job to coordinate the three-day-sightseeing event which was a challenge with all of the differing preferences.

We have a picture at home of the four of us in front of Grand Central Station, taken by an elderly Japanese man we prevailed upon. Katherine has the same smile as in her license photo. She always loved traveling. She had been to New York with her parents when she was in high school. Luke, the other night, pulled out the album she made of photos from both of her trips. On one page is her as a teenager in front of the Chrysler Building posing with her ponytail across her mouth like a brushy moustache. Beside it is a photo of Grace at the same spot with the same pose.

***

Crossing the bridge to Emerald Isle is always inspiring. From the top of the span the panoramic view of the sound with its many grassy islands and water passages below is awesome even after thousands of trips over. Few spots in our state are more beautiful than the sound from this vantage point. There are not many boats to be seen today as spring is taking its time in coming, and the water temp is still chilly. One small yacht is passing under the high rise and heading north up the intracoastal waterway, likely an early return from Florida.

The bridge was completed in 1971 and became a major contributor to development on this end of the island. From the top, in the distance, one can see all the way to the channel which leads to the inlet. The inlet between the island and the mainland community of Swansboro has constantly changed over the years causing the "point" of the island to migrate. Even with a shifting channel, the inlet is a popular passage to the ocean for recreational boaters.

Back at home I call Claude in Raleigh.

"I just got back from New Bern and looking at the Honda," I say. "I understand you spent some time at the garage yourself."

"Yes, there were some questions I had about the accident. Still find it hard to believe that Katherine went to sleep behind the wheel," Claude says.

"That has bothered me too."

"I asked the garage owner if he found any mechanical problems such as worn brakes. He told me he checked them and found nothing wrong."

"Cliff seems to know what he's doing."

"You've not told me where you think she went that evening," Claude says. "I know you have said she did not tell you where she was going, but do you have any guesses?"

"I wish I had more clues, but I don't. Just like you, I need some resolution. They did find a receipt from a fast food place in New

Bern in her car, and I found she stopped for gas that evening in Vanceboro. I have no idea why she was traveling in that direction."

Claude does not speak for a few seconds, clears his voice and says, "Paul, I've tried to not pry. I know it's not easy sharing your marital issues with an in-law, but perhaps this is a time when we can be of help to each other."

After a long pause I respond, "Yes, sir, I think we need to have a talk. There are some things you have a right to know."

"What if I come down tomorrow and we spend some time together. Diane wants to check on the kids. You and I can go over what we've learned."

I agree. "Claude, do you know of someone named Kyle?"

His hesitation is disturbing. Finally, he says, "Let me answer that question when I come down."

He obviously knows who Kyle is. Why don't I know? Katherine was my wife for fifteen years. There should not have been secrets. The words of Frost come to mind, "We dance round in a ring and suppose, but the secret sits in the middle and knows." I'm not sure what Frost intended; I can't stand not knowing.

Claude and Diane have been thoughtful in-laws. They've been available to care for our children when needed and have cautiously managed not to be obtrusive at other times. Not having any other children besides Katherine they built their lives around her when she was growing up. I know it's been hard for them to keep some distance in these years since we were married. Now they have lost their only child and need to be close to their grandchildren.

Claude Rosiere came to this country when he was in college. He grew up in southern France but left to further his education at Penn State. After college he went to work for IBM as an electrical engineer and moved to Raleigh after the company opened its facility in the Research Triangle Park. Katherine adored her father and found his penchant for details charming. He's always been hard to ruffle. Claude is conservative in both politics and lifestyle, frugal and yet generous.

Diane Rosiere grew up in the western part of the state and met Claude at IBM where she worked as a secretary. She's outgoing and has pushed Claude into becoming more sociable. Katherine and her mother were close, but there was always a kind of resistance by the daughter against her mother's overbearing need for control. Diane's very moody, certainly not predictable, and carries the stubborn independence of her ancestors' mountain heritage.

It's time for her parents to know about her depression. It's time for them to share with me what I don't know about their daughter.

The Rosiere house in Raleigh is a photo gallery of images of Katherine. In every room there are pictures of her growing up. Once, while visiting there, I took a few minutes to count the wall-mounted photos of her; I came up with thirty-two. In addition to the ones displayed, there are dozens of albums which are devoted to her childhood. As an only child, she was the recipient of the full attention of her parents.

My mind's crowded with questions. How does the world's most careful driver run a stop sign, whatever time of day or night? Did she meet someone at the Bojangles in New Bern? What does the number 3452 refer to? Who is Kyle? Where did she spend the six and a half hours that evening? Why do people allow love to fade? How can a reasonably intelligent person not recognize he has been so inconsiderate?

I do know this—a person can't stay sane without answers to questions that matter. I think it was Emerson who said, "Knowledge is knowing that we cannot know." I say to old Ralph Waldo, "I can't live with what I cannot know."

Accidental death or not—this is a crime against my sanity, and I must follow the clues to wherever they lead in order to close the case and to gain piece of mind.

I sense that Claude will not rest until he can determine the full story. It's good to have a partner in my quest. My emotional investment is less than that of her parents simply because of years devoted. How many parents reluctantly give their children up to a spouse with anxieties as to how their son or daughter will be treated by their mate? From my experience as a pastor, all too often any trust is misplaced. I was assigned with the well-being of Katherine Rosiere

Brewer. My responsibilities are not met until I provide some answers to her parents as to why I let their daughter die.

***

In our bedroom, my bedroom now, I lay out the items collected from her Honda on the top of her dresser. The piece of paper with the number on it remains a mystery. Three credit cards and her Lowe's grocery allegiance card are in the burgundy wallet. Photos of Luke and Grace abound, and the last family portrait from the church directory is a blatant reminder of the hole which now exists in the Brewer family.

Still in her dresser drawer is the journal. It beckons me, and the pull is strong to explore the intimacies it holds of the mindset of my Katherine. I open it again and begin to read.

January 8

Got an email from Kyle today. He's curious about my life at present. I'm not sure what to tell him. Every other day I try to find the courage to take a break from being a wife and mother, but the thought of shattering our family and hurting the children always forces me to accept my situation.

My situation—that's what I've come to call it. I'm thirty six years old and do not have a career. My whole identity is that of a pastor's wife and mother. This is not enough! I'm educated, talented, and capable. I want Paul to be able to minister well, but why does it always have to be me who sacrifices my wants so he can be the pastor that everyone looks up to?

Do I tell Kyle or anyone else about my suffocating in this situation? I know that anyone in the church would think of me as selfish and spoiled if I were to dare unveil my true feelings. I am Katherine Brewer, the wonderful helpmate to Paul Brewer, the super-pastor. We have the perfect family, just what everyone expects.

This is not that new to me. In the last few months Katherine has intimated her discontent in many ways. I've tried to understand what she's going through but have found it hard to accept she was this unhappy. My take has been that she was going through a passage in her life, a temporary dissatisfaction, something that would pass. Finding her secret journal has magnified my confusion over her melancholy.

In my home library there's a book I've used to help me in my counseling. It's called *Counseling the Depressed* and written by Archibald Hart. I open it again this evening and reread a line I've marked, "Often caused by a combination of physical and psychological influences, depression is like a snarled rope, difficult to untangle and holding thousands of people in a bind of despair and hopelessness."

One thought perplexes me this evening—is it possible that Katherine intentionally drove through that stop sign? I convince myself that she would never do that. Yet, I'm haunted this evening by a quote I remember from Tennessee Williams, "There comes a time when you look into the mirror and you realize that what you see is all that you will ever be. And then you accept it. Or you kill yourself. Or you stop looking in mirrors."

chapter thirteen

CLAUDE AND DIANE arrived about 1:00 today. The children are still at school. We're seated at the round kitchen table with coffee. I've just told them about the journal and the mention of her finding Kyle on Facebook.

"She was in her first semester of college at Meredith when she met Kyle. He was a freshman at N.C. State," Claude begins. "Diane and I didn't know anything about him until after they had been dating for a couple of months, and she asked if she could invite him for Thanksgiving."

"I think they met at a fraternity mixer soon after school started," Diane says. "Kyle was from little Washington. His father owned a car parts dealership there."

Claude continues, "We did our best to let Katherine experience college life as if she had moved three hundred miles away. It was her choice to attend Meredith, only a few miles from our house. Moving her into the dorm was my first realization that my daughter was no longer under our watchful eyes."

Diane now has tears in her eyes. "She would call me several times a week, but I was determined to let her make the contacts, give her that freedom. She didn't mention Kyle or tell me anything about her social life those first two months. Katherine would talk about her suite-mates and her classes in detail."

The combined effort of Claude and Diane is as if the two have rehearsed how they would share this story. I'm mesmerized by the flow of this information which is all new to me; I'm reluctant to interfere with their account.

"We were, of course, eager to meet this boy she was interested in and welcomed him to our home in November." Claude's slight French accent adds to the drama of his storytelling. "I could tell that the young man was not very comfortable in the setting, understandably. I had to caution Diane not to ask too many questions. I remember being surprised by how uninteresting he seemed to me. Why Katherine liked him was not easy to tell. She's always been so intent on her studies. The boy appeared to be a lightweight, not in her league."

"But he was good looking," Diane adds. "He had long hair and a surfer's tan."

"By Christmas it was over," Claude says. "There was no mention of Kyle when she came home those two weeks between semesters. We asked about him, and Katherine announced that she and Kyle had broken up. Paul, I want you to be prepared now for the hard part. I assume she never told you about this."

'She never told me about any of this. I've never heard of Kyle. What's the hard part?"

"We've not thought about any of this in recent years. We've been so happy over her marriage to you," Diane says.

"In light of her journal and everything else, Diane and I feel you need to know the whole story." Claude gets up from the table and walks over to the window, looks out at the street for a minute, and then continues, "About two months into the second semester we received a call from a counselor at Meredith, actually a psychologist, asking if one of us could come by and discuss the treatment for our daughter. The idea that Katherine was seeing a psychologist was a shock. I agreed to meet Dr. Helen Robbins at her office on the campus. When I arrived Katherine was seated in the waiting room with her head down. I asked her what this was all about and she asked me to wait until we went into Dr. Robbins' office."

Claude returns to the table and sits facing me. He runs his hand through his wavy gray hair and straightens his wire rim glasses. "The psychologist was young, in her thirties perhaps. In one corner of her office there were three chairs placed around a small table. She invited

Katherine and me to sit across from her." Claude looks at Diane, and she nods for him to continue.

"Without much preliminary talk Dr. Robbins began by saying, 'Katherine has something she wants me to tell you. I've agreed that it will be easier on us if we begin with my explaining the situation. Katherine has been coming to see me for help in dealing with a traumatic situation in her life. She tells me that you and your wife met Kyle Edwards at Thanksgiving. What you do not know is that Kyle broke off the relationship soon after that, in mid December, and Katherine has come to me for guidance in handling the pain of that breakup.'"

Claude goes on, "I looked over at Katherine who was focused on the counselor and would not make eye contact with me."

"That must have been very difficult for you and Katherine, for her to let you know she was in therapy," I say.

"It was," Claude continues. "I always thought my daughter was emotionally strong. In the counseling center that day I saw another side of Katherine, a fragility I'd not witnessed before. The worst part was still to come. Dr. Robbins explained to me that there was something else I needed to know and that she had advised Katherine to write it out as this would make it easier on all. Katherine handed to me a single piece of paper on which was a paragraph in her neat printing. In a few sentences I was informed that Katherine had had a miscarriage in December. She never told Kyle she was pregnant; only her suite-mates knew about it. She was afraid to tell us and was struggling to decide what to do before the miscarriage, even considering abortion."

I look at Claude and Diane as we sit in silence for what must be a minute. I try to understand why my wife never told me this story herself. I find myself hurting for Katherine those many years ago. It must have been awful telling her parents about the pregnancy and the miscarriage.

"Did Katherine ever talk with either of you about what happened?" I ask.

Diane answers, "not at that time. About two months later she came home one weekend. We were in the kitchen making sandwiches when she said out of the blue, 'Mom, I'm so sorry.' That's all she could get out before her tears started. I didn't want to push her to talk about it. After a few minutes she told me she was so regretful to have disappointed us that way."

"I think a part of her decision to transfer to Campbell was to get a fresh start. Her entire second year at Meredith she chose not to date any," Claude says.

"The Katherine I first met was a very self-assured person. I've never seen any hint of emotional problems until recently." Claude and Diane are attentive as I share this. "A couple months ago she told me she wanted to take a break from our marriage. I just found the private journal she kept. In it, as I told you, she mentions Kyle."

"I'm sorry, Paul," Claude says. "I always thought she must have told you about Kyle and the miscarriage."

"I suppose it was something she tried to forget. She would never even discuss with me her views on abortion."

***

I fell in love with Katherine Rosiere on our second date. We spent that day together at a local park. She brought along a little book called *The Promise of Teilhard* for us to read together. Katherine said that Teilhard was our connection, our common philosopher. We ate lunch, read quotes from the Frenchman, and shared our first kiss.

"The world in itself is not reasonable." Katherine loved this quote and we debated the idea that the world longs for clarity. She was so confident in her philosophical positions. She was so positive. At just twenty years of age she held more inner resolve than most people possess in their forties, if then. I loved her mind, her great interest in all things theoretical.

"I want to teach philosophy in college," she said one day while we were studying in the library.

"You should," I said.

"Seriously, that's my goal. I think I will come into each class and assume the role of Socrates, Spencer, or Heidegger, a different philosopher each day. I will stay in character for the entire class and engage the students to interact with me as that thinker."

Somehow that plan was pushed aside when she became the wife of a mnister and pregnant with her first child. I know she sacrificed much in order to commit herself to me, and our family.

Over the years of our marriage she dedicated herself to the routine tasks of life: parenting, being a supportive wife, and taking care of the house. Philosophy was thrust further into the background, but she never lost her curiosity of thought and was an avid reader. I now know that Katherine regretted she had abandoned her calling to be a teacher of philosophy. She did secure a part time job a few years ago at an independent bookstore at the beach near our church. In those fifteen or so hours a week, she thrived in a world of words and people who love words.

It was a few weeks ago that she first hit me with her intense feeling of unhappiness. Claude and Diane had come for a weekend visit. It was a typical time together, eating out, plenty of attention given to Luke and Grace, and disagreements over politics as Claude's conservatism always caused his daughter to argue her differing outlook. There seemed to be nothing out of the ordinary until her parents left.

That evening, after we were alone, Katherine said without any warning, "Paul, I don't think I can continue to live this life."

I looked at her to see if she was kidding. She looked at me with tears in her eyes.

"What do mean—this life?" I asked.

"I mean us, me in this marriage."

I remember feeling as if the breath had been pounded out of me. The kids had gone to bed. The two of us were watching television in the den. She looked straight at me as I fixed my eyes on a place on the floor.

"This is not working for me," Katherine said. "I'm almost forty years old and have little to show for my life that has meaning."

"You have children." I said. "You have a family. You have your church work in the food pantry. You have an outlet at the bookstore. You have it pretty easy."

"Easy. I have it easy. I'm responsible for three other people who depend on me for almost every detail of their lives. And what do I get in return, certainly little thanks and, for sure, little praise. I need a break from all of this."

"You can't just take a break. Life doesn't work that way. You especially can't take a break from being a mother."

"Why not?"

"Because they count on you." This time my voice is raised.

"Does it not matter what I want?" she asked. Her voice is now quivering.

"What we want is not always possible," I said, trying to calm down.

"You get pretty much what you want. You have your calling, and you receive constant strokes from the congregation. You have your perfect family, your compliant wife."

"And, I have all of the pressures which go with being a pastor."

"Yes, and you expect me to listen to all of your grumblings about church members and feel sorry for you every time the pressure becomes too much. You want me to be there for you. When are you there for me?"

That question gave me pause. I had no automatic response because I'd never entertained the subject before. I remember feeling like a debater without a cue card to prompt my comeback, no ammunition to use as a volley in return. I searched my memory for recent occasions in which I had been the self-sacrificing husband and came up empty-minded.

With feeble force I said, "I've always tried to listen when you needed to talk about something serious."

"Perhaps you have me confused with one of your counselees. My needs, for years, have been the lowest of your priorities."

"Where's all of this coming from?" I asked. "What have I done to make you so upset?"

"It's not what you've done. It's what you haven't done. You just don't get it do you?"

"Don't get what?"

"That I'm unhappy and unfulfilled. If you were not so self-centered, you would have gotten a clue."

She listed several times I'd not been sensitive to her needs. At this point I left the room in frustration. Who was the person I just encountered in there? The remainder of the evening was spent preparing a defense in my mind for my record as a husband. I hoped for some reprieve in which I was granted more time to build my case, even modify my profile. I wished that Katherine would come to her senses and tell me that the charges had been dropped, any interest in leaving having passed like a cloud that moves on out of sight.

I slept little that evening on the couch in the den. I couldn't stop thinking about her indictment. I tried to imagine what my life would be like without her. Did she mean that she wanted to leave the kids with me and go off somewhere? How far would she go? Would she eventually come back for the children? What would it do to the children for her to leave them?

The next morning a different Katherine was in the kitchen fixing breakfast. She was no longer antagonistic, calm and cool instead. She smiled at me, handed me a glass of juice, and said, "I'm better now." What did that mean? I was afraid to ask, not wanting to provoke another tirade, especially in front of the children. Later she said, "I'm not going anywhere." I was relieved to hear that but wondered when the next explosion might occur.

chapter fourteen

CLAUDE AND DIANE have gone back to Raleigh this morning. The children are at school. It's time for me to go back to work. Carla Payne, our church secretary, and Susan, our associate pastor, greet me with warm welcomes. The three of us sit down in my office to allow them to brief me on what I've missed over the last two plus weeks.

We have two church members in the hospital and there's a counseling situation Susan is handling. I can see that Carla's notepad is full. In her mid forties, intelligent, and self confident, she's one of those people skilled in logistics. I'm sure she could keep the church running for a year without my being around but seems very thankful I'm back. Some years ago she was an administrative secretary for a law firm, now applies those skills to her church job, ardent in keeping confidences.

"Paul, are you sure this is not too soon for you to jump into all of this?" Carla asks.

"Probably," I reply. "I've advised myself to take more time. But myself rarely pays attention to my advice. Anyway, I'm here, so let's see what we can get done."

Susan's looking at me with what I would call benevolent wisdom; her dark eyes penetrating. Easy going and yet enthusiastic, she has a full array of people skills. Her job description calls for her to be responsible for our youth and children's ministries, but she has endeared herself to our seniors with her willingness to be a part of their special events.

"Before we get to church matters there's something I need to get out of the way," I say. Both of you knew that Katherine and I were having some problems in our marriage. I didn't talk about it with either of you because I just couldn't. But you both knew. Susan, Katherine told me that she had confided in you, and I'm sure, Carla, you picked up on the conflict. You were both here the day we argued in my office. Perhaps there will come a time when I can share with you what we were going through. I'm not ready yet."

Both of my staff members nod in agreement.

"What about the children?" Susan asks. "Is there something we can do to help with Luke and Grace?"

"My in-laws are going to come back in a few days and stay for at least a month until we can get our family routine worked out. They're getting Luke's room, and he's taking over the den; camping in he calls it."

"That sounds like a good plan," Carla says. "This means I don't have to keep on arranging meals on wheels for you?"

"Sorry to take that fun away from you. Diane's an excellent cook and is looking forward to caring for the kids. Now, what do you two need from me in the way of pastoral duties?"

Both try to speak at the same time, but Susan finally says, "You can handle Agnes."

Agnes Stone is one of those people who craves attention and has chosen the church office as her destination of choice when she wants to be heard. She has a dozen physical ailments and finds a way to mention them all in a conversation. Most any visit by Agnes lasts an hour, and they've become a part of our weekly schedule.

"Thank you for including me in the Agnes duty. I think your sympathy for me has ended too soon," I say.

"We're just trying to let you know that you're missed around here," Carla says.

"Right," I say.

The staff meeting ends with hugs. I wonder if these two women think I'm going to be able to handle all that's before me. On two occasions recently Carla has seen examples of the tension in my marriage. Once Katherine called the church office upset with me, and Carla reluctantly told me of the call after I came back in. Katherine wanted to know where I was. Carla told her I was visiting at the hospital. My wife unloaded on the surprised secretary that I had promised to take my son to his dental appointment and how I could not be counted on in my home responsibilities.

"Paul, I didn't know what to say," Carla told me. "She was very angry and used a tone I haven't heard before from her."

It was only a month ago when Katherine came by the office to remind me that Grace had a school program that evening to which the parents were invited. I told her I had a church finance committee meeting at seven-thirty. I was caught off guard when Katherine raised her voice. "You always let church matters come before your family."

My office door was open. Our office area is very compact.

My first reaction was embarrassment; anyone in the building could have heard my wife's comments. It was an important finance committee meeting and the school function was a PTO program where Grace was singing in a short play. I had remembered Grace's play but had not made the effort to reschedule the committee meeting.

"Why is it that you're willing to let me assume all of the parenting responsibilities?" Katherine asked. "You have known about the PTO meeting for over two weeks. Your priorities are all screwed up. When are you going to learn that your children pass this way but once and missing these key events hurts them?"

Katherine stormed out of the church, and I just sat there considering her accusation. I thought she overreacted. I knew she was right about my giving church matters precedence over family matters on some occasions. When I got home that evening I apologized to Grace for my not being there. She hugged me and said, "That's okay, Daddy."

***

Two hospital visits in the afternoon and then pick up the kids from school rounds out my day's schedule. Once again dinner is provided by one of the church members. Tonight it's meatloaf, mashed potatoes, and chocolate cake. At six the door bell rings and Thelma

Covington, our Jimmy Buffet loving distant cousin, stands there with a smile and an arm full of foil covered containers.

She puts the food on the counter in the kitchen, and says, "I'll bet you this meal is as good as any you've had. Everyone in the church knows that I'm a great cook."

"Your reputation is not to be denied," I say. "Would you like to stay and eat with us?"

"I've already eaten. I'm meeting some of my Parrot Head Club members for a night of dancing. Some say that I'm as good a dancer as a cook."

"A girl of many talents," I say.

"A seventy-two year old accomplished woman. I will bet you that even Diane can't fix a meal any better than this." Thelma leaves on that note.

The children and I sit at the table. The meatloaf is fantastic. Luke has two large servings. Grace only eats potatoes and cake. For them there is no mommy cooking dinner, no mommy calling them to the table, no mommy there to talk about their day.

Grace shares with us how a boy in her class tripped at lunch and his tray flew across the room. "It was both funny and pitiful. His name's Roger, and he does things like this all the time. He's even clumsier than Luke."

"Who says I'm clumsy?" Luke says. "I'm much more coordinated than you, Miss Prissy."

"Hey, guys," I say, "let's curb the name calling."

"How was your baseball practice today?" I ask Luke.

"The coach wants me to play the outfield. I told him I like second base better. He said my arm was too strong for second base."

"Is the team going to be good?"

"We have some good bats. Our fielding is not so great."

"That's because you're such a klutz," Grace says.

"I'm not a klutz."

"Come on now, enough of that," I say.

I am kind of enjoying this little exchange. It's a sign that things are getting back to normal to some degree.

***

Pierre Teilhard De Chardin was a Jesuit priest and paleontologist who received a doctorate in geology. His main interest in life was to demonstrate that science and religion could comfortably coexist. He was in a unique position to bridge the gap because of his training in both the religious and the scientific fields.

Teilhard had an amazing career. Early on he became a Jesuit novitiate, then taught physics and chemistry in Cairo, Egypt. He studied theology in Hastings, England. During WWI he served as a stretcher bearer for the Eighth Moroccan Rifles and received the Legion of Honour for his bravery. He then went on to study geology and zoology at the Sorbonne in France. For much of twenty years Teilhard served the church in China, and was a part of the team which discovered the Peking Man, a major archaeological find.

What Katherine found so fascinating was Teilhard's idea that progress can never be reversed. He believed, "If a thing is possible, it will be realized." She once told me that Teilhard was well ahead of the preachers today who call themselves "possibility thinkers." My wife was filled with what is possible in our lives until recently. On her Facebook page she had a quote from Teilhard, "The future is more beautiful than all the pasts." It was the quote we shared those many years ago, and has always guided my outlook as well as hers, I thought. It's so hard for me to understand how she could ever have let that spirit die. But, of course, she had no choice. She was consumed by depression.

chapter fifteen

I REMEMBER FEELING the pain in my forehead and my mother yelling out, "Karen!" When I recovered from the initial shock of my trauma, I saw Matt bent over in his car seat, the back of the seat facing the ceiling of our Malibu. On the other side of him the window was shattered and my sister's head and shoulders rested on the edge of Matt's upended protective seat, her arms still clutching the brown bear. Then we were stopped, lodged up against the black truck on the guardrail. My mother was in the floorboard moaning, my father trying to free himself from his seat belt. Matt was still crying, louder now. Karen wasn't moving.

Our mid-size car was no match in weight against the twenty-four foot U-Haul. The highway was littered with dozens of wrecked vehicles. I later learned that there were forty-six different cars, trucks, and vans in the final pile-up, and one Greyhound bus as well. The article in the Raleigh paper, which my mother kept, said there were fifty-five people with injuries, eighteen serious, and three deaths. One of those who died was my sister Karen; she suffered a broken neck.

The rain was slowing, and the highway full of emergency vehicles—fire trucks, ambulances, and police cars. People were standing, leaning on cars, or sitting on the pavement. My dad was holding my mom as the medical personnel put my sister in the back of a green and white EMT truck on a bed covered with a white sheet. I held on to little Matt, his arm in a sling. My mother was sobbing into my dad's shoulder. His head was cut and had been bandaged by a young man in uniform.

The U-Haul was a few feet away; its driver, blood on his collar, was talking to a police officer. As far as I could see up ahead there were damaged cars and trucks. An older man came up to my dad and put his hand on his shoulder. He began to pray, and I could see he was wearing a clergy collar. My mother put her hand on the top of my dad's head as he bent forward. I looked at the body of my sister in the ambulance and wondered if our family would ever be okay again.

It was the middle of the day, and far back up the road I could see a line of vehicles all motionless and in order like a funeral precession waiting for a lead car. Matt and I still stood by our damaged Malibu. A boy about my age was sitting in the open door of a truck trying to fix his broken glasses, his left shoe missing. Other children were looking out of car and van windows, some about the age of my sister. I remember thinking that if they were not hurt—why was my sister dead?

In a couple of minutes my father left my mother in the care of the priest and a female medic and walked over to my brother and me. He bent down on one knee, his head bandage stained with blood. He just looked at us and patted our heads. I had never seen my father this sad before. I wanted to tell him it would be alright, but I knew it would not be. He told us to be brave, that he had to help Mom who was still standing at the back of the open ambulance door. Matt held my hand with his good arm and looked up at me as though I could fix it all.

Matt and I sat together on a rain jacket laid out on the wet pavement with another slicker protecting us from the persistent light drizzle. Dozens of people scurried about seeing to the wounded. There seemed to be no end to the pandemonium, and I wondered if we would still be sitting there at dark. Within a few minutes my mother, father, brother, and I were in a van winding our way back up the highway through countless stopped vehicles each spared from the turmoil ahead on the highway by some tiny anomaly in the space/time equilibrium.

Matt rested his head on my mother's lap as the van proceeded up the road against the grain of the traffic. She would turn to look at me in the seat behind her. My father sat beside me holding the teddy bear which had belonged to Karen. He patted the stuffed animal as though to soothe it.

I could only think of my sister alone in the ambulance, no parent, sibling, or special bear to keep her company.

Two hours earlier we had taken a break at a rest stop and Karen played tag with Matt in the thick grass under the tall trees that surrounded the buildings. She was always so agile and quick. Her soccer skills were so good that she made all-stars in her peewee league. She was the best athlete in our family and was my dad's best hope for a sports star. All of his expectations would now rest on his two sons.

The driver of the van was a big man who wore a Yankees cap with a bent brim. He didn't speak but kept looking in his rear-view mirror at his passengers: my parents, my brother, and me. I'm sure I was the only one who saw his intermittent glances which I assumed were the result of his curiosity as to the story of this family which had suffered a horrible tragedy an hour earlier. I could tell right then that this was to be our plight for many months to come—we would become the oddity, a family who had undergone a terrible ordeal, people to pity.

chapter sixteen

THE POET GOETHE once said, "Love is an ideal thing, marriage a real thing; confusion of the real and the ideal never goes unpunished." I'm well aware of that confusion. I thought Katherine and I had developed a reasonable set of expectations as to what marriage involved. I thought we loved each other, but both knew that love must be translated into practical acts of consideration which keep the realities of life from burying the love in a laundry hamper of mundane daily details.

I suppose I was not as caring as I thought I was. The thing that vexes me most is that I don't have the opportunity to repent of my transgressions against her. Since she first told me she wanted to leave, I poured my thoughts into how I could make the changes needed to show her that she was my first priority. Obviously, in those weeks before the accident I didn't make much progress in that attempt.

There's an old joke about a husband and wife who have been married for twenty-five years. The husband's a very reserved farmer who has trouble showing his wife any affection. One day she blurts out, "Why don't you ever tell me you love me?" Her husband thinks about her question for a minute or longer and then responds, "When we were first married I told you I loved you; if I ever change my mind I'll let you know."

That's both funny and ridiculous. People need more reassurance than that, more words of caring. But words were not the issue with Katherine. I told her I loved her often. Her complaint was that I put my church work ahead of family in my consideration. She certainly didn't intend this outcome, but I'm now forced to give parenting a higher priority.

I saw that Luke got on his school bus this morning, took Grace to White Oak Elementary, and now have returned home to get ready for work. For the last two weeks I've not even thought of taking my allergy medicine, but today my congestion is at a critical level. In our bathroom there's a linen closet behind the door with a top shelf devoted to medicine bottles and first aid supplies. My allergy pills are on the front right as they have been since we moved into this house five years ago. Behind them is the bottle of diet pills which belonged to Katherine. I've been through all of her clothes, shoes, and jewelry. It never occurred to me to sort through the items on this shelf which belonged to her. Soon the bathroom counter is covered with an assortment of bottles, tubes, and boxes. At the very back of this shelf, almost at the full extension of my reach, I remove one final bottle. On the label at the top is typed: "Katherine Brewer", below that the word "Lexapro", and at the bottom is "Dr. R. Rosenblum."

I'm not sure what Lexapro is, and I've never heard of Doctor Rosenblum. The prescription was written on January third of this year, over two months ago. It has been refilled once and there are two pills left in the bottle. In the den I open the laptop and google Lexapro. It's prescribed for depression, increases serotonin production in the brain which influences mood. The article explains that imbalances in neurotransmitters play a role in many forms of depression. Serotonin is a neurotransmitter. The side effects are drowsiness, fatigue, and insomnia.

Without telling me, Katherine saw a doctor, perhaps a psychiatrist, and was on medication for depression. This would explain some of her behavior these last few months. I'm not an expert on depression, but I've read a good deal about it and have been asked to help a number of people going through this illness. Most of the time, after a few counseling sessions, I've referred people to those with more expertise. I'm aware that certain endogenous forms of depression have a bio-chemical cause and are treated with antidepressants.

Why did I not see she was in this much pain? One evening in February she just started crying at the dinner table and locked herself in the bedroom for the remainder of the night. My attempts to get her to let me come in were futile, so I slept on the couch. Then there was the night she told me she hated me. How could I be so stupid to miss the signs of her real distress?

Dr. Ronald Rosenblum's office is in a medical park in Jacksonville, a thirty minute drive from my home on the island. Jacksonville's a military town, home to Camp Lejeune, a large Marine base. Highway 24 to Jacksonville is a transitional passage from a tourist oriented community to a military oriented community. Once past Swansboro the road opens up to a selection of mobile home parks and housing developments mostly occupied by Marine families. Coming into the small city the median in the four lane highway is lined with Bradford pear trees; soon the view out the right is of tattoo parlors, military surplus stores, and auto parts places. The auto dealerships are numerous as the young people in the Corps spend their pay on new and used cars. To the left of the highway into Jacksonville the base is the only thing visible as it contains all of the vast acreage from 24 to the waterway and ocean several miles away.

The receptionist is reticent about allowing me to speak to the doctor after I tell her that my wife who recently died was a patient here. The young woman has obviously been trained to filter all requests to see the psychiatrists.

"Listen," I say. "I lost my wife in a horrible automobile accident, and Dr. Rosenblum prescribed medication for her. I need to know if the medication could have caused her to lose control at the wheel." I hand her the bottle.

After looking at the label, she excuses herself and goes through a door behind her desk. In a minute a tall slender man in his fifties appears. "I am Ronald Rosenblum," he announces. "You are Katherine Brewer's husband?"

"Yes, Doctor. I found this morning the Lexapro you prescribed for my wife. I need to ask you a few questions."

"Reverend Brewer, I was so sorry to hear about your loss. I think we should talk. If you will give me ten minutes I can meet with you. I'm on a phone consultation at this time."

I take a seat in a chair across from the receptionist. The walls of the room are covered with pictures of languid landscapes and a row of photographs of the office staff. There appear to be three doctors in the practice. Two other people are seated in the room, a young woman reading a Time magazine, and an older man who is dozing.

My curiosity comes into play as I imagine why these two are here. The young woman may be working her way through a marriage breakup. The older man could be suffering from the effects of retirement and loss of identity. Of course, there are any numbers of reasons why someone may seek counseling. Who would ever guess my purpose in seeing the psychiatrist today?

I decided earlier to call into my office and let Carla know that I needed to go somewhere this morning and would not be at the church until this afternoon. Everyone in the church is willing to cut me some slack now. I know there will come a time when I will need to assume my full duties.

We sit in the psychiatrist's waiting room, the three of us; each anticipating our opportunity to impart our special situations to a doctor. This is where my wife shared intimate details of her life, our life. What did she say about me? Does Dr. Rosenblum think of me as a jerk that had no concern for his wife's well being? Did she shed tears in the very chair in which I'm seated?

After a few minutes I'm ushered into the room where Katherine told a stranger the problems in our marriage. The slim doctor stands by his desk. "Reverend Brewer, your wife came to see me for several appointments. Obviously, the doctor-client privilege is no longer binding now that she has passed away, but it would be unprofessional of me to go into detail over the matters she and I discussed until you and I have established some rapport."

"I understand that," I say. "I'm curious over what she shared with you, but my immediate concern is to make sense of what happened the evening of her death. She ran a stop sign and hit a tree. The highway patrol assumes she fell asleep. I need to know if the medication she was on could have led to drowsiness. Do you think there is any possibility she could have wanted to harm herself?"

Dr. Rosenblum does not respond but looks down at his desk. It's clear that he's not one to speak without much thought. After perhaps fifteen seconds he moves toward me a foot or two. "Your wife was experiencing depression. Her medication does have side effects—in some instances drowsiness is one of them. I do not believe she was suicidal but cannot be certain about that. This is the best I can do to answer your questions for now. Depression is a very complicated matter, and it would be difficult for anyone to know all of what was on her mind that evening."

I can appreciate the psychiatrist's hesitancy to speculate further. He seems to be a very thoughtful man, one who refrains from rash analysis.

"Dr. Rosenblum, did my wife tell you she wanted to leave me?"

The doctor looks at me for a few seconds, searching for the most helpful answer to my plea, I assume. "Reverend Brewer, your wife was struggling with many emotions. She was confused as to how she felt about you, her situation, and her future. What she wanted to do was seek ways to feel better about herself. I think you and I need to sit down for a longer period and talk."

I'm not eager to postpone my search for answers but do not object to his suggestion. We set a time for us to meet in a few days. I can see that he needs to give serious thought as to how to help a distraught husband who has just lost his wife under unusual circumstances.

***

It was a day soon after I became pastor here that Katherine came by the church office to meet me for lunch. We had decided to go over to Swansboro to Yana's, a popular eating place with a 1950's theme. She had waited in the main church office until I finished a counseling session with one of the young women of the church. After my visitor left, my wife came in and sat in a chair opposite my desk. She was in a very playful mood that day.

"Reverend Brewer, could you help me with a problem I have?"

I played along. "Yes, Mrs. Brewer, what is bothering you?"

"My husband was seen meeting another woman in a very private setting. Do you think I should worry about that?"

"Not at all. He's not crazy enough to risk losing a woman like you."

"What do mean—a woman like me?"

"You know, a woman with your looks, your style."

"Reverend, are you making a pass at me?"

"Oh no, I would never make a pass at you here at the church. Let's go to lunch where I can do that properly."

That day we walked the streets of Swansboro taking in the views of this quaint fishing and tourist friendly village built on a bluff overlooking the White Oak River. We looked around at Mrs. Russell's Old Thyme Store and enjoyed the peaceful waterfront where ducks acted as if they owned the place. Juicy hamburgers, great fries, and apple fritters were the menu for lunch at the small, crowded eatery. Elvis watched us from the wall as we ate; rock and roll music competed with the many conversations. Katherine joked and teased me for being so uptight even as I took some needed time off.

What happened to the playful Katherine? I can't remember seeing that side of her for months now.

I always believed in the absurd conviction that Katherine and I were the perfect couple. We were meant to be together and no force could ever separate us. What I never imagined was that an inside enemy would break our bond. As late as last June our relationship seemed to be invincible. We took a five day vacation and left the kids with her parents. We left the beach for the beach as we spent the time at Myrtle Beach in South Carolina and enjoyed the days away. She was ebullient, no hint of depression on the horizon.

In the mornings we walked the sandy shore, in the afternoons shopped at the Boardwalk by the Beach and Blackbeard's Landing. We ate dinner at trendy restaurants and took in a couple of shows at night. There were no church duties, no interruptions.

We ate lunch one day at the Hard Rock Café. Katherine loved the rock and roll paraphernalia and sang out loud as the Eagles song, "Lying Eyes" blasted over the sound system. She had a good voice but was reluctant to sing in public, refusing several invitations to sing in the church choir.

One night we sat on the beach and marveled at the way our lives had been so blessed. Katherine did what she often did and quoted philosophy that night—Teilhard of course, "We are one, after all, you and I; together we suffer, together exist, and forever will recreate each other." I believed we were destined to be a team for many years to come.

***

I've tried over the years to sort out my approach to meeting the needs of people who are experiencing difficulties in how to live their lives. Of course the approach depends on the specific needs of the individual being counseled. I try to consider how I could have helped Katherine if she had shared her depression with me. The truth is that I was too emotionally involved to be objective. Katherine needed to go to someone else.

It's a risky venture for pastors to engage in counseling. A part of our job is to redeem lives, to look behind the facades people use to conceal their real selves. The defense mechanisms we employ to hide who we are often become the means of our destruction. It's never easy to help people who come seeking some relief from their problems, but who, at the same time, often resist the healing they need.

Depression is a challenging problem to work with for any counselor. I remember the words of Harry Emerson Fosdick, "All slaves of depression have this in common: They have acquired the habit of identifying their real selves with their low moods."

For the first fourteen and half years of our marriage Katherine was a positive person. In the last few months her outlook tilted to the negative. One evening in January I overheard a discussion between her and Luke.

"Mom, there's this boy at our school who pushes people around. He's pretty big and is always shoving others, even if they're not in his way," Luke said.

"Has he bullied you?"

"He pushed me the other day when I was standing at my locker."

"Perhaps you should try to stay out of his way."

"That's not easy to do. His locker is two down from mine."

Katherine did not respond for a few seconds and then said, "You're going to find that the world is full of people who are inconsiderate of you. You can't always avoid them."

I was surprised at her counsel but decided not to interfere.

"Mom, should I go see the principal about him?"

"Not just yet," Katherine said. "Unless he hurts you or starts picking on you regularly, you should just let it go."

"Mom, I thought you always told me to stand up for myself."

"Well, maybe I was wrong. Sometimes we are powerless to change others. Life is never easy. In some cases we just have to accept the negatives."

Luke did not say anything else.

A few days later I asked Luke about the bully.

"It's okay, not a big problem."

chapter seventeen

CLAUDE AND DIANE are back with several suitcases. They plan to stay for a while and help with the children. Our two thousand plus square foot house has become much smaller, but I'm pleased they will be here.

Diane's in the kitchen this afternoon preparing Luke's favorite, spaghetti. He told her after he came home from school that none of the church people had brought spaghetti and expressed his amazement over that; in all of the dinners delivered to our door not one family had chosen this dish. Diane got the message.

Claude tells me in private that he has found out some things about Kyle Edwards. "He lives Greenville now and is a car salesman. For the past ten years he's worked at the Toyota dealership. Two years ago he got divorced, and his son lives with his former wife in Pollocksville. I've not made any contact yet because I want to know if you wish for me to pursue this."

"Claude, I appreciate your willingness to look into this. Do you think she went to Greenville the night of the accident?"

"That's certainly possible. I'd like to go up there to see Kyle."

"Do you want me to go with you?"

"Perhaps it would be better if I do this alone. It might be easier on everyone."

I agree with Claude. He will go to Greenville tomorrow. We rejoin the rest of the family in the living room.

Diane's wonderful with Grace. My daughter's excited about having her grandparents across the hall from her. Grace gets undivided attention from her grandmother. I can see that by focusing her love on this little visage of Katherine my mother-in-law has found a way to lessen her sorrow.

I find that I can't talk about Katherine's death with Diane. It's not that she isn't communicative; on the contrary, she loves to talk as much as anyone I've ever known. The simple truth is we're both far too emotionally wounded to bridge the subject now. I'm sure that our mutual impairment would prompt too much pain in any discussion. So, we talk about the children, church, and food.

Diane says, "Paul, I want you to see the recipe book I made for Katherine a few years ago. There should be some meals in here you will want to try down the road."

I remember seeing Katherine take the floral decorated book out many times as she was preparing a meal. In the kitchen, Diane flips through the handwritten pages and stops on a recipe for spaghetti sauce. "This is pretty simple," she says. "It actually was given to me by Claude's mother."

I look at the few ingredients and say, "I think I can handle that."

"Good, Luke will be pleased."

"Luke will be pleased if we eat at Wendy's five nights a week."

"Just the same, you will find several easy-to-fix meals in here. Here are slow cook ribs, and baked chicken. This is the chocolate pie Grace loves."

"I'll give it a try after you and Claude leave."

"You'll do fine. Let the kids help you. Fixing meals together will be good for some sense of normalcy."

"I agree. I'm not sure if I can easily please Grace who is so picky about her food."

"If I can find things Claude likes, then you can hit upon a few for Grace. Claude has always been a finicky eater. I think his French mother spoiled him."

"Thanks for the help. I'll give cooking a shot."

***

Today, Claude's going to Greenville. Last night after everyone else had gone to bed, I again pulled out the journal I found in Katherine's clothing drawer. The mention of Kyle is in a few entrees and not very informative.

January 17

I cry so easily. This morning Grace told me she loved me as she got out of the car at school. I cried all the way to the bookstore and told Marian why my eyes were puffy. Marian is not a person to probe for private information. She has been helpful, however, when I've shared with her some of my sadness over my life. I try not to burden her with my problems but do find her very wise and experienced in the challenges of life. She knows so much about how to find help when a person is in need.

It is best that I pull back on my emails to Kyle. I'm careful to delete all contacts but do not want anyone to know that we correspond. Considered talking to Marian about him to feel her out on what she thinks about our getting back in touch. I've decided that not many people will think that appropriate. My whole life I've tried to behave appropriately. I'm not sure I can sustain proper behavior any longer.

There is so much pressure on me to be the perfect pastor's wife. I've deceived myself for years into thinking that I am meant to be good at this. The thing is—Paul was called to ministry. I was not. I've spent my whole life being the good church girl. Do I have to play that role forever?

Katherine used to tell me that her mother would scold her if she didn't behave in the way expected at church when she was young. One time, as the story goes, she put a piece of gum in her mouth as the service began and discreetly enjoyed the sweet taste of Juicy Fruit. Her mother, sitting beside her, could not see the slight movement of her teeth and gums but caught the aroma, and turned Katherine towards her by putting her hand under the young miscreant's chin. The gum was donated to a Kleenex, and after the worship service mother and daughter had a serious discussion of what is expected behavior in church.

My wife never was a rebel, but she always spoke of her interest in some innocent mischief. On occasion she would enjoy playing hooky from church and let me explain that she was not feeling well as I dropped the children off at Sunday school. One day Luke, when he was about four, told his teacher at church that his mom was going to the hospital when asked about his mother's illness. I'm not sure what made him make up that piece of information. There must have been twenty phone calls of concern that afternoon.

The expectations for a pastor's wife are many. Some churches expect them to volunteer for several jobs in the church. Only recently did I learn that Katherine was burdened by her role. I've read that many spouses of clergy persons develop feelings of guilt when they find they can't meet all of the expectations. Was this one cause of her depression?

Some pastor's mates are introverted which adds another challenge since they are often called upon to sparkle in public settings. Katherine has never had any problems in that area as she is, was, somewhat outgoing. I've seen her charm work on people. She's been able to get close to some of the women in the church due to her knack for warm camaraderie.

I've never considered myself to be a jealous person. This evening I feel a certain disdain towards Kyle Edwards. I remember Shakespeare calling jealousy a "green-eyed-monster". How is jealousy even possible when the one you loved is now dead. Yet, I dislike this man. If I find Katherine went to see him that evening, I'm afraid anger will be my emotion du jour.

Katherine loved to say "du jour." She also loved to say goodbye with the French, "A un de ces jour," which means, "see you one of these days." These were the words Claude spoke when they closed the casket. It's best that Claude go to Greenville by himself tomorrow. I'm afraid of my reaction if I find she went to see Kyle the night of the accident.

chapter eighteen

THIS IS THE first time I've entered the sanctuary since the funeral. I'm at the church alone for the moment. This coming Sunday will be my first back in the pulpit. Katherine usually sat on the second row on my left as I led worship. I situate myself at the podium imagining what it will be like to stand here Sunday without her sitting there. The morning sun is just beginning to strike the stained glass windows behind me and project colors across the room.

Everything is familiar today, yet nothing is the same. Hundreds of services behind me, one like no other before me. Is it too soon? What if I lose my composure? This morning my grief is under control. What if it isn't on Sunday morning?

"You can do it." The voice startles me. Harry Demarest is standing at the side door. "It will not be easy, but you can do it," Harry says.

"I'm not so sure," I say.

"The key is not thinking about yourself. Just focus on the congregation," Harry advises in his deep baritone voice. He's a retired minister who has a second home on our island. Occasionally, he and his wife worship with us. He and I have shared many conversations over the years about pastoral ministry.

"What if I lose focus?" I say.

"Never underestimate what you can do when you're in God's hands," Harry says. "You don't have to do this alone."

Coming from someone else such words would be trite babble, from Harry they smack of experience; he is one who has been in the fire. Some years ago he lost a daughter to breast cancer and, I'm told, stood in the pulpit the next Sunday and delivered a very encouraging message.

"Can you guarantee I have what it takes?"

"Oh yes. But I can't guarantee you will use what you have. That's going to be your responsibility."

The two of us sit on the front row of chairs. Harry looks up at the vaulted ceiling. "I like this sanctuary; it's a nice place to worship. It's simple and yet suggests some complexity, much like faith itself. I'll be sitting out here Sunday, supporting you like many others will be. This Sunday you're going to have our ears like you never have before."

"Thanks, that does not add to the pressure at all," I say.

"So, what else is new? Every time you stand up to preach there's pressure on you to say something that's worth hearing. It's just that this week everyone out here realizes that you know more about life and faith than at any time before. We will be listening to a man who has walked through the storm and stands up there to tell us what it's like."

"What if I choke up?"

"Then the person in the pew will see a man who's human. We will realize that people of faith are not exempt from pain. We will experience the truth that healing is not easy even for those who trust God."

"Harry, like you I've preached that a crisis in life can be an opportunity to grow in faith. I want to be able to tell that to my congregation, but I'm not sure I believe that now."

"We preachers sometimes profess what we have not yet experienced," Harry says. "Have you read Sue Monk Kidd's book, *When the Heart Waits?*"

"No."

"Well, she says we do one of two things in response to a crisis. We say it's God's will and accept it in order to have peace of mind or we fight against it because we believe it's unfair and seek justice. She says there's a third way. We wait, meaning we give it time to allow us to search deep within ourselves. This is how we become whole again."

"I've already tried the first two approaches to my loss. I've tried to accept it but haven't found much peace. I've railed against it and demanded justice. So, your advice is to wait?"

"Advice is discounted. I'm not in your shoes. I do think there is some merit in being patient with the situation and with yourself. I think, in time, you will find a way to overcome your grief and feel whole again."

"Harry, how do you ever let go? Right now, I just want to hold onto every good memory I have."

"Have you ever heard of the diapauses?"

"No, what is it?"

"Kidd writes about the 'mysterious process of metamorphoses' for caterpillars. Some of these creatures do not give in to the cocoon state readily which postpones their transformation into becoming a butterfly. The state of clinging is called 'diapauses'. She says that we humans desperately try to hold onto our old lives when a change is needed."

"Well, I guess I'm in the state of diapauses. I'm holding on stubbornly."

Harry stands up and walks to the pulpit. He looks out over the empty sanctuary. "I can't count the number of times I've stood up to preach and wondered if what I had to say was worth hearing. I look back over some of my old sermons and think—did I really say that? There were those times, however, when I could tell that the message was being received well. You know that experience. The faces give away the level of responsiveness."

"I've had a few of those times," I say.

"Those are the days when it all seems worthwhile. Sometimes we ask a great deal of our listeners. We ask them to go with us into the strange world of the biblical text and make it come alive in today's world. Every person out there on Sunday morning has experiences in their own lives which perplex them. We who preach must let them know we want to grab those experiences and relate them to God's wisdom."

For a minute the two of us remain here in silence. Harry's a wise man. It's possible that his coming by today was prompted by God, a messenger sent to encourage a man with doubts.

***

On the shelves in my church office are many books which I've accumulated over the years. I've read most of them, searched them for sermon ideas, counseling advice, and personal devotions. There are many friends here, people I've never met in person, still, people I know through their writings. Many are ministers who have instructed me through the pages of their printed sermons: Killinger, Claypool, Ogilvie, Campolo, Gomes, Marney, and Craddock, to mention a few. All of these men have been through their dark tunnels.

There's a tap on my door. Susan peeks in and asks, "Paul, could I have a minute."

"Sure, come on in." I feel bad that I haven't given her much time these last few weeks.

"There's something I need to tell you about Katherine. I can't hold this in any longer." Susan does not sit, but instead walks over to a bookshelf and leans on it; her hands are clasped together, her face showing some anguish. She speaks in a measured tone, "Katherine, three days before she died, confided in me that she had been seeing a psychiatrist for depression."

Susan looks at me from across the room waiting for my reaction.

"Yes, I know. I found her medication just yesterday."

"You did? I'm so sorry I didn't tell you before," Susan says. "I thought you had enough to deal with. I realized this morning that you're looking for answers; this might help you."

"It does help in trying to understand her recent behavior. It bothers me that I didn't see that she was in such a bad place."

"Katherine was so good to me. She had me over to your house for dinner all the time; we went out to lunch together and shopping. She taught me so much about dealing with people's needs as we worked together in the church food pantry." Susan moves to a chair across from me and looks straight at me. *"How can a person as together as she was get so depressed?"*

"I don't know," I answer. "It's partly my fault. I put the church before our marriage, before her."

"But she loved being a pastor's wife," Susan says.

"I think she fell out of love with her role somewhere along the way, possibly even with me."

Susan shakes her head. "I don't understand how that can happen."

"It does," I say.

"It's all so unfair, to Katherine, to you, and everyone else," Susan says.

"That's what has been hard for me as well, the unfairness of it."

Susan fiddles with a pen on my desktop, spinning it several times. She speaks without lifting her head, "One day recently she told me that I need to be very careful as to whom I choose to marry. She said I should not assume the person I fall in love with will be my soul mate forever. It made me very uncomfortable—this kind of talk."

"Did you think she was talking about her choices?" I ask.

"I wasn't sure. She had always said that you two were meant for each other. I've never seen a couple so at ease together as you and Katherine. What hope is there for me if Katherine was this unhappy?"

"There is always hope, and you are not Katherine."

Susan gets up and walks to the door. She looks back at me. "It just isn't fair."

I can see that I'm not the only one wounded by the loss of Katherine. I'm in a small group of those whose lives are now framed by this particular sorrow. I remember a quote from Henry Nouwen, "We must learn to embrace pain for something new will be born in the pain." He advised that "we honor our friends by entrusting our struggles to them." His belief was that God will send us the friends we need in times of grief.

I'm so thankful that I don't have to go through this in isolation. Claude and Diane are here to share the load. Susan is a part of the fellowship of support. People like Harry are around to offer advice. As a pastor I'm in a very special position—there's this large family of those who are compassionate and caring. When I stand in the pulpit on Sunday there will be a whole room of those willing to help see me through this dark valley. Across the room hanging on my wall is a framed plaque Katherine gave to me some years ago. It reads, "Friendship is always a sweet responsibility, never an opportunity." Many times my attention is drawn to this saying by Kahil Gibran. I've pondered its meaning often.

chapter nineteen

BEFORE OUR FAMILY moved to the island, and I became pastor of the church here, we lived in Havelock, North Carolina. For three years I served as pastor of a community church in that military town. Havelock is home to the Marine Corps Air Station, Cherry Point, a huge facility of over 29,000 acres. It's said that at one time cherry trees stood on this point of land on the Neuse River. The base has extensive runways, so large that this was an alternate landing site to Cape Canaveral for the space shuttles.

Our daughter, Grace, was born while we lived in Havelock. Katherine painted the nursery a sunny yellow after she found out we were having a girl. "I know people often say they don't care what sex the baby is as long as it's healthy," she said the evening before her ultrasound. "I want a healthy girl."

The church family was very caring; we were overwhelmed with gifts and offers to assist. It was a loving and supportive congregation.

The members were a blend of local residents and the Marine families who passed through the area while on station at MCAS Cherry Point. My three years as pastor involved a great deal of counseling with the military families who were under particular stress related to the nature of life in the armed forces.

Katherine felt a special calling to work with the wives of Marines who were deployed around the world. She started a support group for those in our church in that situation. The Corps did a good job of sustaining the wives of those sent off for long periods of time, but Katherine and a few of the women in our church supplemented this work. She felt a burden to help the younger wives who often were far away from their parents. This wasn't something anyone asked her to do, not a requirement set for the pastor's wife. It started with a nineteen year old girl coming to the parsonage one evening after learning her twenty year old husband had been wounded while in the Middle East. This young woman was from New Jersey, far from family, friends, and emotional support. From then on Katherine went full force in this ministry.

One Wednesday night prayer service she spoke on the ministry. "Sometimes, I think it's clear as to what God wants us to do. A need presents itself, and we're challenged to meet that need. I feel the Lord has placed a burden on my heart to help these young women. Some of them give birth and are far from their families. We can be their families. We can be their support group."

I remember when Katherine showed me a book she had kept from one of her counseling classes at Campbell, *The Art of Helping*. She'd underlined a passage: "Responsiveness is the basic ingredient of human relations. It involves empathy or seeing the world through another's eyes... Responsiveness is the most profound variable in the human condition."

The book is still in our home library, and I just took it off the shelf. One other line she marked jumps out at me, "Initiative begins with a vision of the possible." This was my Katherine, a person who always looked for the possible. How could this woman who had so many insights into life succumb to a deep depression? I hope Dr. Rosenblum can help me with that question.

***

Claude returned from Greenville just in time for dinner. Diane has prepared barbecue chicken in the slow cooker. We all sit down at the table, our new family of five. I can see that Luke likes the feast before us. Grace is a selective eater and chooses to eat only the corn and potatoes. Her grandmother has vowed to help her expand her food repertoire. The battle of wills has been interesting.

The table talk is reserved for questions about the school day. It's Friday and my children are both relieved the week of classes is over. I can't imagine how hard it is for them to carry on as usual. There's no normality when you have lost your mother, the stable center of your life. I can't help but wonder what would have happened if Katherine had simply left as she told me she wanted to do a few weeks before the accident. At least under that scenario there would have been the hope of her return. I'm convinced that if she left it would have been temporary. We're now trying to cope with the permanent loss of the person who was the glue of our lives.

After dinner the children are in their rooms. Both of them like their private time; Luke is usually on the computer on weekend evenings, Grace often drawing. She's a pretty decent artist for a seven year old. Claude, Diane, and I are at the kitchen table again, this time huddled to learn what Claude found out in Greenville.

"I went to the Toyota dealership first thing," Claude tells us. "The sales manager was curious about my inquiry at first but then opened up. Kyle was not working. I found out that he is in Pitt Memorial Hospital in Greenville. The man has lung cancer, and it's at an advanced stage. He may have only a few weeks to live, if that long. He's been in the hospital for three weeks."

"Did you go to the hospital?" I ask.

"Yes," Claude says. "When I found his room, 3452, I realized this was the number on the paper you found in Katherine's purse. I think she must have gone to see him at some point. Kyle was out for tests. A woman was sitting there. I introduced myself and asked about Kyle. She told me she was his sister, and when I explained I had met him back when he was in college she frowned. It was not easy explaining why I was there."

"What did you tell her?" Diane asks.

"I told her that my daughter had recently looked Kyle up and that many years ago she had dated her brother." Claude takes a sip of coffee and pauses before going on. "This brought a strange look from Ginny, the sister. It was not easy telling her about the accident and the journal."

"Did she ever know about Katherine?" I ask.

"Yes, but not until recently. Her brother never told the family about her back when the two were in college. He just told his sister after Katherine's getting in touch with him a couple of months ago."

"Does Kyle have other family?" Diane asks.

"His mother and father are still over in little Washington. He has one brother, older than him, and the younger sister. A few years ago he and his wife divorced. They have one son as we've already found out."

I ask Claude the one question that is most important, "Did Katherine go to see Kyle the night she died. Is that where she went?"

"His sister did not know the answer to that. I asked her if it would be alright for me to wait until they brought Kyle back to the room. She looked concerned and said she didn't want her brother to be upset. She was sure he didn't know that Katherine was dead. He's very weak and the family has tried to limit visitors. I told her how important it was for us to know if that was where my daughter went that evening."

"So, did she let you see him?" Diane asks.

"She suggested I talk to the nursing staff and inquire about his visitors that night. I agreed. At the nursing station I learned that the people on the shift that evening were not on duty now. The charge nurse asked me to describe Katherine. I did, and she told me that a woman fitting that description had visited Kyle one day, but that was before the night I was asking about. She remembered it well because, after she left, Kyle told her the woman was an old friend of his from college and that she now lived at the beach. She recommended I call back tomorrow night when two members of the team working on the evening of the accident would be on duty. They would not give me their home numbers."

I thank Claude for taking on this difficult task. He and Diane check on the children and give me some private time to sort through all of this. My guess is that Katherine went to Greenville the evening of the accident. That would make sense as to why she was on that stretch of road that night. What must have been on her mind on the trip home? There's no mention in her private journal of the cancer or of seeing Kyle. There are some entries which are easier to understand in light of this new information.

January 26

Today I studied Luke as he was eating breakfast. He's so much looks and acts like his father, both tall and thin, both outgoing and handsome. I wonder if there is some kind of revolving genetic cylinder which determines how one child resembles one parent and another child the other parent. Grace has my eyes, mouth, and hair. She also has my reticence to speak before I've first processed what I want to say. I can't remember my health classes where we learned about how the chromosomes are inherited.

What happens when there is a genetic dead end, when a couple does not have children? Does that slot in the chain of hereditary events go unfilled like a lottery number that never is redeemed? I will likely never know the answer to that. One life never truly begins and another ends too early.

There is so much I don't know. I remember Teilhard writing that God does not hide himself from us. I am not so sure about that.

I can't help but infer that Katherine was thinking about her pregnancy when she was in college and the eminent death of the father of that could-have-been child.

chapter twenty

SATURDAY MORNING HAS traditionally been waffle time at the Brewer house. Some years ago Katherine bought a Belgian waffle maker and would usually pull it out on Saturdays. Grace asks me if I can fix waffles for breakfast. Diane volunteers to make them, but I tell her she has the morning off.

The undertaking is an adventure but not a disaster. Luke and Grace sit at the kitchen bar while Claude and Diane take their places at the table. The hot waffles, melted butter, maple syrup, and bacon are presented with a culinary flair befitting Paula Deen. Orange juice and coffee are served, Grace being told no coffee for her. I'm worried that the memories of meals past will surface to provide a sad nostalgia, but there's no sign of gloom. It takes every reserve of emotional discipline for me to suppress sentimentality.

Luke likes strawberry jelly on his waffles.

"Are you going to ruin a good waffle by putting jelly on it?" Claude asks.

"Granddad, just because you like them your way, doesn't mean I have to eat mine that way."

"Don't you know," Diane says, "that your grandfather thinks his way is the only way when it comes to food? He even wants you to cut your waffle one quadrant at a time like he does."

"I like to eat like granddaddy does," says Grace.

"That's my girl," Claude says.

"What a suck-up," Luke says with a hard stare at his sister.

With the final waffle off the grill on my plate the phone rings. It's Susan.

"Paul, I hate to bother you but thought you should know this. Jeff Whitaker has had a heart attack and is being transported to Pitt in Greenville."

"When did this happen?" I ask.

"It was just about three hours ago. They took him to Carteret General, but the doctor there informed the family that Pitt was better equipped to handle the seriousness of problem."

"I will leave in a few minutes," I tell Susan. "This one is my call. You stay put."

Jeff Whitaker's in his early fifties. He's one of our deacons and a good friend. I'm so thankful that my in-laws are here. I can't imagine how I will handle the duties of a pastor after they leave with two children in my charge.

The drive to Greenville means that I will pass through the site of Katherine's accident, if I take the shortest route. In light of the emergency presented this is what I choose to do. At the little rural church I make a left and then a quick right on the road across the way. One would never know by observation that this was the scene of a tragic event if not privy to the knowledge.

On the way it comes to me that Kyle Edwards is at Pitt Memorial. On the early part of the trip my mind has been on Jeff and his family. His wife, Joyce, is herself a nurse. They have a son who's a doctor. Jeff is so proud of his son, Jason, who is on the pediatrics staff at Duke in Durham. When my focus moves from the Whitakers to Kyle Edwards it forces my melancholy to surface.

Pitt Memorial is a huge hospital complex. It provides eastern North Carolina with a first rate medical center.

Joyce Whitaker is in a waiting room by herself when I arrive. Joyce hugs me and says other family members are on the way.

"Air transportation was not available so he came by ambulance," Joyce says. "We've only been here thirty minutes."

"Have they told you anything?" I ask.

"A nurse came out a few minutes ago and said he's stable. I know from my experience it was a massive attack. This was confirmed by the staff at Morehead City where I work. You know that our doctor put him on cholesterol medicine last year. We worked so hard to regulate diet and step up his exercise."

"What happened this morning?"

Joyce gets emotional as she recounts the events. "It was about five and I heard him get up to go to the bathroom. He called out to me, and I found him on the floor by the sink. I knew what was happening. Thank God it only took the EMTs ten minutes to arrive."

We sit on a couch in the waiting room. Joyce is a medical professional, but that does not prevent her from shaking from fear that Jeff is fighting for his life. I'm a professional also with much experience in situations like this, but that does not help me find the most beneficial words to share with her. For long stretches of time we sit in silence, then for a few minutes engage in discussion about her family. Her son calls and announces that he's found someone to cover for him and that he will be in Greenville after lunch. Jim Albright, our deacon chairman, arrives around noon and sits with us.

Jim and Jeff are close friends, golfing buddies. On a couple of occasions I have joined them for eighteen holes at Star Hill Golf and at Silver Creek. Jim is one of the most gracious people I know. A retired insurance salesman, he volunteers at the Hem in Swansboro, a community organization which aids people with food, clothing, and financial assistance. He and Katherine often compared notes on how to help folks on the island. Jim has had heart problems in the past and reassures Joyce that Jeff will come through this.

At two Jason Whitaker arrives. He and his mother engage in a long embrace. At three the cardiologist, Dr. Spencer, sits down on a chair opposite Joyce and Jason. He tells them that Jeff is doing well, considering. He's on monitors and the family can see him in a few minutes. There was some damage, and they will need to observe Jeff for a few days. Jim and I wait for the wife and son to go and see the patient. I make a very brief visit with Jeff and have prayer with him. He squeezes my hand as tears roll down his face.

As many times as I've made visits to hospital rooms, I'm still shocked when a patient is hooked up to IVs and monitors. There is so much paraphernalia—it's both frightening and reassuring. Medical care amazes me, especially in heart situations.

On the way to my car, I stop and wonder if it would be appropriate for me to go up to room 3452. What do I say to Kyle Edwards if he's alert enough to hear me? Claude said the nurses on duty the evening of the accident will come on at seven tonight. Every fiber of my being wants to see this man whom my wife once was so interested in that she needed counseling to get over the breakup. What kind of guy would get a girl pregnant and then break off contact with her? I realize that the man in room 3452 is not the same person Katherine dated in college.

Down several long corridors I come to Kyle Edward's room. The door is shut tightly. First I knock—no answer. Slowly I push the door and wait for some response from inside - none. Opening it further, I see the room is unoccupied at the moment, but it's clear this is a place where serious medical attention is given; beside the bed are several monitors with red and green leds illuminating the dimly lit, drawn curtain quarters. I pull the door closed and find myself relieved. I'm not ready for this encounter yet. As I turn back into the hall a nurse tells me the patient is out for tests. Briskly, I walk back to the elevator and leave Greenville having made my pastoral visit, and spared from an awkward meeting.

The drive back to the coast allows me the time to process all that has happened in the last few days, and I choose not to pass the wreck site again. I decide to go through New Bern this time. The city is the home of Tryon Palace which dates back to colonial times. As I cross the bridge over the Neuse, the downtown is in sight and all of the boats moored there. The Trent River bridge offers a view of the once governor's home in the distance. Downtown churches, such as First Presbyterian, model the Federal style of architecture. The history intrigues me as I wonder what it must have been like to live in those colonial days. I'm forced to explore my past and try to remember what it was like just a year ago when my life seemed to be so secure.

From New Bern down Highway 17, I try to focus on what is best for my children in the weeks ahead. I'm pulled to consider the future, to close my mind to further reminiscing. I suppose I need a catharsis, a purging of my emotions, in order to move on with my life. I read some yesterday from Thomas Moore's *Dark Nights of the Soul.* Moore wrote, "But catharsis also means having sharper ideas, clearer feelings, and a more defined sense of purpose." My purpose now must include helping my children move on with their lives.

chapter twenty one

"MR. BREWER, MY name is Carlton Witcher. Do you know the truth of what caused your wife's accident?"

The caller ID reads "unknown." I try to process who Carlton Witcher is. The name's familiar. "Excuse me, but what did you ask me?"

"Have the authorities uncovered what caused your wife's wreck?"

"Why are you asking me this?"

"Because, you need to know the truth about the events of that evening."

"Tell me again who you are."

I'm an attorney with the law firm of Smith and Witcher, Carlton Witcher. Has someone from the insurance company contacted you?"

Now I realize where I've heard the name. The law firm advertises on television and specializes in personal injury claims.

"Yes, I've talked with my agent. Are you representing State Farm?"

"No, I'm calling to help you. I hope you have not agreed to a settlement yet."

"Listen," I say. "I don't think I need an attorney."

"That's where you're wrong, Mr. Brewer. How do you know that someone else did not cause your wife's wreck?"

"It was a single car accident. She ran into a tree."

"I know that's what they say. However, I've done a little research on your situation. Have you considered that a drunk driver may have forced her to run off the road?"

"Why would I think that?" I ask.

"Because, just one week earlier there was a wreck at that same intersection. A man ran into a woman's car and was charged with a DUI. The woman suffered a sprained neck."

"What does that have to do with my wife's accident?"

"I'm not sure if anything. It's just that the man who was charged lives only two miles from the church there."

"There was no evidence of another car being involved."

"Has the highway patrol seriously considered the possibility? Your wife had a spectacular driving record. Certainly, you must wonder why that should change all of a sudden that evening."

"Mr. Witcher, do you have some information the patrol does not have?"

"Nothing for sure, but I wouldn't rule out that someone left the scene of the accident. It happens all the time. Surely, you want to know the truth."

I've heard of people getting such cold calls from lawyers. It takes some real audacity to make such a call to someone who has just suffered the loss of one close to them. "Mr. Witcher, I'm ending this call now."

"Before you do, let me ask you one more question. Did the investigators on the scene talk to people in that neighborhood?"

"I don't know. I assume they did."

"That's a big assumption. I suggest you ask them. I'm going to send to you some information on our firm in case you decide you do need us."

After I hang up my anger rises over such insensitivity. My first impulse is to call this ambulance chaser back and let him know how much I don't appreciate such an intrusion into my privacy. I stop to consider what he asked me. As much as I dislike his crudeness, I can't help but wonder if there is not some merit in his questions.

***

For most of our married life Katherine was a source of strength. She provided a counter to my feelings of unworthiness. So many times I feared that my congregation would discover my flaws and lose confidence in me. It was Katherine who would tell me that my best quality was my sensitivity to the gap between who I am and what I strive to be. I miss almost everything about her, but for now, I miss her ability to encourage me when I'm down.

Rabbi Kushner titled a chapter in one of his books, "Best Actor In a Supporting Role." I would have nominated Katherine for that award. This, I now suspect, was a contributor to my wife's depression. I saw her as a supporting character in the play in which I held the lead role. Kushner uses a term which I now recall with a sense of guilt, "somebody's somebody." I saw myself as a somebody and saw Katherine as the somebody who supported me. My guess is that Dr. Rosenblum will tell me that my wife resented her supporting actress role. All I know is that I'm now on the stage without her being there to buttress my performance.

***

Claude calls the hospital. The night shift came on duty an hour ago. He speaks to the charge nurse. I'm listening to his side of the conversation.

"My name is Claude Rosiere. I spoke with one of your co-workers yesterday and was told that some of you working this evening were on duty the night of March twelfth and thirteenth. Yes, I'll wait."

Claude nods at me and whispers, "She's checking the schedule for that evening."

The nurse is back on the line. Claude speaks, "One of your patients is Kyle Edwards. I understand that he was on your floor that evening."

Another pause for response.

"I know this is an unusual request, but I need to know if my daughter visited Mr. Edwards on that night. Around midnight on that evening she died in an automobile accident. I'm trying to determine where she went before the accident."

Claude's brow furrows as he listens.

"Yes, my daughter was about five feet six. She had reddish-brown hair. She was thirty-six years old."

I become aware of the times Claude uses "was." Was is past tense. Katherine is past tense.

"Yes, I understand that there are many visitors and it was weeks ago. Could you ask if anyone else remembers?" Claude turns to me. "She doesn't remember the night but is checking with someone named Beverly who was also on duty."

Two minutes pass—again Claude is listening.

"Thank you, Beverly. Yes, that's right—Katherine was from here at the beach."

Claude's expression changes and he touches the phone rapidly with his index finger as if to say this is the one we need to talk with; he's listening for more.

"Do you remember how long she was there? Just a minute please." He covers the phone and whispers, "Paul, I think you should go to the phone in the bedroom."

In a minute I am on the other phone and hear Claude say, "Could you please repeat that, my son-in-law is now on our other extension."

"Sure. As I said, I remember the night well. I was the one attending to Mr. Edwards that evening. At around eight I was surprised when I walked in and found a woman sitting there in a chair in the room. Mr. Edwards was asleep and she was just watching him. She said she was sorry if she startled me. I asked her if she was family and she said 'no, just a friend.' She told me that she had driven up from the coast. I could tell she'd been crying. She got up and walked out as I was checking the patient's vitals. A few minutes later I noticed she had moved to the waiting room. She was still there fifteen minutes after that when I passed by. I don't know when she left the floor. That's all I remember."

"Thank you, Beverly," Claude says.

Claude and I sit at the kitchen table as Diane joins us. The three of us recap what we just learned.

"I don't understand," says Diane. "If she was there between eight and nine, why was she on the road at midnight? How long does it take to get from Greenville to the place she wrecked?"

"About an hour, or a little less," I say. "She must have gone somewhere else."

Claude shrugs his shoulders. "We now know that Katherine was at the hospital that night. We know she'd been there at least once before to see Kyle".

"She was so concerned about other people," I add. "Coupled with her distress over her own life this must have been a lot to handle. I'm so sorry I didn't see the level of sadness she was experiencing."

You can't place all of this guilt on yourself, Paul," Claude says. "Diane and I are so thankful our daughter had you for a husband."

"Well, whatever was wrong with her, I'm a part of the equation."

***

The master bedroom is away from the rest of the house, in a back wing. I've moved my desk and bookshelves in there for the time being since Luke has taken over the den. Tonight, I'm under pressure to complete my sermon for tomorrow. My task is to find a message that will be helpful to the congregation but not too emotional so I can handle it. I'm aware that the people of the church have also suffered a loss.

There is so much for me to process about the night of the accident. I am an inquisitive person by nature—have never been able to abandon my curiosity as to the mysteries which present themselves to me. I tend to probe to the core of each unknown until there is some quantitative explanation. The ambiguities of the accident have made me obsessive in my search for the truth.

On the dresser across from the bed there's a photo of Katherine and myself taken when we were living in Raleigh soon after I graduated from seminary. In the picture we're at Pullen Park by the duck pond on a Saturday. That day we squeezed onto the small train that circled the park, rode the horses on the merry-go-round, and ate hot dogs while watching young families with children enjoy the park together. It was a carefree time, and we cherished this stage of our lives.

Her hidden diary reads like process theology in places. I thumb through it to find one entry which was difficult to decipher.

February 4

I just found a book in Paul's library, With All That We Have Why Aren't We Satisfied, by Clifford Williams. There's a chapter on secret tragedies. The author says that "we all go through life not telling some things to anyone, and we all go through life not telling some things even to ourselves." Much of my life has been lived in secret. Many of my deepest feelings have remained buried.

I have studied psychology and philosophy but have not been able to study my thoughts that well. I have failed to live up to the ideals I have held for myself. I am miserable—I am not that sure why even. I don't know how to escape my misery. Every way out I imagine is fraught with so many negatives. There is no one who knows me, the real me.

I try to push my unhappiness down into the deeper recesses of myself, to repress it. It resurfaces with such force often that I'm afraid of it bursting forth like a submerged ball in a pool. I am reminded of some words by Langston Hughes, "…if dreams die life is a broken-winged bird that cannot fly." Many of my dreams have died and I feel crippled.

Was she this miserable? What were her secrets? You live with someone for fifteen years and do not know them better than this? No, the Katherine in this journal is not the Katherine I was married to all those years.

The knock on the door is like a faint tap on my consciousness. It takes me a moment to change my focus from the past memories to the present reality.

"Come in," I say.

Grace slowly opens the door and stands there in her pink pajamas. "Daddy, I can't remember what mommy told me about the stars."

Most nights Katherine would put Grace to bed with some words to help her sleep. Katherine thought the last words before bedtime were the ones that meant the most. If she was reading a book she would mark her place, verbalize a sentence she liked, and then turn off the lights.

"Do you mean the one about God's promises?" I ask.

"Yes, that one."

"Let me see. I think it goes like this—God's promises are like the stars; the darker the night the brighter they shine."

Grace repeats the line and smiles. "I wish I could remember better. Will I forget mommy when I'm older?"

"Oh, no, I don't think so," I say. "Just keep thinking about the things she said and the way she looked at you. You were so special to her. You were her Grace. She picked your name because she was so thankful God sent you to her."

"I know that. She told me that a hundred times. Grandma put me to bed tonight. I love Grandma, but I wish my mommy was here to do that. She always said the best things."

"I miss her too."

"Will I see mommy someday in heaven?" Grace asks.

"It will be a long time before you go to heaven. Mommy will always be in your heart."

Grace thinks for a moment, "God's promises are like the stars; the darker the night the brighter they shine."

I take Grace back to her bedroom, tuck her in, and turn out the lights. Like Grace, I wish so much that it was Katherine who had this treasured responsibility tonight.

chapter twenty two

WE HAD BEEN on our way from Washington, D.C., heading home to Raleigh when the accident occurred sometime around noon. They took my sister to the Medical College of Virginia which was a few miles from the sight of all of the wrecks that day in Richmond. The rest of our family was taken there as well. A police officer made the arrangements. The emergency room was overflowing with those injured from the pileup on the bridge. The hospital staff was in full-functioning mode. They had just put a cast on my brother's arm.

"Boys, I need to help your mom. They're going to give her a shot to help her relax. Paul, you stay with Matt over in the waiting room." My dad was taking charge.

Almost every seat in the waiting room was taken. Matt and I found two chairs, and he rested his head on my shoulder. I remember there was a basketball game on the television, and at a commercial break an ad for auto insurance came on. I wasn't sure if my dad had insurance and worried about that for a good few minutes. The area was full of people, most from the wrecks.

An old man with suspenders sat in a chair across from Matt and me. His hand was bandaged and he murmured to himself words I couldn't understand. A nurse in green scrubs came and sat next to him. I heard the young woman tell the old fellow his wife was doing well, and he could see her soon. In a few minutes the old guy got on his knees right in front of me, his elbows on his chair, and he started to pray. He said over and over again, "praise God, praise God." His feet extended behind him so that they almost touched mine. I slid my feet under my chair and bowed my head. It seemed like the thing to do.

My father came and found us. He told us Mom was calm now, sleeping off and on. Matt was picking at the white cast on his arm. A man with a Bible in his hand, a minister I assumed, approached and asked my dad what he could do for our family. My father told him we could use his prayers, but we just wanted some quiet now.

Our pastor from Raleigh drove up to Richmond late that afternoon along with one of the deacons from our church. They had come to give us a ride home. The two of them waited with us until all of the arrangements had been made to take Karen's body to Raleigh. Mom and dad sat in the middle seat of the church van, Matt and I in the back. There was little conversation. Matt slept. I wondered how Karen would get back home.

When we arrived at our house after dark my dad went around to my mom's side and opened her door. She stepped out, and he put his arm around her, leading her to the front door of the house. The pastor and deacon assisted Matt and me out of the rear seat and helped with the luggage we had salvaged from our wrecked car. My dad told the preacher that we would be okay, and the two men left our family to cope with our loss that evening.

The next day my mother stayed in bed. Her sister came over to help. She fixed lunch for us, straightened the house, and made sure we did not bother our mom. Dad went down to the funeral home that morning to make arrangements for Karen. When he came back I asked him if I could see my sister. He sat me down at the kitchen table and told me every detail of what would happen next.

"Son, your sister will be buried next to my parents at Oakwood. I picked out a nice casket today."

"Will I be able to see her before she's buried?"

"Yes, they will be ready for us to see her tomorrow morning," Dad said.

"I should have been in that seat," I said.

"What?"

"Karen and I switched seats at the rest stop before the wreck. I should have been in that seat."

My father sat for a minute before speaking. He reached across the table and put his hand on mine; he shook his head sideways. "It was meant for Karen to be there. God has big plans for your life."

I thought about what he said for the rest of the day. What plans could God have for me? Does God choose which child lives and which child dies? I felt as if a great weight had been placed on me. I still do.

chapter twenty three

THE SANCTUARY IS beginning to fill up. From my chair on the platform, I see faces I haven't seen in months. In five years of preaching here—today will be my greatest challenge. I'm wearing my blue blazer and tan pants, not wanting to dress in anything somber. I pulled out the black suit from the closet this morning and vetoed it. That's my funeral suit, the one I wore for Katherine's service. I'm not sure if I will be able to wear it again for a long while.

The sanctuary is packed full with worshippers by ten when the service starts. They have come to worship but also to listen to what a grieving pastor has to say, one who recently lost his wife in an auto accident. Minister and teacher, Fred Craddock, has written that people come to church to overhear the gospel. They need and want to participate in the message. As Craddock puts it, "Participation means the listener…identified with experiences and thoughts related to the message that were analogous to his own." Almost every person here has experienced some loss in their lives. They want to hear what I say after my loss. They want to overhear what I will say to myself.

A quick scan of the congregation provokes memories of many others who have lost loved ones in my six years here. I see the faces of those who have been through separations and divorces. Several of those I've counseled sit out there as well as a few who should have come to me. The room is full of reminders that many know the pains of human existence.

Susan leads in the responsive reading. It's from Psalms twenty-five and twenty-seven.

Leader: Make me to know your ways, O Lord;
Congregation: Lead me in your truth, and teach me,
Leader: For you are the God of my salvation;
Congregation: For you I wait all day long.
Leader: The Lord is my light and salvation; whom
shall I fear?
Congregation: The Lord is the stronghold of my life;
of whom shall I be afraid?

The truth is I'm afraid today. Not that I don't trust God. It's just that I have so many questions, so many uncertainties. On other Sundays I've looked out over the congregation and been keenly aware of my limitations standing before people who look to me for insights into life and faith. This is a different fear today. This is not about abilities. This is about courage. My confidence has been eroded because I was not able to fulfill the most critical duty of my life—caring for the person closest to me in such a way as to save her from the pain which she suffered.

The offering is taken, the hymns are sung, and the time draws near for me to stand and deliver. I remember the words of wisdom from Harry Demarest as we stood here the other day—think of the others not yourself. Harry's seated in the middle on the right, smiling and looking straight at me over the top of his reading glasses. He refuses bifocals, claiming they cause too much confusion for his eyes.

Diane is across the aisle, Luke and Grace beside her. This is also the first Sunday back for my children. Claude sandwiches the two between their grandparents and has vowed a "no fly zone", as he terms it, as far as they are concerned. He intends to protect them from a flood of well meaning condolences. Luke insisted he come today even though I suggested it was still too early for them. Grace made no objections. She has never been one to object.

I raise the microphone on the pulpit to its optimum position for my comfort and fumble with my sermon notes. Opening my Bible to the book of Psalms and inviting the congregation to follow in theirs to Psalm twenty-three, I begin reading the familiar passage. **"The Lord is my shepherd, I shall not want."** The rustling of pages quiets and the words transcend the medium of written word to spoken word as they were originally meant. This text and I are well acquainted and the passage flows from my mouth like a recitation of memory verses. As I conclude the scripture reading I continue:

"May the Lord bless this reading of his word. Let us pray. Father, you have promised to hear the prayers of your people. This morning I ask for this congregation and myself the wisdom to understand the power of your presence in our lives. Help us, O Lord, to know that wherever we find ourselves on the journey of life you are there also. Take away our fear, instill in us the strength to keep on, and assure us of your abiding love."

The congregation raises its collective heads. This is the moment of expectation, the one time when speaker and listener are engaged in the dance of readiness. For the next minute the preacher has them. They will soon begin to go off into their own tangents of thought, sometimes prodded by the words of the sermon, sometimes into wistful daydreams or plans of events to come. This is my chance to secure their attention for a longer period. Do we in the pulpit seek to shock, amuse, or startle in order to hold them with us for a minute longer? Do we attempt to be so clever so that their interest is held in order to see where this is all going, or do we demand their ears through some warning of impending damnation if they dare ignore what follows? I begin with a personal story.

A few years ago I visited an Episcopal priest friend of mine in the hospital who was stricken with a rare form of cancer. He had been at Duke for a number of days on the floor where malignancy is the order. He was very appreciative of my visit and told me of the many people from his church that had made the trip to Durham to support him. He told me that his days were filled with tests and treatments, with a parade of friends, relatives, and even other patients on the floor. He told me that when the door was closed at night and he lay there with only the occasional check by a nurse, he was so thankful that he was in the arms of God.

This morning I want to address those times when we walk through the dark and lonely valleys of life which test our courage and faith. T. S. Eliot, in one of his poems, over and over repeats one phrase—"Falls the shadow." He reminds the reader that the shadow times are a part of life. This is why the twenty-third Psalm is so beloved. Almost every person who has lived a few years can identify with these words, "Yea, though I walk through the valley of dark shadows"—the most accurate translation of the Psalm.

One way of looking at the twenty-third Psalm is as though it were a day in the life of the sheep. In the morning the sheep awaken to find the ever present shepherd on duty and are assured their needs will be met another day. The shepherd leads them to find food, water, and a secure place to rest. At times they pass through narrow openings between the rocky cliffs, dark and foreboding.

The Psalmist declares that in those shadowy channels the sheep do not fear as long as the shepherd is leading them. He speaks the words of assurance and comfort, "For Thou art with me." We humans, in those darker and frightening passageways of life, are comforted by the promise that God is with us.

One of the most interesting aspects of preaching is the opportunity to make eye contact with members of the congregation as you look up from your notes. There are always some who acknowledge your glance in some way such as a smile, nod, or a certain other sign they are intent on hearing the message. This morning, before the time for the sermon, I search the sea of faces and halted my survey briefly on several whom I know have been through the darkest of valleys in their lives. Jackson Lewis recently was diagnosed with lung cancer; Patricia Wilson lost her mother a couple of months ago; Lawrence Deville's wife left him after thirty years of marriage. Each of these has personal knowledge of the valley times.

The story is told of a French general who one morning before a big battle was shaving and his hand began to tremble. He spoke to his fearful body with these words, "Tremblest thou, vile carcass, thou wouldst tremble more if thou knewest where I am going to take you this day." We all tremble in the face of imminent danger, but those who believe in a caring God are calmed by the promise of his presence.

The sermon deals with the most serious of subjects. I realized in preparing it that there needs to be a breather where it can be lighter, a pause to allow the heaviness of the air in the room to settle. The experienced preacher is aware that some humor can cause the listeners to enjoy a sigh in the middle of sober oration.

Many children are afraid of the dark and are reassured by words of comfort from a parent at bedtime. A young mother put her two young boys to bed and turned off the light. She then washed her hair and changed into her flannel bathrobe. A towel was wrapped around her head and cream applied to her face. She heard one of the boys cry out and went to their room where one child said he was afraid and wanted some light to be turned on. She told them there was nothing to fear, tucked them in again, left the hall light on, and cracked the door. After she left one of the boys said to the other, "Who was that?" I'm not sure how comforted they were by the visit.

There are some muffled laughs and many smiles in the congregation. Others are silent and unflinching, possibly trying to picture the scene in the illustration.

Fear of the darkness represents some of our deepest anxieties. So many people find themselves in places and situations where death, despair, depression, failure, or disappointment has put them in one of those dark valleys. William Styron's autobiography called *Darkness Visible* is an example of one of those gloomy passages in life. He suffered from manic depression and describes it this way: "In the middle of the journey of life, I found myself in a dark wood, for I had lost the right path."

The Psalmist again and again reassures us that God is with us in those dark woods. Martin Luther wrote these words to his friend Melancthon, "I am against those worries which take the heart out of you. Why make God a liar in not believing His wonderful promises when he commands us to be of good cheer, and cast all of our care upon him."

I'm aware that most every person here is waiting for me to share a personal word of my recent loss. I decided last night that I would not be able to do such and hold it together. Therefore, I work around the edges of my dark times. It's my hope the people out there will understand my reluctance to mention Katherine yet still infer from what I say that underlying this message is my need to cast my sorrows into the lap of God.

We Christians are not exempt from fear. We still shudder at the prospect of entering a dark valley. The baseball great, Satchel Paige, may have spoken for most of us when he said, "Don't look back, something may be gaining on you." I agree there are those times when we are overtaken by those things in life which we most dread.

What are we to do? The advice of the Psalmist is to keep on going with the knowledge God protects us. "Yea, though I walk through the valley of evil." I take from this we are to keep walking, keep moving on, and keep living our lives.

Christian writer, Eugene Peterson, in his book *Over the Wall,* has a chapter on grief. The book is about the life of David of the Old Testament. Peterson writes, "Death is not the worst thing. The worst thing is failing to deal with reality and becoming disconnected from what is actual." In other words the worst thing is to stop moving on.

Peterson also frames the David story in the idea of wilderness. It was in the wilderness that the shepherd guarded his sheep. Again words from *Over the Wall*—"In the wilderness we're plunged into awareness of danger and death; at the very same moment we're plunged, if we let ourselves be, into an awareness of the great mystery of God and the extraordinary preciousness of life."

In the Psalm the shepherd brings his flock home and prepares a table for them. Even when foes are pressing upon us provision is made for us to find the security of the Lord's Table. God's care exceeds even the most we can expect from him. Not only does He protect us—He makes arrangements for us to find the spiritual food which sustains us.

On a personal note—I have been through the dark valley. We all have or will. I so appreciate the support you have given to me. I appreciate God's loving arms surrounding me. I appreciate Christ, my shepherd, walking beside me.

The point is that in the darkest of times we learn the greatest of lessons. Let us not fail to make the best of the periods of passage through the dark valleys. Let us not fail to grow closer to God when we are most aware of his presence. Let us be thankful when we are thrown into the arms of God that he is there to hold us.

The closing hymn is Martin Luther's "A Mighty Fortress Is Our God." The congregation, at first, sings with a stupor as if comatose from the gravity of the moment. As the power of the music and the meaning of the lyrics take hold, they awaken to the opportunity to testify in pooled voice the grandeur of the timeless hymn—**"We will not fear, for God hath willed His truth to triumph thro us."** At the conclusion of the singing, I ask Harry Demarest to offer the benediction.

I open the front door of the church to welcome the fresh air and ocean breeze to enter the foyer. The minister shaking the hands of those who exit is a long standing tradition. Today it's both a burden and a relief. Some tell me of their prayers for me in the last few weeks. Some thank me for the sermon and tell me that it was what they needed. Others grip my hand or hug me as though words could not do justice to the occasion. What a release to have made it through this time of immense emotional pressure.

Back in the church office I put my Bible and sermon notes on my desk and prepare to go home. Susan comes to my door. She has tears in her eyes and just stands there.

"Hey, what are you crying for?" I ask.

Susan walks over to me and hugs me. The embrace is brief as she steps back and says, "I just remembered my first Sunday here. Katherine came up to me after the service and invited me to lunch. She said I should consider myself a part of your family."

"I think she felt you were," I say.

"I know. That's why I can't imagine how you lose a part of your family and go on with the routine of life. How do you ever fill that void?"

"If I had a good answer for that today, I would tell you. I lost my sister when I was ten years old. I still think about her all the time. Katherine, my sister, and my dad all now inhabit that part of my heart which aches for my losses. I doubt all of this is helping you. I'm sorry. I'm supposed to be the one with assurances here."

Susan dries her eyes with a tissue and says, "You're really not very good at consolation, are you?"

"Not one of my strengths, it seems."

"It's good to know that you have some weaknesses. I was beginning to think you too perfect to work with. It was a very good sermon."

"Thanks. I'm relieved it's over."

"I can imagine, but next Sunday is only a seven days away."

"I know."

chapter twenty four

I⊤ WAS OUR first Sunday at Havelock. Katherine, Luke, and I had just moved into the parsonage a few days earlier. The church family pounded us before we moved in; they stocked the kitchen with canned goods, the fridge with milk, eggs, and meats. It was a pleasant surprise. Katherine was overwhelmed. She appreciated the thought and the array of goods but said she felt like this was some kind of home invasion. It was our first experience with a parsonage and a pounding.

After the worship service Sunday, two of the families insisted that we go out to eat with them. Katherine was hoping we could have a private lunch at home, but we went out. That evening there was a welcoming reception where a cake with butter cream icing was cut, and again the congregation showed us how happy they were to have us with them. Later that evening we were finally home in the parsonage—on the church property in sight of the church buildings. We sat on our furniture which was placed in their house.

"You had a great sermon this morning," Katherine said.

"I'm glad this day is over. It's good to be at home," I said.

"Home in the proverbial fishbowl," she said.

"More like the aquarium at Pine Knoll Shores. We are the fish in the tank and the congregation watches us go about our business."

"Thankfully, we fish have some privacy at night," Katherine said as she playfully stood in front of the drawn drapes, holding them tightly closed. "I really do like these people. I just hope they don't like us too much—give us some breathing room."

"They will. It's just that they want to make sure we feel welcome."

This was not the last of such discussions. The congregation was very supportive of us. They continued to gift us, invite us, and honor us. Katherine, all the while, fought for some separation. When Grace was born the outpouring of affection was overwhelming. There was no shortage of offers to babysit, and Grace was the princess of the church nursery.

One afternoon, Mary Alice Jenkins called Katherine and asked if she could come over for a few minutes. Mary Alice was the wife of one of the deacons, Marshall Jenkins. Katherine welcomed her in and the two were talking about family when Mary Alice announced the real purpose for her dropping by. She told Katherine that from then on she, Mary Alice, was going to be her protector. She told my wife that she and her husband, Marshall, had realized the pastor's family did not have enough privacy, and they were going to make sure we were no longer smothered.

When I came home that evening Katherine was in a very good mood and told me of her visitor. The next day Marshall came by my office. He proceeded to share what he and his wife had decided.

"Paul, Mary Alice and I have been taking note of the way our church family treats you folks. We have come to see that the people here are too eager to presume upon you. I don't want to keep us from being supportive, but we need to give you some space. It's just that you're our first young pastor with young children. I've talked with several of the deacons and we all realize that living so close to the church is ripe for overindulgence. I promise you that we will make changes to slow down our intrusions into your private times."

I thanked Marshall. After that there were no drop by visits to the parsonage. Those who did plan to come over always called in advance by at least an hour. People continued to invite us to their homes or out to lunch on Sundays, but there were always weeks in which there were no invitations. We began to call those weeks "unsocials". Katherine learned to love the warmth of the people and her unsocial periods.

***

The philosophical question which has been debated for centuries is: are people the same person over their entire lives? I remember Katherine posing this to me while we sat on the end of the Bogue Inlet Pier one warm spring evening a couple of years ago. As a small boat passed on the horizon, she reminded me of Plutarch's Ship of Theseus. The early Greek, Plutarch, asked a probing question—if a ship were to be replaced plank by plank over time would it be the same ship after everything had been substituted? Many years later the English philosopher Thomas Hobbes brought up this analogy as he pondered whether or not people change their basic selfhood.

Katherine's take on the age old discussion was that human beings are in reality a point of view. "We use our point of view to make sense of our thoughts and our experience," she said. "Over their lives people change their points of view to some degree."

In my reading I've come to see the impact which depression makes on our point of view or our perception of the world. The depressed person sees themselves as defective, also deprived. Their perception is that they have limitations which have hampered their selfhood. They become different persons than they were before the depression. They see the world as being unfair to them. I have no doubt the Katherine of the past few months was not the Katherine of some years ago. My question is not philosophical, however. My question is practical—how much did I change over the years, and how much did I contribute to the changes in Katherine?

***

I'm drained of energy this Sunday afternoon. My shirt was soaking wet when I arrived home from church at twelve; I changed into a knit one after freshening up. Diane has prepared a lunch of hot chicken salad. Claude has offered a "well done" and Luke a thumbs up over my message. Grace simply sits on my lap on the couch and leans her head back as though the morning has been exhausting for her as well. Katherine would usually, on these afternoons, give me a rating of my sermon. It would range from B to A-. She explained once that I never did poorly so as to warrant a C, and I was never perfect, thus the grading system with A- at the top. I was satisfied when the message received her A-.

Sunday afternoons were what Katherine called "Sabbath rest". She tried her best to keep me from working. Both in Raleigh and Havelock there were evening services or Bible studies to go back to, however.

One Sunday last summer Katherine, Luke, Grace and I went to Fort Macon State Park for a few hours. The park is on the far end of the island from where we live. There's a public beach with a bathhouse and refreshment stand, also the refurbished Civil War fort along with a visitor's center. Luke loves the fort; his interest in the Civil War has been keen since he was only four. Grace gets bored at the fort but loves the beach.

Fort Macon was built in 1832 to guard Beaufort Inlet at the east end of Bogue Banks. During the Civil War, the fort was bombarded by the Federal troops and surrendered, thus allowing the inlet to be used for Northern shipping. The town of Beaufort across from the fort has many preserved houses from the colonial period. Grace loves the Fudge Factory on the waterfront. Katherine always insisted that we stop in at the Rocking Chair Bookstore when we were strolling through town. Luke likes to visit The Old Burying Ground in that small town where many Revolutionary and Civil War soldiers are interred. My son has memorized the inscription on one of the graves:

> The form that fills this silent grave,
> Once tossed on Ocean's rolling wave,
> But in port securely fast.
> He's dropped his anchor here at last.

I remember that day with our family at the fort well; it was the very first time I suspected that my wife was unhappy with her life. Luke was checking out the "dungeons" as he called the inner belly of the brick works. Grace was seated on a set of steps going to the top battlements drawing on a pad she bought in the gift shop. Katherine and I were standing beside one of the cannons on the parade grounds. She was silent and pensive. I asked her if something was wrong.

"Do you ever wonder what life would be like if we had never met?" she asked me out of the blue.

"No, not really," I replied. I meant that I had never given it serious thought. Of course I had, at times, looked back and posited such a scenario. What married person doesn't?

"I just wonder if you and I had taken separate paths would our lives have been fulfilling in different ways," she said.

"There would not be Luke and Grace," I said. "I can't imagine wanting to undo the circumstances which brought them into the world."

"I know that. Perhaps there would be children from other marriages, possibly even a son and daughter with some of their traits but not exactly them."

"Why are we discussing this?"

"Because I need at times to consider the alternatives to my actions, to the life I'm living. Most women envision different scripts for their lives."

"Do you mean fantasize?"

"That word has base connotations," she said. "Visualize is a better term."

"Do you regret our getting married?"

"There you go again using the more corrupt word. One can speculate without regrets."

She never did answer my question about regretting our marriage. She turned off the discussion of the matter like one twists the handle of a sink faucet. Grace announced she was ready to go to the beach and thus ended the conversation of alternative lives.

We looked around for Luke; he was not to be found. Grace went with Katherine as they started around the fort to the right. I began to head in the other direction. There are dozens of rooms, some with displays of fort life, and others hollow and still dark. In a few minutes we met back at the entry—no Luke.

Steps go up to the parapet on the inner fortifications. I climbed to the top and looked out across the fort, making my way around the perimeter again. As I progressed along the top I peered into the moat below and to the outer ramparts. From my vantage point I could see out over the sound and the inlet to Beaufort. Still, no Luke to been seen anywhere. The three of us decided to check out the welcome center. Inside the main foyer, Luke was standing by a window display of weaponry. He had a small audience as he was leading an impromptu guided tour of the facility. He had been to Fort Macon so many times that he could be on the staff.

We collected Luke and spent an hour at the beach then headed home down the island, passing through communities such as Pine Knoll Shores and Salter Path. Salter Path was once a small village of settlers from the mainland who were referred to as "squatters" since they resided on the land without deeds. It's believed the community got its name from the fishermen who passed by the house of the Salter family on their way from the sound to the ocean. The small houses of the descendants of the squatters today are surrounded by high-rise condominium units. The changes here are stark reminders of what development has brought to these coastal communities.

Change is on my mind these days. It has been pressed into my every waking moment. It dominates my perception like blinders which narrow one's focus. I can't get out of my head the song written by Bernard Ighner called "Everything Must Change". I heard it on the radio this week performed by Simply Red:

Everything must change.
Nothing stays the same.
Everyone must change.
No one ever stays the same.

chapter twenty five

THE PHONE RINGS. It's sergeant Tolliver from the highway patrol. "Reverend Brewer, there is someone who has information on your wife's accident. She's coming to my office in an hour. Could you come up to New Bern and meet her?"

"Do you mean now?" I ask.

"I think you will want to hear what this person has to say as soon as possible."

"I'll leave in the next few minutes. By the way, Sergeant, have you considered that there could have been another vehicle on the road that night at the time of the wreck?"

"We have. There's no indication of that. I think when you meet the person coming to my office some of your questions will be answered."

I tell Claude and Diane about what the patrolman said. They agree I should go.

Crossing the bridge it's clear that the weather is turning warm as a number of boats are traversing the channel and others are beached on the sandy edges of the small islands below. The wind is still today and the water so glassy that the boats appear to be sitting on the surface of a mirror.

On the mainland side of the bridge Highway 58 crosses Highway 24 at Cape Carteret. It's about a twenty minute drive from here to the small village of Maysville. In Maysville I turn right onto Highway 17 and head towards New Bern. In the sleepy little town of Pollocksville a bridge crosses the shaded Trent River as it winds its way toward the coast.

Passing through these quiet communities in eastern North Carolina on this Sunday afternoon reminds me of a story my dad once told me. A friend of his used to spend most weekends fishing from the Bogue Inlet Pier at Emerald Isle. He and his wife would drive down from Raleigh on Friday nights in their camper and return home on Sundays. The camper was a shell on the back of a pick-up truck with beds inside where he and his wife slept.

One Sunday morning around eleven they packed up to leave the campground and head home. The fellow had fished late into the night as the spot were biting that evening. He was very tired and asked his wife if she would mind driving. She said she would drive, and then he asked her if it would be okay for him to lie down in the back on the bed and tale a nap. She was in the truck cab; he climbed into the shell using the door at the rear. He decided he would be more comfortable if he slept in his boxers and tee shirt.

His wife made her way up the same route I have just traveled, except before Pollocksville she turned left to head towards Kinston. In the sleepy, small town of Trenton she stopped at the red light in front of the courthouse, about twelve fifteen in the afternoon. Her husband in the back woke up with the movement of the vehicle halted, and still half asleep, stepped out the back door. The light changed to green and the driver made the left turn not knowing her tired spouse in the rear had gotten out. She headed up the road to Kinston. Meanwhile, her husband stood there in the street in his underwear and quickly became wide awake as he took in his predicament. Several proper ladies coming from the Methodist church were shocked at the sight of this disheveled man in his underwear.

As my dad told the story, a young man in a sports car pulled up to the intersection, offered the fisherman a ride, and they headed off in pursuit of the man's wife. She had a good ten minutes head start and in Kinston decided to stop for a brief visit to a grocery store to pick up items for their dinner when they arrived back at home. She decided not to wake her husband in the camper. While she was in the store the sports car passed without the husband realizing his wife had stopped. Since they never caught up with truck, the young man agreed to take his passenger home.

The fisherman arrived home to find his wife not there yet. He thanked his chauffer and bid him farewell. Since the fellow in his underwear did not have a key to get in he waited in a chair on the front porch for his better half. A few minutes later she turned into the driveway, and spotted her husband whom she thought was still asleep in the back of the vehicle on the porch. Startled at the sight she ran through the back wall of the carport.

I've told this story many times even though I'm sure my father might have embellished it some. Once I used this as a sermon illustration in a message which asked where God is in relation to us, making the point that God is ahead of us waiting for us to catch up with him.

***

Pulling up in front of the patrol station, I'm apprehensive about what I'm going to face. Tolliver says he has some new information about the night of the accident, someone for me to meet.

Lenora Watson appears to be in her early fifties. She's seated in Sergeant Tolliver's office and is introduced to me. Her flowered dress accentuates her plus size body. She stands up to shake my hand. The patrolman offers me a seat across from her.

"Reverend, Mrs. Watson called this morning with information about your wife's accident," Tolliver says. "I would like for her to tell you what she told us. Go ahead, ma'am."

"Reverend, let me first say how sorry I am about your wife. I know that her death must be hard on you," she begins.

"Yes, her loss has been difficult for our family," I say.

She folds her hands in her lap and looks at the sergeant then me. "Reverend, my father is not the man he used to be. A few years ago his mind began to slip. At first he would just forget a few things, but lately it's gotten worse. We moved him into our house last year, cause we didn't believe he was able to live by himself."

I'm not sure where this is going but shake my head to signify that I'm listening to her with interest.

"You see he has dementia, the doctors say. This makes him so confused that he often forgets where he is. We have to watch him closely or he might wander off somewhere and get hurt. A couple of times he's slipped out at night and neighbors have called us to come get him."

I adjust myself in the chair as to be in a better listening position. "I have known some people with dementia. I think I have some idea of what it's like for family members. This must be a great challenge for you."

"Pastor, the Lord has indeed placed a heavy burden on my husband and me, our children too. I'm not saying that God has done this to harm us, just that he's testing us this way."

"Tell the Reverend about the night of the accident," Tolliver says.

Mrs. Watson alters her position so as to face me directly. "You see, that night was one of those times when we thought Pop was in his room asleep but found that he had gone out the back door. At about midnight my son, Trevor, called and said that Pop was at his house a mile away. He had walked up the road and was spotted by a neighbor of Trevor's. We were scared to death when we learned of this."

Mrs. Watson fidgets with the purse on her lap then looks at me with an expression I can't place. "My father was there when your wife wrecked, there at the church. A few days ago he told my husband that he saw what happened. At first Clyde, my husband, didn't know what Pop was talking about. He's hard to understand since his mind started going. When he described the car yesterday as he told the story again, my Clyde remembered the one your wife was driving. Everyone in this community remembers all about the accident. It was such a terrible thing."

Lenora Watson opens her purse and takes out a tissue before she continues her tale. "He was there, Reverend. He saw the whole thing. I'm so so sorry; I think Pop may have caused the accident. He was likely walking down the road and caused your wife to take her attention off what was ahead—the stop sign. Least he told Clyde and me that she had to swerve to miss him."

The sergeant adds, "It looks like he might have walked out in front of Mrs. Brewer and startled her that night. If he is remembering right, he was there that evening and may have been in the middle of the road."

Could it be that this old man with dementia did cause Katherine to miss that stop sign? This could have caused her to run into the tree?

"Mrs. Watson, I appreciate your sharing this with us," I say. "It's very helpful to know more of what happened that night."

Lenora Watson stands up and walks toward me; I stand as she takes my right hand in both of her hands. "I'm so sorry, so sorry. My father would never hurt anybody on purpose. He's a good man."

"I understand," I say.

Mrs. Watson leaves the office. The sergeant asks me to stay for a minute. "Reverend, I would like to interview this old fellow in order to make sure we have all of the information. Would you like to be there when I talk with him?"

"Yes, I would like to meet him. It might help me with some resolution in my questions."

"Good, perhaps we can do this on Tuesday," says Tolliver.

I call Claude on the way home and tell him about my conversation and about Mr. Salley. I can tell that the news helps him just as it has me.

In a sermon once I used a quote from Julius Caesar, "In war, events of importance are the result of trivial causes." I would add to that to say that in much of life events of importance are the result of trivial causes. An old man walks onto a highway at night and may have caused my wife to lose her life. It was such a senseless death. Is there any death which makes sense?

You can't be a pastor without accepting that death is in your job description. The conducting of funerals takes priority over every other pastoral duty—schedules are changed. In Pascal's *Pensees* there is a credible assessment of the place of death, "The last act is tragic, however happy all the rest of the play is; at the last a little earth is thrown upon your head, and that is the end forever." How do we play our roles in the earlier acts knowing what the final scene will be?

My mind seeks to adjust my appraisal of the accident at the church. If what Mrs. Watson said was true, it means that Katherine did not hit the tree on purpose. It also means she did not fall asleep. It was a matter of unfortunate timing. It is not all that satisfying to blame timing on our troubles in this world. There are occasions, however, when a fraction of a second means the difference between life and death.

chapter twenty six

As I HEAD home from the patrol station I come to a realization—I have spent so much time trying to solve the mystery of Katherine's accident that I have not given adequate attention to my grief. Grief can't be ignored for long; it must be met and dealt with in order for one to move on in life. It's a weight that's always there and makes everything difficult because it hampers our mental agility which is needed to navigate the twists and turns of life. Grief is like the sandbur that lodges in our sandals; it pricks us and prods us to see to it. Otherwise every task is a greater challenge.

I remember the day my father took me with him to Oakwood Cemetery when I was about eight years old. The only one buried there at the time was my grandfather who had passed away the year before. It was the Fourth of July and Dad wanted to put a small American flag on granddad's grave. My grandfather, Charles Edward Brewer, served in WWII in the Navy and was on a ship in the Pacific at the battle of Guadalcanal.

After he carefully placed the little flag by the headstone, my dad turned to me and said, "Son, we should never stop grieving. We should always keep a small kernel of grief in our hearts for those we love, just enough to remember now and then what they meant to us."

I remember this very clearly because he said the same thing a few months after Karen died as we stood over her grave. Sometime soon I need to go up to Raleigh and visit Oakwood. It's the place where much of my sorrow is laid to rest. Perhaps I can leave some of my inner turmoil there but not all of it. Some of it will always be with me.

I've wondered about savants. Do some of them remember every emotional pain they ever experienced? I know that savants have a specific field of recall such as music or math, but what if one could remember every painful emotion they ever felt? I speculate about this because I think I might have a special ability to grieve, far beyond what my father advised.

***

Katherine was late coming home. It was six in the evening and the children and I were waiting for her as we were to all go out to dinner. This was about nine months ago. We had planned to go to Morehead City to the Sanitary restaurant. Luke loves the place for this is where the sport fishing boats come in and unload their catch of the day.

Katherine had run over to the church to meet Susan and help a family with food. The summer day was hot, and we were all dressed in shorts. Grace had her favorite cap on, the one which she had gotten from the Sanitary at a previous visit, pink with the restaurant name in white letters. She also liked to eat there because of the views of the seagulls out the windows as we ate. We had invited Susan to go with us.

It was six-fifteen when Katherine walked in the door. She was crying. The children and I watched as she sat down on the couch in the living room.

"Why are you crying, Mom?" Luke asked.

Katherine sat there, tissue in hand.

"Katherine, what's wrong?" I asked.

After a few seconds she sobbed, "This world is wrong. Life is so unfair."

The four of us were now all sitting; Grace was beside her mother stroking her hair. Katherine was attempting to pull herself together. Luke was struggling to sit still as his mother's emotional mood had caused him to be uneasy.

"Did something go wrong with the person you met?" I asked.

Just then the doorbell rang. Luke bolted up and let Susan in. She walked into the room to witness the emotional scene.

"Did Katherine tell you what happened?" Susan asked.

"Not yet," I answered.

"It was a mess," Susan said. "You would not think this could happen in our country."

"What?" I said.

Katherine finally is calm enough to speak. "They said they were from South Carolina and had come to the island to find a friend who lives here. The friend had moved and they didn't know what to do, so they stopped at the church."

Susan joins in, "Their car's old, a Ford I think. It looks like it couldn't go another mile. Paul, there were three kids. Their clothes were filthy and their bare feet were dirty black. My guess is the girls were two and four, the boy maybe seven. I was there alone in my office when they first showed up so I called Katherine and Jim Albright."

Katherine stands up and secures another tissue from the kitchen counter and returns. "The mother was tiny, only about five-three. She wore a halter top and grungy white shorts. The guy, her boyfriend she said, was out of it. I didn't smell anything on his breath, but he was intoxicated or on drugs. She was driving."

"So, they were asking for food?" I said.

"Yes, and anything else we could provide," Susan said. "We started to call you, but Jim drove up. I was relieved because the guy, Jerry, was getting loud and demanding we give him gas money. Jim took him aside while we talked with the woman. She said her name was Marlene. According to her, they had been driving all day and had not eaten since yesterday. The children were so pitiful."

Luke was sitting next to Susan and taking all of this in without speaking. Grace was still beside her mother and fully engrossed in the story. All I could think of was how upsetting this must have been for Susan and Katherine.

"Where are they now?" I asked.

Jim had them follow him over to the Best Western in Cedar Point," Susan said. "He said that the Hem or the White Oak Ecumenical Ministry often helped people in situations like this and arranged for a night lodging. He volunteered to sign for the room until he could get reimbursed and get them a tank of gas."

"Paul, the car was grubby, trash piled up inside, empty drink bottles in the floorboard," Katherine said. "Those children looked to be so hungry. The younger of the girls, Shana, had sores on her arms and legs." Katherine began to cry again as she talked. "We gave then canned goods from the church pantry and then followed Jim to the Foodlion where they bought some milk and bread to take to the motel."

Susan added, "Marlene went with me into the grocery store while Jim and Katherine stayed with the others by the car. The woman went about her business as though this is a common event for them."

"It probably is." I said. "When I was in Havelock we had transients like this stop by the church quite often. It's a way of life for some."

"The smallest girl hugged me while we were in the Foodlion parking lot," Katherine said. "She didn't speak a word, just held onto me. The boy was afraid—of the boyfriend, I think. The skinny kid had a big bruise on his left arm. Jerry, the jerk, had the audacity to ask Jim if he had any cigarettes. Jim didn't answer him."

Susan said, "I wanted to call the cops on him; Jim advised we help them as much as we could and see that they move on. Supposedly, they're heading to Virginia tomorrow where Marlene's mother lives."

"You did the right thing," I said.

"I don't think there is a right thing in a situation like this," Katherine said.

The five of us went as planned to the Sanitary for Luke and Grace's sake. Susan and Katherine were in no mood to eat out, however. They were thinking about the children at the motel. Sometimes ministry is rewarding. Sometimes it is heartbreaking. Sometimes the two go together.

chapter twenty seven

THE FUNERAL SERVICE for Karen was hard on everyone, especially my mother. For weeks afterwards she would sit for long spells without saying a word. Sometimes she would just stare at Matt as though she had to make sure he would not disappear. I tried to be as good as I could be so as to not upset her even more. One day, about a month after the accident, by mistake I fired my BB gun at a neighbor's window. The neighbor told my dad. My father took me aside and gave me a long talk about how we all had to be careful to not make life any harder on Mom. I took my air rifle and put it in the back of my closet where it stayed for many months.

Karen was a quiet child who entertained herself much of the time. My Grace reminds me a lot of her. After my sister died my mother refused to let anyone change anything in her bedroom. The ruffled bedspread with the yellow flowers remained on her bed along with her stuffed animals, except for the one she had with her in the wreck. That one was buried with her. Besides stuffed animals she loved airplanes; several small models sat on shelves. She claimed she was going to be a pilot when she grew up. The door to my sister's bedroom remained closed, as did my mother's mind about using the space for any other purpose.

Some nights I would slip into Karen's room and sleep there on the floor beside her bed. I would imagine she was still alive, and we were having one of our two person slumber parties as we did before. The word "before" became one I frequently used; everything about our family life was divided between before and since. There seemed to be no now. It was as if life in the Brewer family was a timeline with a major break in it—a wide gap which separated our world between happy or before and sad or since. Sometimes I would have nightmares in which a form of the wreck would be the center of the scenario. If I woke up afraid I would never go to my parent's room; I would not tell them of my dreams. My suspicion was we all had our nocturnal reveries.

***

My mother lives close to my brother and his family in Raleigh. She lives alone now since my dad's death. She retired from her job as a dental assistant a year before Dad died and cared for him in his bout with cancer. Every month she goes by herself to Oakwood cemetery where she places flowers on the graves. My brother convinced her to let him accompany her last week. He called me the next night.

"Paul, we went to the cemetery today and Mom told me she believes that our family has been singled out by God to bear many burdens. She said we were like the Kennedys with all of what has happened in their family."

"Thanks, Matt; I appreciate your going with her. Did she cry much?"

"No, she was calm and told me she has a ritual. She says the Lord's Prayer over our grandparent's graves, Karen's grave, then Dad's, and now Katherine's. Evidently, this has been her routine for many years. It's the darndest thing. She puts a flower in the little vase, calls their name, and then says the prayer. After that she just stands there as if to wait for some word from heaven."

"What did you say to her?" I asked.

"I just stood aside and watched. When we were ready to leave she took me by the arm and said, 'Son, it is our plight to withstand sadness and let it touch our hearts without taking our hope away. The Lord calls his own to him and expects us to adjust to his will.'"

"Where do you think that came from?"

"I thought it was something you taught her. You're the preacher. I'm a building contractor. This is your area of expertise."

"Well, Matt, I think our mother has her own ideas about things."

"That's for sure," Matt said.

***

My dad could be profane at times. He had an expression which he used often, "hot damn." After I finished at seminary and was ordained into the ministry he would try his best to not use profanity around me any longer. When I was a boy the "hot damn" expletive was very common. I remember well the first speeding ticket I received. I was seventeen and a senior in high school. I was going to my part-time job at a grocery store when I was pulled for going forty-eight in a thirty-five. With fear and trembling I told my father that evening about my transgression. He let out a series of "hot damns" and then made it clear that I would pay the ticket out of my earnings.

One week after Katherine and I moved to Havelock, he and mom came for a visit. He could not grasp the concept of a parsonage, the idea that he church owned the house and a progression of pastors lived in it. On his second day there he spied a loose shingle on the edge of the roof, got a ladder out of the garage, and proceeded to climb up to fix it. I was walking over from the church and spied him up there with a hammer in his hand.

"Dad, what are you doing?" I asked.

"I'm taking care of things that need to be taken care of," he said.

"But, Dad, there's a church maintenance committee which fixes things around here."

"So, where are they? I've found three things today that needed repair."

"Dad, you're going to get hurt."

"This ain't no big deal," he said.

He began to drive a roofing nail into the shingle but missed and hit his thumb. I heard a loud, "hot damn." My father, holding his thumb, then looked around and over at the church about sixty yards away. "Anybody over there?" he asked.

"No, I don't think so," I said.

"I'm sorry, son. The truth be known, God don't mind a curse word now and then, long as it don't contain his name."

"And, you got that from what source?" I asked.

"From the book of common sense. One of those not in the Bible."

My father loved Katherine. He called her "Plato" and enjoyed goading her into a discussion of what Socrates or Aristotle taught. He was not college educated but did read some, and after he got to know my wife he studied some philosophy so he could discuss it with her. He liked to ask our resident philosopher things like: which came first the chicken or the idea of chicken. He loved Aristotle's more sensory view of the world as opposed to Plato's theory that the idea comes before the physical. Sometimes he would confound my wife with his mixture of Charles Brewer wisdom and classical philosophical concepts.

My dad never would talk about the accident on the bridge. My guess is he felt he was at fault—better reflexes on his part could have saved Karen's life. I would sometimes find him sitting with her photo in his lap. He would not cry, but the level of emotion in the room was akin to a nuclear reactor on the edge of meltdown.

Charles Brewer rests at Oakwood now beside Katherine Brewer. This may not be solid theology, but my guess is that they are also sitting side by side in heaven discussing Pauline theology from a lofty perspective. I doubt the "hot damns" are common on the golden streets.

chapter twenty eight

I HAVE AN eleven o'clock appointment with Dr. Rosenblum on this Monday morning. I'm very apprehensive. Katherine shared with this psychiatrist her deepest feelings and many aspects of our life together. He knows things about her I didn't know which is disconcerting. I suppose my real qualms about this meeting are that I'm afraid I will learn things I don't want to face.

The drive over takes about thirty-five minutes. My mind races with thoughts of what my wife revealed in the private journal. It was written by a person troubled over the course her life had taken recently. She was hurting from the feeling she had given up too much to gain what she had. Will I find out from her counselor that she did indeed hate me for this?

The doctor does not smile. He has a wide mouth, but it doesn't betray any emotion. His eyes, however, are raised and lowered with almost every exchange of words. Sometimes one eye is demonstrating a contrasting shift from the other. I can't tell if this is some minor affliction or a practiced method of communicating responses. Perhaps he has a mild form of Tourette's syndrome.

Dr. Rosenblum is Jewish. This doesn't bother me. I'm actually pleased that he has a faith perspective for his counseling. He asked me before I left his office the last time if that was a problem for me. I told him no. As I wait for my appointment with the psychiatrist I can't help but remember something I read a while back about Jewish culture. It said that many Jewish people do not answer the question, "How are you?" with a positive come back. I find myself usually responding with "fine" when asked about my well being. The tendency among some Jewish people is to say, "not bad" or something like that. Boasting about health is thought to bring bad luck in some cultures. Here I am in the office of a psychiatrist where most patients are not in the best frame of mind when they enter. I'm certainly not fine today.

The inner office is large with a number of still-life paintings on the wall, each depicting a different approach to the same setting of fruit on a table. I wonder if this is some kind of Rorschach test where the apples, oranges, and pears are meant to elicit particular responses based on the placement in the bowl.

"Reverend Brewer, how are you today?" the psychiatrist asks as he enters the room.

"I'm okay, considering," I say. "How are you?"

"Not bad. Do you mind if I call you Paul?" Dr. Rosenblum asks. "I would prefer if you would use my first name, Ron. We're here today as colleagues."

We're here today because I'm the husband of a someone who was unhappy with her life. I do appreciate the colleague idea, however.

"Okay, Ron, first names will be easier."

"Perhaps we could begin, Paul, by you telling me what it is that you would like to know about my conversations with your wife?"

"Well, to be honest, I didn't know that Katherine was seeing you until a few days ago. I was surprised that she saw the need for counseling. I still don't understand why she sought out psychiatric help."

"Katherine was depressed. You probably know that millions of people in our country suffer from depression and that a higher percentage of them are women. You also know that a large percent of pastor's spouses become depressed over their roles at some point."

"I know all of that. I just didn't know that my wife was one of those women, one of those pastor's wives with role issues, one of those statistics."

"Your wife was in a high risk group; depression is a very complex disorder. It would be easier if I could tell you that one thing caused Katherine's problems, but I can't. I met with her five times and we were just beginning to explore all of her issues. Let me ask you, what signs of her depression did you see?"

"I found out the last two months before her death she was very unhappy with her life. I was blindsided when she told me she wanted to leave me. I knew she was not the same recently but had no idea it was so serious she felt the need to seek therapy and to separate from me."

"That must have been a shock," Ron says. "You know it took some courage for her to come out and tell you that she might want a break from the marriage."

"Yes, she was trembling that night when she said it. I felt like someone had just torn away my heart. I knew she was hurting, but so was I. A part of me wanted to hold her; another part of me wanted to put my hand over her mouth and tell her to not say anymore."

"What did you do?"

"I don't remember everything. I think I just sat there hoping it was some kind of glitch in my comprehension. I couldn't look at her. I'm sure I didn't handle it well."

"She told me you became angry at first."

"Yes, I guess I did. I'm not that good with surprises. Give me some time and I can think more clearly."

"Have you ever felt that kind of anger with her before?"

"No, not that I can think of. She's always been easy to live with. I would say that I was more frustrated than furious that evening."

"So, did the two of you work through the idea of her leaving?" Ron asks.

"No. I guess I closed off the discussion. She acted the next morning as if the whole thing had not happened. I was hoping it was just some momentary emotional hiccup that hit her. I didn't forget, however, the question she asked me that night—'When are you there for me?'"

"Do you think you were there for her?"

"I've been turning that over and over in my mind since that night, especially since the accident. I thought I was considerate of Katherine during our marriage. I guess she didn't see it that way."

Again Ron just sits and looks at me. I assume he's giving me time to reconsider my answer.

"Sure, I've been very focused on my ministry," I say. "I admit there were times when I was so involved in my work that I didn't give my family enough attention."

"Katherine used the word 'neglect' in our sessions. Would you agree that you neglected your family?"

I see that this is not a discussion between colleagues. The psychiatrist is treating me as a counselee. He's probing for my sensitive areas. "Ron, I can't relate to the word 'neglect'. I did not neglect Katherine. I made a concerted effort to spend time with her and the children. I can appreciate that you're trying to help me see what our problems might have been. I think Katherine grew up being the center of the attention of her parents which deeply influenced her outlook on life."

"Are you saying she was spoiled?" Ron asks, looking straight at me.

I don't answer immediately. There were times in our marriage when I thought her behavior was the product of her parent's doting on her. That was early on in our years together.

"My wife is dead. I loved her very much. I will not call her names or say anything derogatory about her. Obviously, I wasn't as good of a husband as I should have been. Any opportunity to mend my ways has now passed. I'm here today to understand how I missed the beginning signs of her depression. How could I have not seen this coming?"

Ron looks at me for at least thirty seconds, again without saying anything. Finally he asks, "Paul, do you remember the discussion you and Katherine had a few months ago about her teaching?"

"Sure, she was offered a job at the community college."

"Did you two argue over that?"

"We discussed it and decided it was not workable."

"When was this?" Ron asks.

"In the summer. The position came open for the fall semester."

"I think that may have been a turning point for your wife."

"Did she tell you it was?"

"I think it was an important matter to her. She saw it as an opportunity to fulfill one of her dreams."

"But she was the one who decided against it," I say.

"Maybe, she thought she had no choice."

"It would have placed even more pressure on our family."

"Yes, she felt it would not have been easy. I think she really wanted to try it."

"She told you I ruled it out?"

"Yes."

"Wow, I don't remember it that way."

"You asked me before if I thought she was suicidal. I don't believe she was. I would be very surprised to find out the accident was a result of some plan to hurt herself."

I tell the psychiatrist about what we learned yesterday, about the old man who may have walked out in front of her at the site of the accident. He seems relieved that there's some explanation to her wreck and asks me a few questions about how I found this out. We then return to our discussion of Katherine's depression.

"Paul, most depression is a consequence of a feeling of loss. Depression is usually reactive, reactive to a perceived deficit. Katherine told me she had lost her hold on almost every aspect of her life."

"I was unaware this was happening. With all of the demands of my work I missed the signs."

"I'm sure there is plenty of pressure on you in your vocation. Likely, there are times when the stress is too much? You see, the pastor's wife is the secondary, innocent, victim of these stressors. The ministry brings great demands on the spouse as well."

"I'm very much aware of that. I know that Katherine had to suppress her true feelings at times. The lack of privacy in our lives was troublesome to her. I wish now that I'd been more aware that these things were bringing her down all along."

"Paul, you know that one person can never discern for sure how someone else feels, especially those who are depressed. The fact is the depressed person is themselves confused about what they feel. It's no wonder that a husband or wife misses the clues. The indicators are often hidden behind the lack of communication on the part of

r. The depressed person seeks reassurance they're under-
____e they are, at the same time, trying to mask who they are."

"That's what bothers me most now. I didn't understand what was happening to her," I say. "I, of all people, should have been more aware."

"There is one thing you and I have in common with our respective faiths, the Old Testament Psalms, Ron says. "Psalm 69 is a favorite of mine. I call it the psychiatrist Psalm. It's about depression. I keep it on a card here in my desk and look at it often. I don't usually make it a practice to share my religion with my clients, but you are not my patient. Would you mind if I read a part of it?"

I don't remember this Psalm and say, "No, I don't mind; I'd like to hear it."

Ron reads from the card, "Save me, O God; for the waters are come into my soul. I sink deep in mire, where there is no standing: I am come into deep waters, where the floods overflow me. I am weary of my crying: my throat is dried: mine eyes fail while I wait for God."

The sadness reflected here causes a lump in my throat to form. Was Katherine this miserable? "I remember now some of this Psalm from my study, especially the part about the floods overflowing me."

"Sometimes people get to the point where there is no reasonable escape from their despair," Ron says. "There is one other thing which Katherine shared with me. It was an old wound that recently opened again. She said this was her one big secret she kept from you. I've been thinking about this since our first meeting, and have decided we must talk about it."

"Are you referring to the miscarriage?"

"Yes. So you know about that?"

"I just learned of it from her parents. She never told me about it."

"She said she could never find the courage to tell you. I think it was a traumatic part of her life which she never completely dealt with. Recently it resurfaced when she heard from the guy she dated back then."

"Do you think this triggered her depression?" I ask.

"I think it was a part of the cause. I told you her emotional health was a complicated matter. I'm pretty sure she never got over the guilt she felt over the pregnancy. Do you see, Paul, all of the forces working on your wife? She still had emotional pain from years ago. She felt you were not as attentive to her as you once were. She regretted giving up her career choices by settling in as a pastor's wife."

"I see all of that now. Still, how does a person get this depressed in such a short time?"

"It's likely this all was brewing for a few years now. She managed to keep it from showing. The truth is that from the day we are born, we start losing. By making some life choices, we forgo the opportunity for others. We lose certain freedoms, and we lose some of our self-confidence as our limitations become more evident. Quite often, depression is fostered by this sense of loss. The feeling of deficit accumulates and then triggers despair in some. Katherine's depression was reactive, a slow reaction to many perceived losses."

I nod as though I understand. It's clear that our session is about over. The psychiatrist has summed up for me the extent of Katherine's troubles. Dr. Rosenblum shakes my hand and pats me on the back as I leave the office. The still-lifes on the wall catch my attention as I depart. Which of them reflects my confusion?

My return from Jacksonville is not only a car trip but a mind trip as well. There's so much to think about. Ron Rosenblum was very helpful, and I appreciate his effort to guide me through my grief and questions. It will take me a while to process all I've learned about Katherine. I went there to better understand what happened to her. I left there wondering what happened to me. Is it true that I became this insensitive, career focused jerk who did not take the time to notice the signs of my wife's distress? How many sermons have I preached on being considerate of others? On top of all of the many other names I've called myself in the last few weeks, I now have to add hypocrite.

There are many people who believe that Christians do not get depressed. I've read studies which show religion has little bearing on the numbers. The old spiritual expressed it well, "Sometimes I'm up, sometimes I'm down—standing in the need of prayer." It's crucial that we dismiss the myth that our faith will always result in lives of joy and happiness. Faith does bring joy, but it does not always protect us from depression. Moses, Jacob, and Paul all became depressed. I recall the words of Jeremiah who said, "God, I have lived a moral and upstanding life but to what benefit?"

Ron Rosenblum has prompted me to think back to the time last summer when Katherine told me that she had been offered a teaching position at Carteret Community College in Morehead City. I was aware she had sent her resume to the college the year before when they advertised for an opening to teach a night course. It seemed like a good possibility for her at the time.

I was working on a sermon in the den one day last July when she came in and asked if she could interrupt me. I try to remember that afternoon now as Ron thinks it was instrumental to her dejection. I think she was nervous as she brought the subject up.

"Paul, I received a call today from Dr. Weisner at the community college. She wants me to consider filling an opening they have on the faculty."

"I didn't know there was a position available now," I said.

"They announced it a few weeks ago. One of the teachers took a faculty spot at Chapel Hill. My resume was still on file and they called to see if I was interested. I told them I might be. It would be an opportunity to make use of the Master's degree I finished while we were in Havelock."

"I don't remember you telling me about this job before," I said.

"I didn't. You had a funeral that week, and I assumed they would look at other candidates."

"Is it a night course like last year?" I asked.

"No, this is a full time position. I would essentially be the philosophy department. I would teach three or four courses a semester."

"Four courses. How in the world could you handle that?"

"It would not be easy, that's for sure."

"Katherine, you have the children to consider. Your few hours at the bookstore are workable, but this would be too much on you, on us."

"I looked at the fall schedule of classes," Katherine said. "Two are in the evenings when you could be home. None are on Wednesday evening when you have church."

I remember the measured excitement in her voice, and the calculations in my mind of how this could possibly work. It would have certainly created a lot of chaos for our family. Life is made up of hours, a finite allotment of them. Where would she find the time to do all of this?

"What do you think?" she asked.

I don't remember exactly what I said. I believe it was— "I think it would be too much on us all."

She just sat there.

I do remember saying, "You know that the church must be our number one priority."

Katherine responded to that with, "Of course, the church must come first. I've honored that rule for fifteen years. This is something I can do that will be worthwhile, my contribution."

"You make valuable contributions to our community now," I said. "You give of yourself through the church. I don't think your teaching full time is workable. Luke and Grace will suffer."

At this point Katherine stood up and looked at me with an expression I took as being acceptance of what I had said. I don't remember her saying anything as she left the room. I recall spending a few minutes trying to imagine her taking such a demanding job and deciding she would come to see the impossibility of it working.

The next day she told me that she had turned down the position. I told her I was sorry that it wasn't practical and that she had made the right decision.

Katherine loved to quote Aristotle when he said, "Philosophy is the science which considers truth." I'm confused as to what was the truth of my relationship with my wife. I didn't see myself as denying her opportunities to fulfill her dreams. Now I think I did force her to miss out on realizing her desire to teach. The thing is—she would have been so good at it.

chapter twenty nine

THERE IS A deep pile of messages on my church office desk. Carla and Susan have handled all they could, but some matters are the responsibility of the pastor. Jeff Whitaker is still in the hospital in Greenville. Madge Roberts is at Carteret General for tests. Carter Moore, chairman of the properties committee, needs to talk with me about a heating and cooling issue. The regular deacon's meeting is tomorrow evening and Jim Albright needs to go over the agenda with me. There's bulletin material to prepare, numerous calls from well wishers to return, and Marian from the bookstore where Katherine worked has a paycheck for me to pick up.

Susan has a couple of counseling situations to share with me. We meet in my office. Susan acts a little more upbeat this morning. My son, Luke, has a crush on her. He asked me some time ago why she wasn't married. I told him I didn't know. What I didn't tell him was she was almost married once, but the guy chickened out a month before the nuptials. She has never talked about that with me but shared the details with Katherine. My wife said that Susan and the fellow was not a good match. She was brought up in church; he was not a church attendee until he met Susan. Katherine was determined to play matchmaker, but Susan has been reticent to go out with anyone she didn't know well. Our church has only a few single guys, most over sixty.

"I suppose you want a raise since you are handling so many of my duties," I say.

"You have been a slacker recently, and I could use a new car," Susan replies.

I will bring that up with the finance committee but don't hold your breath."

Susan is quick with a comeback, "I've already spoken with David Prescott on the budget planning team, and he has assured me that adjustments will be made." She smiles.

"So what have I missed?" I ask.

"You may not want to hear this, but Della Lowrimore has asked for financial assistance again."

I swivel in my chair and bite my lip. "How much has the church helped them in the last year?"

"We've paid for rent and utilities on several occasions, about three thousand from our local missions fund since last summer. Jim Albright has spoken with several deacons and feels we should put a limit on what we do for them. He will discuss it with some of the other deacons."

Della Lowrimore has two children, a boy ten and a girl eight. Her husband, a boat builder, left her about a year ago and does not pay child support. She works in a local retail store and doesn't make enough to make ends meet. Our church tries to help local families in trouble, but there does not appear a way out for Della. She gets county assistance, but her rent is too high. She refuses to move from the house she and her husband rented on the island, a very expensive place to live.

"That's a tough situation," I say. "What other good news do you have for me?"

"Steve Blair has run away from home again," Susan says. "This is the third time. His father wants you to refer some counseling for him. I don't think he trusts me to handle this."

"Where is Steve now?" I ask.

"He's back at home, but he and his father argue all the time. His mother tries to intercede, and is afraid Steve is going to get in trouble with drugs or something else. At thirteen he's a real challenge for his parents."

"I'll give Ted Blair a call. Anything else?"

"Sam Welch came by the other day to complain about the songs we sing in worship. He's upset that Michelle picks the same hymns to sing too often. He brought in a spread sheet where he has plotted her music choices over a year period. According to Sam, we've used one hymn six times in that period. He's also printed up a list of the hymns we have not sung during that year. We do not sing enough blood songs, he says. He questions if Michelle is not energetic enough to serve as our music minister."

"So, how did you handle that one?" I ask.

"I told him we are considering doing away with the hymnal and going to all praise songs like some churches do. I said it was time we move to a more contemporary style of worship. Sam liked the idea—just kidding."

"Right, I can see Sam Welch standing up and clapping his hands to "Our God Is a Mighty God". He's so traditional that he objected when we took the doxology out of the order for a few weeks. My guess is that you really told him you would pass on his suggestions to Michelle."

"Yes, I did what any good associate minister does—pass the buck. Michelle said she will try to placate Sam."

"Tell me there are no other sticky situations."

"That's it for now. So, how're you doing?"

I tell Susan about my meeting with the psychiatrist and about the old man who probably walked out in front of Katherine the night of the accident.

She's quiet for a few seconds and then says, "I have a confession to make. I was not sure that Katherine didn't set out to hurt herself."

"Why did you think that?" I ask.

"Because, she told me that when she was in college she once thought seriously about taking her life."

"When did she tell you that?"

"A few weeks ago she invited me to the house for lunch while the kids were at school."

"How did it come up?"

"We were talking about our college experiences. I told her I had this guy who wouldn't leave me alone, and made me uneasy every time I left the dorm. She then told me that she had some serious relationship problems her freshman year and one night contemplated suicide. She never told you that?"

"No."

"I now feel so bad that I wondered about her accident. I should have known that she would never do that to you and the children, to herself."

"I think you're right. The wreck was an accident."

Susan leaves and I contemplate what she has told me. Will there be an end to the revelations of Katherine's past, the details of which I was oblivious?

***

It's one in the afternoon and I feel I must go back up to Greenville to visit with Jeff Whitaker at the hospital. Joyce called this morning and told me that her husband had a bad night. So, I'm on the road again.

Jeff is still in ICU and hooked up to all kinds of monitors. I know that it's best if I don't stay too long and tire him out. He tells me that he's worried about Joyce staying up there all of the time. She refuses to go home. Their son is busy at Duke but did spend Saturday night with him.

"Paul, I have a great support group. My wife, my son, the deacons from the church, and my sister are all keeping close tabs on me. You don't have to take the time to come up here and see me."

"Jeff, you're a church member and a friend. This is my job and it's what I want to do. Besides, I kinda like seeing you in that hospital gown. You see, I'm jealous that you always dress so impeccably."

"I asked them for an Izod gown, but they told me they couldn't afford designer hospital wear. I'll bet this thing will cost me more than a half dozen of my knit shirts."

We have a prayer, and I speak with Joyce a few minutes before I leave. She's handling it all well.

With some audacity I take the elevator to the floor where Kyle Edwards is being treated. I ask at the nurse's station if he has any visitors and am told no. The person on duty tells me he comes and goes, out of it most of the time. I tell her that I'm a minister, feeling somewhat bad about the semi-deception since I'm not his minster.

The door to his room is partially open, and I can see this thin man with little or no hair turned on his side so his face is toward me. His eyes are closed, oxygen rhythmically seeping into his nostrils. For a minute or two I stand here at the door to the room and try to imagine what Katherine felt as she stood here that night. Did she cry when she saw how pitiful he looked?

I'm not sure what I would say if he were to wake up—perhaps, "I'm the husband of Katherine Brewer who died in an auto wreck because she felt the need to come see you." Clearly, that would not be fair to a man who's on his death bed. What's fair anyway? Is it fair for a vital man to contract cancer at less than forty years? Is it fair for a mother to die in an accident on a dark road because she feels the need to reconnect with someone who hurt her years ago?

There are a few greeting cards on the bedside table; a couple of plants sit in the windowsill. Curiosity grabs me and I venture over to the array of cards which are folded open. There are four to be exact: one from the car dealership, another has "from Mom and Dad", a third with a brief note from his son. The final card is signed "K." This last greeting has a one-line line generic message, "A misty morning does not signify a cloudy day."—Ancient Proverb.

I'm now close enough to Kyle to hear his labored breathing; it's the sound of a body struggling to steal a few more weary moments of being. Cancer is such a sour killer. Everything about it is unpleasant from the loss of hair to the sallow epidermis. I have had too many encounters with this morbid intruder. Cancer is death spelled slowly.

I can't count the times I've visited people in hospital rooms. This is the strangest of all. I don't know him but know his situation well. He's dying. I've stood beside the beds of dozens who were near death. Somerset Maugham once wrote of death, "My advice to you is to have nothing whatever to do with it."

I go back to the nurses' station and ask if Beverly is here. I'm told that she just started afternoons today and is on the hall somewhere. In about five minutes she approaches me in the waiting room.

"Reverend Brewer, I'm Beverly Wilson. They told me you were here to see me."

"Yes, I'm sorry to interrupt your duties. You spoke with my father-in-law the other evening about my wife visiting here. I was on the other line when you two talked."

"Yes, I told him your wife was here on the night she had the accident. I'm so sorry about her death. Is there something else you would like to know?"

"I was hoping someone might be able to tell me what time she left," I say.

"Like I told your father-in-law, the last time I saw her was in the waiting room over there about nine."

"Who else was working your shift that evening?"

Beverly thinks for a moment and says, "I'm pretty sure Deon was the nursing assistant on duty that night. He's here today. Let me find him for you."

I wait for Deon, hoping he remembers the evening and can tell me more.

"Yes, sir. What can I do to help?" He wears a name tag which reads: Deon Jackson, Certified Nursing Assistant. Deon is slender and probably about twenty-five. He has a tattoo of a mermaid on his left forearm.

"Mr. Jackson, Beverly tells me that you were on duty the night of March twelfth. My wife came here that night to visit a patient, Kyle Edwards. On the way home she was killed in an auto accident. Do you remember seeing her that evening? She was…"

"Yes, sir I remember her. I heard about the accident. I'm good with faces. I don't forget many, a gift my mama says. She had kinda reddish hair and was wearing a black sweater. The thing is she was very upset that night, sat in the waiting room a long time with that boy."

"What boy?" I ask.

"The skinny kid, the man's son."

"Whose son?"

"The Edwards fellow in 3452. The boy comes here a lot. He and your wife talked for over an hour."

"Do you remember what time she left?"

"Can't say for sure. All I know is she was in the patient's room for a while, then the boy came back from the cafeteria, I think, and the two of them sat and talked in the waiting room."

"Did the boy leave when she did?"

"I think so."

I thank Deon and head for my car. Katherine talked with Kyle Edwards' son? He may have been the last one to see her alive.

***

It was August, two years ago. Hurricane Eunice had been brewing for days far out in the Atlantic. People who live at the coast have learned to watch the weather channel with an eye out for those named storms which head for the Continental United States. After a few days of constant north-westward movement, the projected path of Eunice was a possible landfall in the Wilmington area. This would mean that our part of the coast could be on that dreaded right side of the storm. Eunice was true to course and headed right for the Carolinas.

The evacuation order was given in the afternoon and by early the next morning most tourists and locals alike had left. Eunice was assumed to be a category one storm. Katherine and I had evacuated the year before, only to return after a false alarm as that storm stayed well out in the ocean. One scenario or track for Eunice was that it might do the same and just skirt our coast. We decided to stay on the island and chance this category one; a two or three would have been another matter.

The first strong rain bands of Eunice hit at noon with the eye predicted to pass nearby at around midnight. She did not veer but set her sights clear upon us, now a category two. At five a tree limb broke off across the street and hit a transformer. The power for our neighborhood was now out well in advance of the main thrust of the storm. Luke said that at least we did not have to anticipate it going out over night. We broke out the candles and the flashlights, ate our sandwiches, and hovered around the little battery powered television to monitor the reports.

Katherine was always a storm nut. She mocked doom and despair predictions and saw such times as thrilling, times for family togetherness. At eight she broke out the Scrabble game. We were captive gamers who now were under the direction of hurricane scoffer, Katherine Brewer. The wind howled, the candles flickered, the rain blew steadily against the windows, and the tiles were placed on the game board. Grace placed her word on a bonus spot—"dark", a fitting choice. It was not totally dark in our house, just a little dim.

At eleven we decided to turn in and try to sleep. I worried about the roof; Katherine said, "There's no need to worry. Remember the sermon you preached titled, 'Wait to Worry.'"

I remembered and asked, "Do you believe everything that a preacher says?"

"Not everything, just the things I want to bring up when he fails to heed his own advice," she said.

At about two in the morning a loud crash woke me up. Disoriented in the pitch dark, it took a minute for me to realize that there was no power and that I needed to secure the flashlight beside the bed. When I turned it on, I saw Katherine sitting on the floor by the closet.

"What are you doing over there?" I asked.

"I don't know," she said.

"Are you afraid?"

"Maybe."

"I thought you were tough where storms are the issue."

"It's just that constant roar of the wind," she said. "While you were asleep the eye passed over. For a few minutes it stopped and then started again, this time from the other end of the house."

"What do you think hit the house?" I asked.

"Must have been the top of the oak over by the kitchen."

"I'll go check it out."

Grace was standing at the door to her room with her pink flashlight shining down the hall.

"It's going to be all right," I said.

"What was the noise?" she asked.

"Not sure. You go back to bed and I'll look around."

As I directed the beam of my light to the kitchen window it was no doubt the tree, or part of it, was now on our roof. All I could see out the window were oak branches pressed closely. There did not appear to be any ceiling leaks at that point.

Back in our bedroom, Katherine was now sitting up in the bed with her battery powered lantern. The devil-may-care storm mocker was obviously still very upset. I held her for a long time until she finally fell asleep. I stayed awake for another hour worrying about our house and the church buildings. It was a night to remember.

chapter thirty

I THINK WHAT I miss most is the sound of her voice. Katherine and I talked to each other a lot. I miss her smile, her touch, her hair, her eyes, but I miss hearing her the most. She was not really all that verbose, but when she would speak on a subject dear to her she could be loquacious. If the topic was our children, she would wax on forever. Katherine loved to share stories of their quirkiness or of their clever sayings. Grace has always furnished fascinating material for our discussions as this child who speaks so little has expressions which are so charming. One turn of phrase often used by our daughter has been, "what just happened?" This would come anytime Grace would be surprised.

Of course Katherine loved to talk about philosophy. I remember the time she read the novel, *Sophie's World*, and would not stop sharing parts of it with me. It's about a girl who keeps getting letters which introduce her to philosophical thought. My wife never gave up her love for Teilhard. Her favorite quote of his was— "You are not a human being in search of a spiritual experience. You are a spiritual being immersed in a human experience." I can't count the times she reminded me of that quote.

It's her voice on our home answering machine still. Claude has suggested that it might be good if I replaced it. I know it is not best for callers to still hear her voice. I agree to erase it; for now I will keep her cell phone so that I can listen to her voice.

Every morning Katherine would call our dog, Crocker, to his breakfast. She was not a dog person, but she was Crocker person. These were often the first words she would speak in the morning, and I loved hearing her talk to him as though he were human. I wonder what goes on in his dog brain now that he does not hear her voice.

We all miss her. There should be a vacancy sign in the window of our house, not to signify an empty room but an empty spot in our hearts.

I remember a story I once used in a sermon illustration about a man who used to frequent a service station in the days when attendants came out to assist you. A boy named George often filled his tank for him and cleaned the windshield. For several visits the man noticed that George was not there to render the service. Finally the man asked, "Where's George?" The station owner replied, "George doesn't work here anymore." The customer then said, "Who's going to fill his vacancy?" The manager replied: "George didn't leave any vacancy."

I suppose there are people who move away, quit, or even die, who are not missed. That's sad. Katherine is missed.

***

This morning I feed the dog and wake up the children. Diane is still asleep, Claude left an hour ago on a quick trip to Raleigh. The school bus comes early for Luke. Breakfast is Rice Krispies, banana, and raisin toast. Grace will eat the toast but remove the crust; she loves the cereal and fruit. I will take her over the bridge to her school and then come back to get ready for the day myself. I used to jog most mornings while Katherine got the children ready. Perhaps there will be a time when our daily routine will allow for that. Diane gets up in time to help Grace get dressed.

I'm on the road again, this time up to meet Sergeant Tolliver and go to the home of Lenora Watson. We're going to interview her father, Omar Salley. I'm nervous about pressing this seventy-eight year old, dementia ridden man, to recall the night of the accident. Hearing his story, however, could be essential to my knowing what caused Katherine to wreck that evening.

Mr. Salley is a short, lean, African American. He's sitting in a leather swivel rocker, wearing a wool shirt and high waisted work pants. He doesn't stand up when we enter the room but does wave at us as if we were long missed acquaintances. His hair's mostly gone, and his black rimmed glasses have thick lenses which magnify his dark eyes.

Mrs. Watson explains to us that some days her father can talk lucidly but on other days gets so confused he can't make a sentence. "Today he's not so bad, but he may get emotional and freeze up. This is a part of how the dementia affects him," she says.

The sergeant and I nod that we understand.

She calls him "Pop" and stands beside him with a hand on his shoulder. I can see the resemblance between father and daughter though she's almost twice his size. She explains that he was not always this frail and that he was a dairy farmer who spent his life working hard. "He still likes to go out and walk among the cows in the field. He seems to be happiest out there."

"Mr. Salley, we are here to talk with you about the automobile accident two weeks ago," Sergeant Tolliver says. "Do you remember that night and what happened?"

The older man looks at the uniformed officer and then up to his daughter who is still standing beside him. "Who's this?" he asks.

"The highway patrolman, Pop," Lenora says. "Tell him about the woman at the church, the car wreck."

There's a long silence. Mr. Salley looks at everyone in the room and tears begin to water his cheeks. He takes off his glasses and rubs his eyes with the back of his hands. He looks out a window in the direction of the church which is only a mile away from the small frame house where we all await his words.

"It was my fault," Mr. Salley says. "I didn't mean to be in the road. I jus' got confused. Some nights I can't get to sleep and has to walk. I seen the car comin', but I ain't much for doin' nothin' fast. I couldn't see the driver. Heard my daughter later tellin' her son the paper said it was a woman. She died."

Sergeant Tolliver speaks, "You told your daughter, sir, the driver turned to keep from hitting you."

Mr. Salley looks over at me, "You her husband?"

"Yes, sir," I answer. "My name is Paul Brewer."

"I didn't mean to cause no wreck," the old man says. "I am very sorry."

It strikes me that several dozen people have said those words to me in recent weeks, but this time they are not words of empathy; these are words of contrition and regret.

"Yes, sir," is all I can think to say.

"I watched the car cross the road over to the church. I saw it hit the tree. I was fearful. It was dark, but the pole light shined through the trees. I knowed the driver was hurt bad. That car must have bounced back ten feet."

His daughter rubs his shoulder and is now crying.

Mr. Salley looks at Tolliver, "Then I seen the boy get out the car. He jus' stood there for a while, then walked away."

The old man is beginning to get mixed up, I think.

"What boy?" Sergeant Tolliver asks.

Mr. Salley looks around the room again and settles on me. "The boy that was ridin' in the car with your missus."

"Mrs. Watson, you did not say anything about a boy," Tolliver says.

"I've never heard this before," Lenora Watson says.

"Someone was in the car with her?" I ask the old man.

"That's right, a young fella, thin white boy."

"Are you sure about this?" Tolliver asks.

"I ain't sure about much, but I seen the boy. Seen him under the night light."

Into my mind pops the expression my daughter uses, "What just happened?" The old man seems to be lucid. Why was someone else in the car with Katherine? Who was it? Why were they not hurt? I remember sitting in the passenger seat of the Honda in the garage and being amazed how there could be so much damage on the driver's side and so little on the other.

"Pop, why did you not tell us about the boy before?" Lenora asks. The old man nods his head. She looks at me and says, "I'm not sure he's remembering right."

"Am so," Mr. Salley says. "As God is my witness, there was this boy in the car. He got out, went around to the driver's side, then walked over to the church."

"What did you do then?" the patrolman asks.

"Me, I jus' turned around and kept walkin'. I figured someone would see to the person in the car. Didn't know then it was a woman."

Sergeant Tolliver tries to ask more questions; the old man's tired and not willing to say more. He just shakes his head no, and his daughter explains that this is the way he is sometimes. "He just can't keep his concentration for so long."

Mr. Salley slumps in the chair, head in his hands. His frail body seems to be swallowed by the leather rocker. His daughter kneels down in front of him and pats him on the top of his head.

The patrolman and I walk out onto the porch. The sergeant says, "That someone else was in the car is hard to imagine. The old fellow was adamant, however, that he saw someone get out of the wrecked vehicle that night."

"I think I know who the boy may be," I say to Tolliver. "My wife went that evening to visit an old friend of hers in the hospital at Greenville. The boy in the car was probably the son of Kyle Edwards, the patient. I just learned that the young man and Katherine talked at the hospital that night. He lives with his mother in Pollocksville."

Sergeant Tolliver writes this down. He promises to get back to me soon.

I stop again at the little white church after I leave the Watson house. Standing out in the yard I try to picture the scene that evening. The old man is across the road, over where the stop sign is. Katherine swerves to miss him; she then realizes she has overlooked the stop sign and turns hard to the left, probably thankful there's no oncoming traffic. Before she can make any other adjustments or hit the brakes she has crossed the ditch, and the trees loom before her; she realizes that a collision is imminent. Knowing her; her mind is racing as to whether she brushed the old man with her car, what about the boy in the seat beside her, and possibly wonders will she survive the impact if she hits one of the trees ahead. In that tiny fraction of time before everything turns dark, her thoughts are bombarded with several fragmentary pieces of concern.

There was no time to contemplate the meaning of it all, no time to meditate on what Teilhard called the "principle of the conservation of the personal." Katherine would often say that we humans are so incomplete. I found this Teilhard quote in her private journal, entered only a few days before her death:

> "In broad terms it may be affirmed that the Human, having become aware of its uncompleted state, cannot lend itself without reluctance, still less give itself with passion, to any course that may attract it unless there be some kind of discernible and definitive consummation to be looked for at the end, if only as a limit."

Once she told me that she would, on her death bed, contemplate the mysteries of the universe and end her days on earth with some definitive philosophical appraisal of the meaning of life. I wish she could have had that opportunity. She would have loved to pass from this world in quiet meditation. That was not her fate, however.

***

Diane's watching television when I return; Claude has gone to Lowe's lumber to get a part needed to fix something for Luke. I wait to talk about the boy in the car until Claude returns. I sit on the couch with a diet Pepsi in my hand and join my mother-in-law in watching CNN.

Diane lowers the volume, "Can I ask you something, Paul?"

"Sure!"

"Did my daughter ever tell you that I once left Claude before she was born?"

I look at this sixty year old woman who is always so active and vocal. She and I have talked often about the children. She loves to regale about her childhood over in the mountains and of her two older sisters who formed with her a singing trio when they were young. The group sang in churches in the area. She's never shared any intimate aspects of her married life with me, however.

"No, I've never heard about that," I say.

"I only told Katherine about it three years ago. Do you remember when we went to Charlotte together on the shopping trip?"

I shake my head yes.

"Katherine was shocked when I told her that her dad and I were separated for three months. It happened when I was only twenty-two and had been married just two years. Claude was wrapped up in his work. He had insisted that I quit work since he was making good money. I got bored. Don't worry; I'm not going to embarrass you with a story about an affair. I just did not feel appreciated and decided to do something dramatic to change my situation."

My eyes get wide as I listen. "Where did you go?"

"I went to stay with my sister, Mildred, in Chapel Hill. Whenever it comes up now Claude calls it my holiday."

"What did Claude do?" I ask.

"Oh, he didn't make much of a fuss. He would call me each night and ask how I was doing. We would talk for fifteen minutes and he would always end the call by saying I miss you."

"What would you talk about?"

"He'd tell me about his day at work, and I'd tell him what was going on with my sister's family. It was all very ordinary."

"How did you get back together?"

"One Saturday Claude called in the morning and asked me if I would like to go to a movie that afternoon. I agreed to go. We went to see High Noon with Gary Cooper and Grace Kelly. After the movie we went to dinner, and then he took me back to my sister's home. When we pulled up in front of her place he calmly said, 'Diane, you need to come home, for your sake and for mine.' There was a quiver of emotion in his voice. I went in, packed my bags, and we drove back to our house. The next day he told me I was his girl and that he would do his best to be a better husband. That was the end of our separation."

"That's amazing. Just like that. May I ask if you ever wanted to leave again?"

"Paul, every wife, every husband, has times when leaving comes to mind. All couples have their bad periods. Sure, I thought about it a few times over the years, but I've never forgotten the fear in Claude's voice when he told me I needed to come home. It was such a matter of fact statement, but behind the words there was a delicate pleading that broke my heart. I could not ever do that to the man again. I'm telling you this to say that Katherine may have told you she wanted to leave, but it was probably not a forever thing."

I thank Diane for sharing this with me. Within a few minutes Claude comes home. I can't help but look at the man in a different light. He has some idea of what I was going through with Katherine. I wonder if Diane, in telling Katherine this, planted some seed that she could take a vacation from our marriage for awhile.

chapter thirty one

LUKE AND GRACE are sitting on the living room couch with a small book. They're both laughing when I walk into the room.

"What's going on?" I ask.

"We're just looking at this book about strange facts," Luke says.

"You should read some of these, Dad," Grace adds.

"Okay, let me hear one."

Luke begins reading, "Some turtles can breathe through their butts. These butt-breathing turtles have the ability to stay under water for extended periods by sucking water in through their cloacae…"

"That word means rear-ends," says Grace.

"I'm not so sure I like you reading that kind of stuff," I say.

"Oh, Dad, this is just science," Luke argues.

"What's the title of this book?" I ask.

Luke reads, "Are You Kidding Me?"

"That's the title?"

"Yes," says Luke. "These are fun facts that seem like they can't be true."

"Where did you get the book?" I ask.

Grace says, "Mom brought it home from the bookstore a few weeks ago, before she …" Grace stops and looks at me.

"Do you want to hear another one?" Luke asks.

"Sure, fire away."

"We have more bacteria living inside us than we have cells. Our bodies have about 100 trillion cells and almost two quadrillion bacteria."

"Isn't that amazing, Dad?" Grace asks.

I agree that it is. It's good to see Luke and Grace enjoying something. They've both been so down the past few weeks, understandably so.

"Don't worry, Dad," Luke says. "I'm not letting Grace see the ones in the book that refer to sex."

I take the book from him. "I'll be the judge of what you and Grace can't see."

"Come on, Dad, Mom let us look at all kinds of stuff," Luke says.

I almost say the standard line—"well, Mom's not here now". I catch myself and instead say, "Let me just go through it and see what's in it. Maybe I'll learn something new."

My two children watch as I take the book to my room. There are so many aspects of being a single parent which I've yet to consider. There were so many facets of parenting which were Katherine's area of expertise. Katherine was always buying books. She must have spent half of her pay at the bookstore. I didn't mind for I loved to read what she brought home. She often took Luke and Grace with her to shop at Bogue Sound Books on weekends—they grew to love books as much as Katherine did.

One of Katherine's favorite books was *Peoplemaking* by Virginia Satir. She loved the opening lines where the author said that when she grew up she wanted to be a "children's detective on parents." Virginia Satir's stated goal was to help families find a "better life together." Katherine was a serious reader on parenting. She told me on several occasions that the key to being an effective parent is being able to manage change. She also felt that our job as parents was to see that our children have positive self-esteem.

I know that my children were instilled with much self-worth by their mother. They will have to live the rest of their lives without her guidance, but they'll never lose what she planted in them. They'll be able to call upon that reservoir of positive traits she taught them, ingrained in them, and lovingly nourished in them. Katherine had the amazing knack of communicating her acceptance of who our children were through her choice of words, her facial expressions, her open armed gestures, and her caring actions.

The thought occurred to me today that if Katherine had indeed taken her vacation from her roles as parent and wife she might have dipped into that reservoir of self-esteem she left with Luke and Grace and caused them to question all she taught them. Her death may have prevented this possibility. This is a terrible thought—that my children are better off that she died instead if she left us while she was alive. My guess is that one reason she fought the urge to leave was her consideration of what it would have done to the self-images of Luke and Grace.

I remember one evening we were all watching Jeopardy after dinner. Katherine and I often tried to outdo each other answering the questions. The children usually rooted for their mother. That evening one of the categories was "Philosophers". Luke said, "All right, Dad, you're toast tonight."

One of the answers, I remember well, was "This thoughtful philosopher is best known for this statement, Cogito ergo sum." Katherine quickly called out, "Who was Rene Descartes?" Luke high-fived his mom.

Under the category, "Lakes and Rivers"—The answer was, "The river most mentioned in the Bible." To our surprise little Grace yelled out, "Jordan". Luke said, "Wrong, you didn't make it a question." Grace began to cry and her mother soothed her spirits.

I was behind by a few dollars by the time of "Final Jeopardy" when they announced the category: "Actors and Roles." Katherine had run the philosophers category while I did well on naming the rivers and lakes. Luke brought a pencil and paper to both of his parents for the final answer.

"Sam Shepherd played the role of this real-life character in the movie, *The Right Stuff*." I smiled as I wrote down my answer while Katherine was slow to enter her response. "Remember to make it question," Grace advised her mother. Two of the real contestants answered correctly: "Chuck Yeager" while one guessed "John Glenn". Luke collected the answers of his parents. He revealed mine first which was correct. The suspense was thick as Luke unfolded what his mother had written. He was superb in hiding his emotion as he calmly announced, "The winner in our family Jeopardy this evening is Katherine Brewer, the new champion."

Grace stood up and danced as she sang, "girls rule." Luke seemed conflicted over the side he had chosen after that. Later Katherine told me that Augustine said, "I think therefore I am" long before Descartes.

chapter thirty two

It's JOHN WILLIAMS on the phone, the pastor of the church where Katherine's accident happened.

"Paul, I thought I might check on you and see how you're doing," John says.

"Well, I'm trying to adjust, to get back to work. It's not easy. I appreciate your thinking of me."

"You know, Paul, it's not a sign of weakness to take the time you need to grieve."

"I know that, but keeping busy seems to help."

"Oh, it helps," says John. "There still needs to be private time. I sound like the old meddling fool, don't I?"

"No, more like a sympathetic sage with a whole bunch of experience."

"Then, let me tell you—from my experience these first few weeks can be mighty hard. After my wife died, every time I turned around there was some reminder of her. I would eat something and remember she liked this food. I would hear people talking about a subject totally unrelated to her death, and it would cause me to remember a conversation I had with her. Every song I heard or television show I watched, reminded me of her in some way."

"I know what you mean."

"That never seems to stop, but it does become less intense," John says.

"I hope it becomes less severe with me soon."

"Paul, the word is out in our community that an old guy down the road from the church here may have caused your wife's wreck. I just heard of it today. I suppose they have made you aware of this."

"Yes, John, I just learned of it. Do you know the man?"

"I don't know him personally, but I've seen him walking beside the road on a couple of occasions. His granddaughter cleans our church. The old man has dementia. Listen to me call him old man. Not much difference in him and me, other than the memory loss, and I'm not far behind on that score."

"I've talked with him. He feels bad about that night," I say. "I certainly can't blame him."

"They're good people, Paul. The granddaughter is really broken up over your wife's death and her grandfather being there. Sometimes, I wonder how a set of circumstances such as this works out the way it does. Preacher to preacher, do you think God blinks and stuff happens during that fraction of a divine bat of an eyelid?"

"I won't preach on that; I do conjecture such at times."

"I've been preaching for almost fifty years and still don't know what to tell people when some senseless tragedy occurs. I think I must be out of the loop when it comes to insight from God on such things. I catch myself saying 'I'm sorry' to them. I know that's not what they need to hear from their pastor. I guess what I mean when I say that is – I'm sorry I don't have something better to say."

"Same here. Being on this side of the calamity does help me see how important it is that empathy requires a more focused response," I say.

"I've learned one thing in this area over the years—don't assume you know what people are feeling. I try now to let them share what is really going on before I offer a response. So, let me try that with you. Does it help you to know that your wife's accident may have been caused by Mr. Salley wandering around late at night?"

"Yes, it does help to know. I never really believed she crashed into the tree on purpose but knew she was distressed that night. If it was a result of her swerving to miss the old fellow then I can settle that issue. There are so many other matters left to settle, however."

"Unsettling is a word I find myself using often," John says. "I hope you will find a way to get past your troubling questions. If you need someone to listen as you work your way through them—I have some time on my hands."

I thank John for his call and his concern. I think I may just presume upon his wisdom again.

***

It was two years after the accident in Richmond before our family took another vacation. In the fall we took a trip to the North Carolina Mountains, to Boone and the Blue Ridge Parkway. My mother wanted to see the colors of the changing leaves; my father, I think, made the trip in hopes that it would cheer up my mom.

I was twelve at the time, Matt was seven. We were still a family with a gaping hole in the middle, but we were making progress in accepting the loss of Karen. Mom had just that summer finally turned Karen's room into a home office for all of us to use. It was strange seeing the furniture replaced, and the stuffed animals donated to goodwill. Dad and I actually boxed all of the small stuff up while mom was grocery shopping, her suggestion.

For almost two years, sadness defined our every activity. For the first time we were setting out to enjoy some time away. Since I was only twelve, my grasp of our family dynamics was not very astute. I knew enough to realize that this trip was meant to be therapeutic, that word not in my vocabulary yet, but the concept partially understood. My dad never let on, but I sensed that he was anxious about the trip. I can now imagine what was at stake for him—the pressure to make sure there were no problems on the road, nor any reminders of our last family trip out of town.

I had a talk with my brother before we left, trying to make him aware that his behavior needed to be almost perfect. This was my attempt to intercept his normal brattiness. He had become very spoiled as Mom doted on him, a natural consequence of losing one of three children and filling the void with more attention on the youngest. Since my sister died, I had become the extension of my father's paternal discipline. There was no allowance for any mischief on my part as my adulthood started that rainy day on the bridge.

The scenery on the parkway was fantastic. Even Matt marveled at the colors and the views from the roadside overlooks. No one would ever have called my father eloquent, but he waxed well on the wonder of God's creation on that trip. "Boys, this is the hand of a loving creator at work," he said as we stood peering out over an expansive valley below Grandfather's Mountain. "We're as close to heaven as you can get right here." Matt corrected him in that there were other points on the parkway where the elevation was greater.

My mother smiled and said, "Son, your dad meant that seeing such beauty is an example of God's design."

I was impressed by my parents' take on things and gave Matt a look so as to remind him there are times for children to be seen, not heard.

"Paul, you said a while back that you would like to be a preacher when you grow up," Dad said. "Well, boy, there is no better place to get the call to preach than right here in God's natural world."

"Charles, Paul will get his calling in a church service, not on a mountain," my mother said.

Dad agreed with her, probably not wanting to spoil the moment. He had learned how to keep things on an even keel since the accident.

My father announced that he wanted to go over to Blowing Rock and see the view from there. My mother agreed to the side trip. It was an adventure for Matt and me as we climbed up one of the huge rocks. Mom and Dad sat close to each other across on a bench as we explored, and everyone seemed to really enjoy the day. I remember thinking there was a chance they might be happy again.

On the way back to Boone, Mom announced that the motel had an indoor pool and that we could swim that evening. She sat in a chair beside the heated pool as Matt and I had the water to ourselves. Dad stayed up in the room watching football. Our mother seemed to really take pleasure in this time with her boys. She teased Matt for his "fish face" as she called his expression in coming up from beneath the surface. I hoped this was the end of her melancholy.

The motel had views of the mountains on each side. The distant peaks loomed like "citadels of nature's eternal majesty," as Dad put it. I assumed he read that in one of the brochures he had picked up. Every aspect of the trip went smoothly. Matt behaved, there were no close calls on the highways, and every subject which came up was pleasant.

I realized on the trip that our family was back to as close to normal as we could be. There was always going to be an empty space in our lives. We would never forget the day of the accident. We were people of loss, but we were also a people of gain as our bond was tighter because of Karen's lasting connection holding us together.

chapter thirty three

Tonight is the monthly deacon's meeting. The church is a community of believers, people engaged in shared ministry. The deacons are individuals with their own needs but who are charged with seeing to the needs of others. Jim Albright opens the session with prayer.

After the minutes are read and the old business is handled, the time comes for reports. Brad Thompson reports on the ministry situations that exist. He mentions Jeff, still at Pitt Memorial, and three others. The deacons have been keeping on top of these situations. I'm proud of how they have assumed responsibility. I look around the table and my heart is warmed by the commitment of these laypersons.

Susan reports on the ministry with children. Two new families have started coming to our church, each with young ones. Our congregation is growing and the need for more workers in the education program is presented. There's a financial report and one from the properties committee. Each deacon is given the opportunity to share what's on their mind; most pass. Doris Cromartie says she does have a concern.

"Mary Bettleson is a neighbor of mine," Doris says. "Mary came over the other day and told me that she and her husband, Ed, are thinking about leaving our church. She said they're unhappy that our church is not conservative enough."

I can see that several of the other deacons are frowning. My guess is that they do not want anything controversial to come up tonight. It has been a challenging few weeks for everyone in the church.

Jim speaks up, "Doris, I appreciate your bringing that to our attention. I will talk with the Bettlesons."

"They want to meet with the pastor to discuss this," Doris says.

"I think, for the time being, we deacons can handle such matters," Brad says.

"I'm just telling you that they're pretty upset. I know they can be difficult at times, but we should make an effort to address their concerns."

"Doris, I will meet with them," I say. "I'm aware of some of their issues and think it is a matter for the pastor."

"Paul," Jim offers, "I think this is not the time for you to have to deal with this."

"The agenda lists pastor's time next," I say. "This is where I usually share what's on my mind. There are a few things I would like to say. Folks, this has been a difficult time for all of us. I appreciate so much what you leaders have done. This church family is so considerate."

The other nine people are all still and very attentive.

"First, there's something personal I need to say," I continue. "If I were in your shoes I would be asking this question—how will Paul be able to pastor our church now with his wife gone and two children to care for? I've asked myself that question, of course. My answer is——I'm not sure. But that's not very helpful; so I feel the need to offer a better response. I have a little book in my personal library written by another minister many years ago. It's called *Tracks of a Fellow Struggler*, written by John Claypool. He wrote the book after his eight year old daughter died. I reread it this week."

I stop for a moment and take a sip from the cup of water in front of me. Most of those at the table adjust their positions during this break.

"One thing I've learned from this book is that I should not make any quick decisions. More is going on in every event in our lives than we first realize. God is not finished with this situation yet, not finished helping me through it. If I were forced to plan my future tonight, I would most likely say—there's no way I can go on with all that's on my plate. But I'm finding that every day a new resolve bursts forth in me, some new smidgen of courage. What I ask of you who are charged with leading this church is some time to allow God to have his way."

Jim takes the opportunity as I pause my thoughts to speak. "Paul, every one of us is wants to give you all the time you need."

"Thanks, Jim. I do appreciate that. This is not something I can simply think through and come out all right. John Claypool put it this way, 'I am called to live in order to know rather than know in order to live.' I simply have to move forward and hope to be able to work it out."

"Isn't most of life trial and error?" asks Brad Thompson.

"I suppose it is," I reply. "I've usually planned my agenda and then went ahead trying to make it work out. Now, I don't know what agenda to plan."

"I don't want to be impertinent," Susan says. "I am the youngest one here, and I have lots to learn. It seems to me that every one of us at this table is going to have to feel our way through this situation. For sure, Paul, you are the one who lost your wife, but each of us feels this loss in our own way. Katherine was our friend, our fellow church member, and if you don't mind the analogy, our first lady. I certainly don't know what it's going to be like without her as we try to move on."

I can tell that there's a nonverbal consensus in the group, an unspoken "amen" expressed. For a few seconds no one seems to want to follow what Susan said.

Finally Jim speaks, "As I see it, we deacons are charged with helping Paul and the congregation through this time. I say we look on this as an opportunity to participate in an experiment of trusting God. Paul, you have taught us the church is a laboratory for testing out the Christian life. I, for one, am willing to engage in the mysterious process of investigating how one gets through a period of grief in a body of believers."

All around the table there are similar pledges of willingness to use this as a learning experience.

"I like the spirit of cooperation," I say. "There are some things, however, which fall to the pastor. One of those is to counsel with unhappy church members. I will speak with the Bettlesons, Doris. This is likely a very sensitive matter."

"Thank you, Paul," Doris says.

The meeting ends with hugs of support, not just for me but for each other. Emotions are overflowing, and the spirit of cooperation high. I'm encouraged, yet very much aware that in the great experiment we are to engage in—I am the x factor.

***

Last night after I returned home from the deacon's meeting, Claude and I discussed the possibility that Omar Salley did remember the events of the night of the accident clearly. Claude, in his earlier investigation, had found that Kyle Edward's former wife lives in Pollocksville on this side of New Bern. We both wonder if the son still lives there with her. Claude placed the call and found Patricia Edwards at home. He explained that his daughter had died in an auto accident. She knew all about the Katherine's death. He asked her how she knew, and she said she read about it in the papers.

The next part was a little tricky as Claude asked her if she knew that Katherine had been to see her former husband that evening, March twelfth. She said she did not know that. He asked if it would be possible for him to come up and talk with her about Kyle. She was very accommodating and suggested they meet in New Bern at her office on her lunch break the next day. Claude said he would like to bring his son-in-law with him. Again she agreed.

***

Patricia Edwards works for a law firm in New Bern. Claude and I meet her in front of her office building at noon. She's an attractive woman likely in her late thirties, tall and slender. She invites us to go with her to a coffee shop nearby. This is certainly one of the most awkward lunches of my life. She expresses her condolences over Katherine's death and then asks us why we wanted to meet with her.

"Mrs. Edwards," Claude begins. "Paul and I have learned some things about my daughter's accident which are confusing. We were hoping you could help us with one of those things."

"I don't see how I can help," Patricia says. "I only know what I read in the paper."

"Mrs. Edwards, I appreciate your willingness to meet with us," I say. "I found a journal my wife kept and learned from it that she had known your former husband years ago while in college. We just found out that she had been to see him in the hospital, and she was there on the night of her accident. We also learned that your son was at the hospital that evening, and she talked with him."

Patricia Edwards looks shocked and pulls back away from the table. "Someone said that she talked with my son?"

"Yes," Claude says. "Someone on the nursing staff saw them in the waiting room down the hall from Kyle's room."

"Kenny has been to see his dad on several occasions. Why are you asking about him?"

Claude and I look at each other, not sure where to go with this conversation. Patricia picks up on this and says, "What? What are you afraid to say?"

I choose to answer her. "Someone saw a boy in the car when my wife ran into the tree that night."

"Oh, my God. You think my son was in the car?"

"We're not sure," Claude says. "It's possible."

"My son has not been injured. How could he have been in the car?"

After a pause, I say. "The passenger side of my wife's Honda was not damaged nearly as much as the driver's side." My instincts tell me that Patricia knows more than she lets on.

"My son's a good boy. He was very upset when his father and I separated and divorced. He's so very concerned about his father now."

"Does your son live with you?" I ask.

"He does."

"Would it be possible for us to speak with him?" Claude asks.

"No, I don't think I want you to do that," Patricia Edwards says as she stands up.

"Mrs. Edwards, the highway patrol is going to want to talk with your son. It might be less threatening if we could head that off," Claude says.

She sits back down and looks around the room. It's clear that she's very upset about all of this. After a minute she speaks. "I work for three lawyers. I would like for you to come back to my office with me. I want one of the lawyers to advise me as to what to do."

We agree to go back there with her.

At the office of Brown, Foster, and Wiggins we wait while Patricia Edwards speaks with Jonathan Foster. In a few minutes Foster invites us into his office. He's in his early forties, dressed in a button down collar shirt and wearing a UNC necktie. Mrs. Edwards is seated in a chair beside his desk. We are invited to sit in two other leather chairs across the room.

"Patricia has filled me in on your conversation at the coffee shop," Foster says. "Let me say that I'm very sorry about the death of your wife and your daughter. So, you think that Patricia's son was in the car that evening?"

Claude answers. "All we know is that he was seen talking to Katherine at the hospital that night between nine and ten, and that an old man who lives near the accident site says he saw a young man get out of the car after the wreck."

"Even if he was a passenger in the car there's no crime in his leaving the scene," the attorney says. "Passengers are not held responsible."

"Mr. Foster, this is not about getting the boy in trouble," I say. "All I want to know is what happened that evening. I need some closure on my wife's death. We think someone walked out in front of her on the road and caused her to miss the stop sign. If the boy was in the car, he might be able to tell us if that is correct. I can understand his being afraid and leaving that night."

The attorney asks us to wait outside while he speaks with Mrs. Edwards. In a few minutes he comes out. "Gentlemen, I will arrange for you to speak with the boy. It will have to be tomorrow. He's at school now, and we will want to discuss this with him when he gets home. Mrs. Edwards wants to be of help. She understands your need to know what happened."

Claude and I leave New Bern and head back to the beach. On the way we recap the situation. I can appreciate that Kenny Edwards will be very reluctant to tell his story if he was in the car with Katherine. Why was he with her is what I question.

"I wonder how the boy got home?" Claude asks.

"My guess is that his mother knew all about that evening. Like many mothers she's trying to protect her son."

"I suppose she agreed to meet with us to find out what we knew."

"Possibly out of guilt feelings as well."

Claude says, "I think I can now appreciate better what detectives must go through as facts come to the surface slowly in their cases."

"It makes you speculate as to what else we will learn about that night."

chapter thirty four

WHEN I WAS sixteen, one evening a friend and I went bowling in Raleigh. I had just gotten my driver's license. I took my friend home and, as I was backing out of his driveway, I hit a car parked across the street. There was no street light and the car was black. I've always been pretty adept at making excuses for myself. That night I went back to my buddy's door and told his father what had happened. It was after eleven and there were no lights on at the house across the street. My friend's dad said he would, first thing in the morning, tell his neighbor what had happened and give them my name and phone number. I went home.

The next morning as I sat at the breakfast table with my parents and younger brother, two Raleigh policemen came to our door. They had a warrant charging me with leaving the scene of an accident. It seems that my friend's father did not get up as early as his neighbor that morning, and the neighbor went out to get his paper and saw the sizeable dent in the side of his car. He called the police before my friend's father had a chance to tell him what happened. After the police left our house, my dad let out a series of "hot damns".

My father went to court with me two weeks later. By that time the warrant had been reduced to failure to report an accident, a lesser charge. My friend's father had written a letter to the court explaining what had happened. The result was a day of work missed by my dad, a lecture given to me by the judge, and a "prayer for judgment" ruling by his honor. I've often thought of that ruling by the judge. Not many people ever pray for judgment.

***

The bookstore near our church is a favorite spot of mine. The rough hewn wood floors creak, and the pine shelves form private nooks for intimate browsing. A wide range of literature is available from the latest bestsellers to classics which have stood the test of time. It's a treasure trove for those who like to read and for those who like to explore new adventures and enter new worlds.

Katherine worked at the store, part time, for three years. She enjoyed the opportunities to peruse the new book arrivals and read between waiting on customers. Marian Davis is the owner and manager. Marian and Katherine became close over the years and enjoyed working together. Marian's a tiny woman with an expansive IQ. Katherine often came home amazed that her boss was so well rounded, a renaissance woman, as my wife put it. Marian does not go to church but is keenly interested in religion. She's told me on several occasions that she's a spiritual agnostic. Katherine told me that her boss's childhood experiences with an authoritarian Pentecostal pastor turned her off from organized religion.

I sit in the small office at Bogue Banks Bookery. Marian has Katherine's last paycheck for me which she has cashed out. She apologizes that retail pays so little and that she was not able to compensate Katherine for what she was worth. I tell her I understand and that Katherine would probably have worked here for free.

"Paul, your wife was a rare find," Marian says. "She was so bright and so interesting. We had some fascinating discussions. I miss her so much."

"I know," I say. "She thought a lot of you."

"What happened to her?" Marian asks. "In the last few months she changed. Her enthusiasm vanished as if it had been drained from her through a transfusion. She was still pleasant at work with the customers, but as soon as she was not waiting on someone a cloud would surround her and her demeanor would grow sullen."

"She was depressed. She went to see a psychiatrist."

"I know," says Marian. "I made the recommendation. He had treated another friend of mine. One day I sat down with Katherine here in the office and told her she needed some help. He came highly recommended."

"I've talked with Dr. Rosenblum. I'm pleased that he was her doctor."

"Good, I didn't want her going to someone who would tell her that her problem was she didn't have enough faith. Her problem was not religious, whatever it was. I could not stand the idea that someone would tell her that God does not want her to be sad and that Christians should not be depressed. Now, don't get me wrong, Paul. There's something to be said for faith in God."

"Marian, you're a wise woman, and I would not be surprised if there is some evangelical pull lurking around in that agnostic heart of yours."

"You're wasting your time if you intend to make a convert of me, Reverend."

"Maybe, but I happen to know you have quietly slipped into our church a couple of times for worship and sat up in the balcony. I chalk that up to curiosity."

"Just wanted to see what you were made of, Paul."

"At this point I'm pondering that myself. It's tough losing your wife, more so when I consider the possibility that I was a major contributor to her unhappiness. Anything you can tell me about that, Marian?"

"Are you asking if she talked with me about your relationship? Well, I can tell you that she never did. All I know is that she was very unhappy about something or somethings. I do know this—being intelligent is no guarantee that you're able to handle all the things this life hits you with. There's a book on the psychology shelf over there which I'm sure you've read, *The Road Less Traveled*. It begins with these words, 'Life is difficult.' By golly, that is an understatement. Katherine was married to a good man. It just shows that there are no guarantees in this life."

"I know," I say, "that we should never take for granted that everything is going to work out right if we just love someone enough. I now realize that a person can care for another and still not have the needed level of sensitivity to meet that other person's needs."

"Come on, Reverend Paul. There's no need to punish yourself like that," Marian says. "Have you read Sam Keen?"

"Yes, some."

"Well, you may remember he says that we must begin everything we do 'by acknowledging the inevitability of failure.'"

"That's a pretty dour view of life," I say.

"Not dour, just real. If I were a pastor like you and a couple came to me to get married, I would counsel them that they are going to fail at being a good spouse. I would add, however, that the key to making a marriage work is to be thankful for the times they overcome their failures. Like Keen says, 'the most significant index we have of the stature of a man is the amount of pain and tragedy he has been able to bear and still rejoice in the gift of life.'"

"Are you preaching to me now?" I ask.

"I'm just sharing a little of what I've read with you."

"Katherine said that the two of you often talked philosophy," I say.

"She was fascinated with the history of thought. She would complain that our philosophy section in the store was too small. I would tell her that most people who come to the beach want to read a romance novel or a good mystery. She would say we were missing the opportunity of introducing them to existentialism, mainly joking about that."

"She told me that you added some philosophy titles at her request."

"That I did. She reminded me of what Sartre said – 'existence precedes essence'. I asked her what that had to do with anything. She said I would not ask that question if I had more philosophy books."

After leaving the store I reflect on what Marian said about failure being a given in life. I must somewhat agree with her. Marian is wise. Someone once told me that in order to face life after loss you need the right company. I now feel that need. I require people who will not minimize my loss. I want people around who will be frank with me, hopefully frank and sympathetic. Marian is such a person.

***

The private journal haunts me. It represents a
my wife's psyche that was hidden from me. In its pa;
which were a part of a person who lived in the same
I lived, but who inhabited a place in which I was no

February 18

*Today I perused the books at the store trying to find some insights which
may help me escape my sadness. I tried to remember the nature of the forces which
shaped Owen Meany's poignant life. I searched my recollection for Dostoevsky's
winter of despair. I touched the spine of Catcher in the Rye and thought that even
the worst among us are precious.*

*How would someone write my story? Would it be a comedy or a tragedy?
Would I be the heroine or the villain of my own life? Why is there so much
sorrow in good literature? Why is life so difficult? My story is not worthy of telling. I am a secondary character in my autobiography.*

*My life is a paradox. It is absurd. I live two mutually exclusive lives. In
one I am a wife and mother. In the other I am a free thinker. There is no real
freedom when you are part of a family. There is no room for family if you wish to
think for yourself. I feel like I'm in the old classic paradoxical joke—If a woman
tries to fail and succeeds, which did she do?*

It tears me up to think of Katherine in such state of mind. I
wish she were alive today for my sake, that I had the opportunity to
help her through her inner turmoil. I wish she were alive today for
her sake, that she could have come to a place of inner peace.

***

One of the books Katherine brought home from the store was
Rollo May's, *Love and Will*. I find the copy on our living room bookshelf. In it she marked a passage: "To love means to open ourselves
to the negative as well as the positive--to grief, sorrow, and disappointment as well as to joy, fulfillment, and intensity of consciousness we did not know was possible before."
I read further in the chapter and find a sentence which stops me
cold. May wrote, "For death is always in the shadow of the delight
of love." He is not just talking about physical death here. He asks if

.oving relationship does not destroy the person who entered into it. When we give up the center of who we are, do we ever get our original self back? He writes that we no longer have any guarantee of security after we love another.

chapter thirty five

TONIGHT IS DINNER and Bible study at the church. As Luke, Grace, and I enter the fellowship hall I smell the ribs cooking. Claude and Diane have also agreed to come. This will be a a night off in the kitchen for my mother-in-law.

Josie Greenfield, in her late eighties, is our most senior member. She approaches me with her usual engaging smile. "Pastor, my prayers have been with you. I thought so much of Katherine."

"I know, Miss Josie. She always loved you, and she especially liked the pecan pies you made for the church dinners."

"My ministry is my cooking. My pies are baked for the Lord. As it says in the Psalms, "Accept my offerings of praise'. My baking is my offering."

"I'm sure God values your gifts," I say.

"Pastor, if you ever need someone to talk to, you're welcome at my house. I know I'm old and some see me as only Josie the good cook, but I've not just lived long, I've lived many experiences. I lost two husbands, three sisters, and four children. Me and the Lord have had some serious talks over the years. I have some real practice with death. I would like to share with you a little of what I've learned."

"Thank you, Josie. I will take you up on that offer." It seems everyone I talk with knows something of what I'm going through.

The study for the adults this evening is a continuation of a series on the Beatitudes of Jesus. I started this a few weeks before Katherine's accident, and until a few days ago had not given thought to continue it. This is my job, however. I am Paul Brewer, pastor, and until the good Lord shows me some sign of a new role for me; this is what I do. It's just that I'm no longer Paul Brewer, husband; God has allowed a change in that distinction.

Before the study it's customary for me to entertain prayer requests from the people gathered. Usually there are the declarations of friends and family who are not well and expressions of concern for recovery. Often there's a death of someone in the extended family. Sometimes, a member will bring up a matter of financial need or a hope for reconciliation in a squabble. The typical prayer list can include a couple of dozen needs. There's no lack of prayer needs mentioned this evening from battling cancer to loss of jobs.

I remember a story of a pastor who stood up one Wednesday at one of these prayer times and heard a procession of examples of good news. Someone spoke of better health after a long illness, another of a perfect child being born, and there was the announcement of a positive turn in finances. This was not typical of such sessions—all good news. The pastor recorded each of these for the prayer to follow and then asked, "are there other prayer requests." He was not accustomed to all the positive sharing and became a little concerned there might not be the need for the usual intercession for bad news. Then someone mentioned the death of a distant relative, and the pastor said without thinking, "Finally, some bad news, thank the Lord." This, of course, surprised his parishioners. I can't imagine a prayer session without need for God's intervention being revealed.

The Bible study goes well and the students are attentive. It's almost like the many times I taught before the Katherine's death. I realize that I've come to think in terms of before the accident and after the accident. It's though my life has a clear dividing line that cuts through the middle of every experience to place events in one category or the other like one sorts piles of laundry to be washed. Is this to be my new way of organizing memories, before and after that night, the one which parted the pages of my existence?

Claude and Diane take the children home. I stay until everyone has gone and lock up along with Susan who has led the youth group meeting tonight.

"How did it go?" She asks.

"It was okay," I tell her. "The people were very intent, it seems, on ensuring this be a typical service, nothing out of the ordinary."

"They simply want to help you adjust," Susan says.

"That's an interesting idea—adjust. How does one regulate emotion? How does a person amend the total constitution of their life?"

"I'm sure you've told many people how to do that in your counseling sessions," Susan says. "You do it one day at a time."

"Yes, one day at a time, one long day at a time. Katherine was the center spoke of my life. I can't imagine all of the days ahead when I will have to alter everything I do."

"I've never been where you are now, but I think you might better stop imagining the distant future," Susan says.

I sense she wants to hug me, knows she can't now. It's an awkward moment as I can tell she's becoming emotional trying to support me.

We're standing outside the door to the education building. The pole light illumines the parking lot, now almost vacant. The night is still, and in the distance the ocean roars as the waves crash on the dark beach. As we each move to our cars, I assume this will be my routine for some time to come—living my life in two competing tenses, past and present.

***

When I arrive home there is a message from Jonathan Foster, the attorney in New Bern. He asks that I call him tonight on his cell.

"Hello, Reverend. The reason I asked you to call is that I've arranged for you to meet Kenny Edwards tomorrow at 4:30 after he gets out of school. Could you come up to Pollocksville where he lives?"

"Thank you, Claude and I will be there," I say.

"Patricia has asked me to be there as well."

"That would be fine. We do not wish to admonish the boy, only let him tell us what happened."

"His mother is very concerned about all of this. She thinks her son is having emotional problems over the accident."

"I can understand that."

"Patricia is a little worried about your father-in-law. She's afraid he will be too intense in questioning Kenny."

"Claude is a thorough person but not insensitive. I can promise you he's interested in Kenny's well-being."

"That's good to hear. We will see you at 4:30 tomorrow."

***

The nighttime is the hardest, of course. It's somewhat easy to be fearless in the daytime, not so easy at night. My bed is one-sided. The other side was hers. I never unmake it, never roll over to it. It remains unused. The only sounds of slumber are my own, no muted snoring from the other side, no interruptions from another body turning to change positions.

I've begun a ritual. Before I go to sleep I open her private journal and read a passage or two. I'm aware this is not helping me make progress in letting go. I've never liked that term—letting go. It implies that if I held on it would make a difference. I don't have the option of letting go or of holding on. My only choices are to either remember or forget. In her journal I seek only one thing—to find out who she was those last weeks of her life.

February 25

I desperately seek meaning for my life. A part of me says I have all I need. I have a family, husband, children, parents, church family, and friends. How unappreciative I am for not being more thankful for them. Another part of me says there must be more. How to find the more is my problem.

Today, Paul was more attentive than usual. I found myself resenting that. It simply reminded me of how it was in the beginning when he and I were equals in our relationship. We were two people sitting on a see-saw taking turns at applying our influence as to the movement of our lives, the ups and downs.

I feel so selfish, but who will see to my needs if I don't myself? I am discontented because there is no one who cares about me, the inside me. I am frustrated because my role is to care for others without much reciprocity. I am a person too!

How did I not see Katherine was so miserable? How did I not see that her identity had been suppressed?

chapter thirty six

We live in a beautiful place. The ocean and sound offer magnificent opportunities to enjoy nature. On the mainland, just across the bridge from our island is the Croatan National Forest. It contains almost 160,000 acres of pine forests, salt estuaries, and pocosins. The forest is bordered by the Neuse River, the White Oak River, and Bogue Sound. Luke and I have hiked some of the trails in the forest.

One day last September, Katherine and Grace decided they would go along with us; Katherine suggested we pack a picnic lunch. Luke was not too happy with this female intrusion into our male bonding routine, but he relented when he saw the array of food prepared, especially the toll house cookies. The four of us set out to hike to Patsy Pond. Luke wore his standard hiking shorts and tee shirt from the North Carolina Zoo. Grace came out with her pink ballet leotard. Luke refused to go until she changed.

We parked in the lot off of Highway 24 and set out on the yellow trail. Grace wanted the blue trail because she likes blue better than yellow, but Luke said the blue trail was for sissies. Katherine and I were enjoying the sibling disputes. The walk was uneventful until we came to the first small pond where Grace proceeded to throw a pine cone at a turtle basking on a log. Luke advised her that we were not there to disturb nature.

The virgin long leaf pines shade the sandy trails. We were hoping to see a red-cockaded woodpecker and perhaps even a bald eagle which populate the area that time of the year. The large pond which is at the half-way point of the hike has crystal clear water. We spread a blanket on the ground for our lunch break, and Katherine broke out the sandwiches, fruit and cookies.

The Katherine in the woods with us that day was enthusiastic, cheerful, and sporting. She marveled at the serenity of the forest and the feeling of isolation from civilization even though we were only a mile in from the highway. She listened as Luke shared his knowledge of the woods, some made-up, some acquired. On the way back she jumped up and down when a woodpecker did indeed land a few feet away in a tall hardwood tree.

Luke said as we returned to the car, "Mom, would you like to do this again?"

"Yes, indeed," his mom answered. "You are the best hiking guide in the world."

***

No matter how early I rise, I am never up before Claude Ros-iere. The man's a machine. He's a sixty-three year old creature of habit, a lover of routine, a paragon of discipline. His god is efficiency, and he calculates every decision with engineered thoroughness. For thirty years, each day from Monday through Friday he made the trip from Raleigh to the Research Triangle Park, leaving home precisely at seven-thirty each morning. On Saturday mornings he spends the hour from seven-thirty until eight-thirty in his home office taking care of his personal business. I'm sure the man has never paid a bill late and never missed a discrepancy in accounting matters.

He's sitting at the kitchen table dressed in his usual light blue button down shirt and navy blue slacks. The one thing missing in his retirement regimen is the necktie so dutifully worn each work day. A glass of orange juice sits in front of him, a napkin neatly folded to the right of the glass. A pad of yellow lined paper and a ball point pen rest on the table with printed notes in numbered sequence.

"What are you working on?" I ask.

"Trying to determine a timeline for the minutes after the acci-dent," Claude says. "When we talk with the boy today, I'd like to be prepared to account for the progression of events. From all we have learned there must have been only three to five minutes allowance for the boy's departure from the scene."

"I'm still amazed that he wasn't injured," I add.

"He likely made the exact body movements needed to prevent the impact from applying force to his head or upper torso. NASCAR drivers have developed instincts which they employ in collisions which minimize the damage to their bodies in those high speed collisions."

"And, the brunt of the force was on Katherine's side," I add.

"Yes, she was too busy trying to correct her steering to be able to focus on protecting herself. The full inertia of the car impacting the tree came directly at Katherine and she was caught in what they call "the crumple zone.""

Every time I envision the accident, I imagine the horror of those brief seconds. I'm also sure that her primary concern at the moment was her passenger.

"You know," Claude says, "I think this boy has had a very traumatic experience and will not be eager to share it with us. I think he told his mother what happened or she helped him get home. She did not ask us the right questions for one who was oblivious of all that took place."

"I picked up on that too. It's hard for me to imagine the boy's fear. He didn't even know Katherine; she was a stranger to him until that evening."

"All the same, the boy should have stayed by the car until the police came," Claude asserts.

"Let's face it, not everyone is as responsible as you are."

Claude acknowledges my compliment with a slight smile.

***

On the way to school Grace tells me she has a school play in two weeks. The play is about The Underground Railroad. I ask her if she knows what it is.

"Duh, Dad. I'm in the second grade. We've studied about how the slaves ran away to freedom."

"I just don't remember covering that in school until maybe the fifth grade," I say.

"You know, it wasn't actually a railroad with trains and all. They just called it that cause trains were the way people traveled back then. I need to have a costume. I'm one of daughters of the plantation owner. Grandma says she'll make an outfit for me. You'll get an invitation to the play."

After I leave Grace at White Oak Elementary and head to the church, I worry about how I will handle all of the parent responsibilities when Claude and Diane go home. I have no experience in making costumes.

I have an appointment this morning with the couple who want to talk with me about their unhappiness with our church. They've been worshipping with us for almost a year. Ed Bettleson's retired from a career with DOT. He was an engineer in charge of bridge projects. Ed's a large man; I estimate he must weigh around two hundred and fifty pounds and is at least six feet-two. His wife Mary appears to be a slight hundred and twenty, no more than five-five. She also worked for the state in the Department of Revenue.

I'm aware they harbor some concerns about our church not being conservative enough. They're here this morning to ask me a few questions. Eastern North Carolina is conservative politically and religiously. We have, however, a wide variety of church backgrounds represented in our congregation. This is not uncommon for churches in resort areas where people from all over settle after moving to retire.

The fact is—Ed and Mary are not pleased with their pastor. They will likely accuse me of not being the right kind of pastor. I've been in this position before. It is expected of me to listen to their complaints and try to appease them. I feel the great majority of those in our congregation are supportive of my ministry style, but hope that I have the sensitivity to work with those who are used to other styles. Pastors are supposed to keep their cool under fire.

"Reverend, we hate to bother you with our problems in a time such as this for you, but we feel we should share what's disturbing us," Ed says.

"Ed, I'm glad you and Mary have come by. There comes a time when one must get back to their duties. Please, sit down and share with me what your concerns are."

They sit beside each other in the two chairs across from me. Ed's wearing a knit shirt with a small Duke logo over the pocket. Mary's in a long navy blue dress. I begin by asking about their children and grandchildren. Mary is very willing to give me a full account of names and ages.

"Our son and his family were with us last weekend," Ed says. "They didn't make it to church. My daughter-in-law was afraid our granddaughter was coming down with something. She's the type of mother who frets too much over any little sniffle."

"Ed, that's not fair. The child was a little feverish," Mary says.

"I'm just saying she has the tendency to blow things out of proportion."

I break in, "I asked both of you to come by because I've heard that you are having a difficult time adjusting to our church, maybe to my style."

Ed nods at Mary and sits back in his chair.

Mary seizes her cue to proceed. "Pastor, we've noticed that in our eleven months here you've not preached on the devil or hell one time. Do you not think those are important subjects to address from the pulpit?"

"Mary, I want to use my opportunities in preaching to deal with matters that will be helpful to everyone in living the Christian life. I try to relate biblical passages to those things which we all encounter in our daily lives."

"So, you just don't want to preach on Satan, damnation, or judgement?" Ed says. "Isn't there a need for apocalyptic preaching?"

I anticipated such a question. "I believe there's a need to point out the consequences of living a life that goes against the grain of the universe as God has designed it."

"I don't know about that kind of stuff unless you're talking about sin," Ed says. "We live in a fallen world."

"You don't seem to talk enough about specific sins like adultery and abortion," Mary adds.

"I think that may be a fair assessment," I say.

"Is this not a God fearing church?" Ed asks.

"Ed, this church is full of people who love God and who do not want to go against the will of God. It's important, I think, that I focus on ways to help us make our own individual faith decisions."

"We come from a church in Durham where the pastor calls a sin a sin and makes no bones about it," Ed says. "He preaches on the power of the devil often. We like many of the people we've met here, but this just isn't what we're used to. We need to hear powerful, biblical preaching that will step on people's toes."

"Ed, I value the Bible as much as you do. We simply approach it from different perspectives."

"I didn't know there were different perspectives," Ed says. "The Bible is the Bible. It says what it says."

I'm well aware that some people see the scriptures this way. I feel the need to answer Ed's concerns without misleading him as to my approach to ministry. "Ed, I appreciate your biblical view. There are, however, many people in our congregation who have had very different church backgrounds than yours. I hope we can minister in such a way as to be supportive of various views of our faith."

Ed shakes his head side to side. "Doesn't do anyone any good if you water down religion so that it fails to heed God's judgments on sin."

Mary speaks up, "Reverend Brewer, we can't change how we feel. I'm sorry. We do not feel spiritually fed when we worship here."

"Pastor, it seems you may be one of those who don't take the Bible as God's literal word," Ed says. "You don't even read from the King James."

"That's right. I prefer more modern translations."

Ed gets up and walks over to my bookshelves. He pulls out a New English version of the scriptures. "This is not a real Bible," he says. He puts it back and turns to hear my response, arms folded across his massive chest.

I feel that he is challenging me, trying to provoke me.

"Sit down, Ed," Mary says.

Ed smiles and does as his wife asks.

I reach behind me and pick up a Greek New Testament from the credenza. I open it on my desk and point to it. "Ed, this is a real Bible." As soon as I say it, I realize this is not helping. I've let myself get angry, surprised that I did. I breathe deeply in order to calm down.

Ed looks down at the open Greek text. "Sorry, I can't read that one."

Mary puts her hand on his arm. "Pastor, I'm afraid that we are taking too much of your valuable time."

"I can understand if you're not comfortable worshipping here," I say. "I hope you will give our approach some more time. You two have friends here who want you to remain a part of our fellowship."

Ed looks at his wife and then at me. "Reverend, it's best if we try some other churches in order to find one more like what we're used to."

Mary says, "Pastor, I believe you're a good man, and I'm very sorry about the loss of your wife. I just wish you and this congregation were more concerned with getting people right with God."

Ed is through talking. He stands up and shakes my hand. He leads his wife to the door, her looking back at me as they exit. They're encountering what many in our country experience in their search for a church family—it's not easy to find the right fit. The thing is—a church like ours cannot change its stripes to suit every person who seeks our fellowship.

Pastoral ministry requires tact and caution in responding to the variety of religious points of view. It also requires patience. Patience, I find, is harder to come by in the aftermath of my personal loss. A few years ago Katherine gave me a plaque with the words of Teilhard on patience. It hangs on the wall behind my desk here. I turn to give it another look. Teilhard's advice is, "Above all, trust in the slow work of God." He wrote, "And yet it is the law of all progress that it is made by passing through some stages of instability…"

I'm passing through a time of instability; that's for sure. I do feel God's hand leading me and pray for his guidance.

chapter thirty seven

I OPT FOR some personal therapy. My lunch break today shall be on the water in the solitude of my kayak. One hour of paddling is what I need. The sound is a little rough; the wind usually picks up this time of day. My tiny boat slips through the surface tide, however, crossing the northward ripples of current as if they don't exist. The steady motion of the blades pushing the water is a reminder that out here it's my power against the forces of nature. Today, I'm the winner in the contest, not always the case. This is what I like about the kayak—it's pure human will which makes it go, the mind instructing the arms to maintain a steady rhythm of applied force.

The marina has little activity this day. There's not a power boat to be seen moving in the passage out to the main waterway, so I cross without any interference. Once, this was the channel for the ferries which brought people and cars from the mainland. This was before the bridge was built. In those days cars would line up on Sunday afternoons to leave after a weekend on the island. Some Sundays there would be a two hour wait as each ferry could only carry twenty plus vehicles. My dad has many stories of the ferry days and the "Hoi Toiders" who manned the big boats. Many of the crew members were from what is called "Down East" and spoke in the old brogue. Progress demanded that the old way be replaced by the more efficient new way. Always progress comes at the cost of nostalgia. To long for a past day is to want to undo what can never be undone.

I'm reminded of what Thomas Moore wrote in *The Soul's Religion*, "The wish literally to restore a golden age of the past is self-protective. It is rooted in the death principle, not life." We can't go back to a time of our choosing and stay there—this is not the reality of life. There are those in the church who want to retreat to a past in which values were simpler. They want a time when crossing the sound was by the slow moving ferry and not the swifter bridge. This is to wish that life be stagnant. As painful as change may be, it is the way God designed the universe.

I remember another body of water. Katherine and I visited Walden Pond a few years ago on a trip to Boston. We stood where Thoreau once stood and Katherine remembered a quote from the man who lived there for a while in isolation, "Things do not change, we do."

"I think the man was wrong," I said "Look around. The modern world has closed in on Walden Pond. A mile or so away is an office tower."

Katherine picked up a small stone and tossed it into the pond. "When I first read Thoreau I dreamed of spending a summer here alone with my books. I would take long walks and contemplate my place in the world."

"There are times I wish you and I could retreat to a place like this and close out the rest of the universe," I said.

"I imagine the kids would want to come along. You and they would want to have television and video games, me too. The man who lived in the cabin up there should have said, 'Things change us.'"

No place is change more evident than out here on these ancient barrier islands. These islands were formed when the climate became warmer and the sea level became higher. The dunes were shaped as wind pushed the sand, and the marshes developed on the back sides of the isles. The balance between sea level and marsh level is ever adjusting.

Some days when I'm out here on the water I choose to park my kayak and walk through the marsh. At times the mud begins to ooze around my water shoes as I step where there's less root material. At low tide these islands look like vast flat meadows. At high tide it's a sea of submerged grass, each blade of grass potentially a refuge for the creatures which cannot stand submersion in salt water for long. Daily life in the salt marsh is a parable of the fluctuations which occur in the lives of people, of families, as they encounter the ebb and flow of life.

Today a long-billed marsh wren fusses at me as I move too close to her nesting area. You would think she has a deed to the Spartina alterniflora where her eggs must reside. A clapper rail slips between the grass stems, hard to spot in the thick growth. A Melampus snail is attached to a grass stalk. My son studied them in school and tells me they have lungs and can hold their breath for an hour. They have an internal tide clock which prompts them to move up the stalk every six hours.

I wonder why God has not placed within humans a natural clock which regulates our grief so as to allow it to expire at some preset time so the pain abates and we can more easily move on with life.

***

After my talk with the Bettlesons earlier, Susan and I spent a few minutes going over church matters. She asked me how it went with Ed and Mary. "They're not happy with our church," I say. "They long for what they left. I see it all the time in those who retire to the beach. They come from a place where they are comfortable but give that up for the dream of a new life where they can leave behind much of what they did not like about their old life. The problem is they also leave behind the things they did enjoy."

"Why do so many people make that choice?" Susan asks.

"I think people vacation at the beach and enjoy the break from their normal routines. They imagine being on vacation all of the time but when they arrive here for retirement it's not the same as vacation. This becomes the new routine."

"We sure do have a wide variety of backgrounds in this church," Susan says. "How in the world do we assimilate so many varied faith experiences?"

"We try to moderate our approach to church without sacrificing the essentials of what church must be. The struggle for ministers has always been what to emphasize as being essential."

"Are you saying that here we need to water-down our theology so as to make it amenable to a more diverse congregation?"

"No, not exactly. It's just that wide doctrinal divisions within a group of believers require some walking a tight rope in order to maintain unity."

"And what if we fall off that high wire and plunge to the ground?" Susan asks.

"There is always that risk in ministry."

***

Katherine and I were having lunch at Rucker-Johns one day about a year ago when we were approached by Mike Gallant, one of our church members. He proceeded to sit down beside me in the booth. Mike has a bold personality and takes some pleasure, I think, in his abrasive nature.

"Katherine, if you don't mind, I have a church matter to discuss with the pastor," Mike said. "I will not take too much of your time with your busy husband."

Katherine smiled and continued eating her salad.

"Listen, Paul, we need to do something about our collections," Mike said. "You need to be more forceful from the pulpit on stewardship. There are people out there who are holding out on us. When I usher and pass the offering plate I can tell who steps up and who doesn't. I suggest you preach a series of sermons on tithing to the church."

It's not easy having a discussion with someone who's sitting beside you in a crowded restaurant booth. Mike's a large man and I felt pinned in by both his physical and verbal presence. "Why don't you come by the office tomorrow and we'll discuss this," I said.

"I'm sure your wife does not mind if we conduct a little church business right here. After all, we don't pay you for long lunch breaks."

Katherine put her fork down and looked over at Mike. "Would you like to join us for lunch?"

Mike gave her a broad grin and said, "Thanks, but I've already eaten."

"Well, Mike, we are just beginning, and Paul deserves a few minutes away from church talk."

Mike did not pick up on the obvious hint or perhaps ignored it and continued, "Paul, we're never going to build a stronger church without more emphasis on finances."

The waitress appeared and asked if we needed more tea. She asked Mike if he would like anything. Before he could answer, Katherine said, "He's just here for a minute. He's getting ready to leave. Right, Mike?"

I was shocked by her boldness; Mike too, it seemed. He looked across the table at my wife who was resolutely eating her salad without looking up. Mike and his wife, Joanna, have eaten with us before on a couple of occasions, and we've been with them at church social functions. We've been somewhat close, but Katherine had never been this audacious with Mike before.

"I guess we'll talk about this later," Mike said as he got up from the booth. "Katherine, I hope you enjoy your lunch."

After Mike left I looked at my wife for a long minute. She finally acknowledged my stare. "It worked, didn't it?"

I was surprised by her confident wit.

***

The night of the accident is never far from my need to remember. I run through the events of the evening over and over, trying to imagine what I could have done differently. When Katherine walked out the door while we were eating supper, I should have gone out to stop her. Any other response on my part could have broken the chain of events which led to her death.

About nine that night Luke came into the living room where I waited for Katherine to return. "Dad, where did mom go?"

"I'm not sure, son." I answered. "She didn't tell me where she was going."

"Is she going to leave us?" he asked.

His question so surprised me that I almost choked. "What makes you ask that?"

"It's just that she has been acting strange lately, and I heard her tell Grace today that she must listen to you after she's gone. Grace probably thought she meant gone for a few hours. I think she meant gone for a long time."

"Luke, your mother has some problems. She's trying to work through them. It may take her some time."

"What kind of problems?"

"I think she's unhappy with parts of her life."

"Is she unhappy with me?"

"Oh, no, son. She's unhappy with many things but not you and Grace. She loves you both very much. Sometimes people become sad for a while and need to work on being happy again."

"I don't understand," Luke said. "Is she unhappy with you?"

"She may be."

"Then, you need to do something. You need to find a way to make her feel better. You need to keep her from leaving us."

"I know," I said. "I will."

Luke went to his room. I remained on the living room couch looking out the window, phone on my lap.

That evening I went into our bedroom and checked to see if any luggage was missing. I wasn't sure if she intended to come back after the way she left. All of the bags were still in place, but does a person who's extremely upset think rationally enough to pack for their departure?

I have a theory now. She went to Greenville to see Kyle and say goodbye to him again. His son came into the room, and her focus was changed to getting to know the boy. He was the representation of what might have been. That's as far as my theory goes. I can't be sure she was planning to come home that evening after she dropped him off at his house; I suspect she was.

How often in life do we make plans for the future, and they are disrupted by an unpredicted turn of events? How often do we meet a new person and that alters the direction of our lives? Is God the divine mover who places these events or people on the board in such a way as to force us to revise our strategies? I've never been all that good at chess because I have trouble seeing far enough into the future to map out my moves. I certainly can't visualize how others will hinder or facilitate my plans.

chapter thirty eight

I ARRIVE HOME at two-thirty. Claude has gone to pick up Grace from school before he and I plan to head up to Pollocksville to meet Kenny Edwards. Diane's in the kitchen brewing coffee. I sit at the kitchen counter on one of the wooden barstools.

"Are things okay at the church?" Diane asks.

"Things are fairly normal," I respond.

"And your time on the water, was that helpful?"

"Yes, I was able to do some thinking."

"I've also done some thinking. I'm trying to imagine how you, Luke, and Grace are going to manage after Claude and I leave. I'm glad we can help out, but this is not a good situation for the long-run. The three of you need to get used to being a family without us interfering."

"I don't think you're interfering," I say. "It's good to have you around."

"Just the same, we need to go soon. Paul, I know there were times when you must have felt that I was too much into your family business. Katherine and I talked almost every day, and I was never one to hold back on my advice. My daughter was very bright; she was also very spoiled. I know it was my fault. I doted on her from the time she was born until she married you. After she was married I suppose I still tried to control her to some degree."

"Diane, you were just trying to keep your daughter close."

"Sure, close. I never trusted her instincts. She was always too much into abstract thoughts, never practical enough. When she was seven years old she still had an imaginary friend. She and her friend would engage in conversations where they would debate such things as the nature of love and evil. A seven year old working on the problem of evil— can you figure that?"

"With Katherine I can." I reply. "She loved the world of the mind."

"Yes, and she let it take her to places which were not good for her. I spent much of my time when she was a teenager trying to teach her to be realistic about life."

"From where I stand you did a good job. Katherine was a wonderful wife and mother. She managed to run a household well and still delve into her intellectual endeavors."

"Until she found it all to be too much," Diane says. "I have a pretty good idea of what caused her depression. I think she got to a point where it was all not that meaningful to her."

"I haven't thought of it that way, but it makes sense. I just wished that I could have been more sensitive to her needs."

Claude walks in with Grace and our conversation ends.

***

We were married on Valentine's Day weekend. The church was decorated with red roses, several dozen red roses surrounded by white wisteria. Where is the line between tacky and tasteful? That's a matter of degree more than anything else. To my mother-in-law degree is a word that means all out. The sanctuary was so enthusiastically adorned that there was hardly room for the wedding party to stand. I must admit it was breathtaking— so was Katherine. Her floor length gown was white, covered in layers of lace, the bodice just revealing enough so as to tease the imagination.

There are those moments in life when adjectives have not been invented to describe the joy we feel. We search our vocabulary for expressions to do the moment justice but are wanting for utterances which carry enough impact to be worthy of delivering. I don't remember today a single part of the vows we wrote for the occasion, but I do remember the feeling with which I spoke them. I did fully intend to fulfill what I promised.

Our honeymoon trip was to Williamsburg. We were poor, perhaps more accurate, prudent. It was her choice. It was freezing and rainy—not a problem. We made history in that most historic of towns, our own history. In the patches of sunshine we walked the colonial streets and imagined what life was like in those hard but glorious times. We were bathed in the past but focused on the future.

On the way back to Raleigh from Williamsburg, I ran out of gas. Katherine did not fuss about it: she simply pointed out that I have a tendency to not take care of the details in life which are important. Thankfully, a gas station was close by. Two other times in our fifteen years together we were stranded because of my oversight. Each time my wife would analyze my propensity to overlook those little matters which are the minor essentials of life. I think she inherited from her father the eye for detail which allowed her to be careful and disciplined. She was more rational than her mother thought she was.

On our anniversary this year we ditched the kids for the evening and stole away for a romantic dinner. It was Valentine's eve as the calendar fell. The Katherine who joined me that night was not the same person who stood in the middle of a rose arbor fifteen years earlier and told me in a voice husky from emotion that I was her everything. I ordered a dozen roses and had them delivered to the restaurant ahead of time, a gesture of hope that we could overcome the distance which had divided our relationship like a seismic rift since the year began.

I chose Wilmington for our getaway in order to have some privacy. The small Italian restaurant was perfect and the red flowers filled the tiny table. She cried before the meal came. I could not tell if they were tears of joy or of sadness. During the dinner she was passive, unresponsive, and distant. My would-be romantic evening was overturned with thoughts of estrogen and progesterone levels, monoamine oxidase and neurotransmitter stages. These were the things I had researched when I suspected she was going through a depression. Today I wish that I had confronted our enemy that evening instead of trying to mask it with red roses and faux intimacy.

I have read there is a tai chi exercise known as "Push Hands." Two people face each other and touch palms very lightly. A circular movement is begun as the two lean and sway. The goal is to find a balance between pushing and giving in to pressure. You try to detect any imbalance in your partner and find a way to give way to it. I detected an imbalance in Katherine but could not find the right sense in myself to help her stay upright.

***

In the car to Pollocksville this afternoon Claude and I discuss our approach with Kenny Edwards. We have every reason to believe that he was in the Honda with Katherine on the night of the accident. We are also reasonably sure that he will be reluctant to discuss the night with two strangers. Sergeant Tolliver with the highway patrol has agreed to let us bridge the subject with the boy as opposed to a uniformed officer questioning him.

The small town borders a lazy river, and the house owned by Patricia Edwards is on the riverfront. It's old and once served as a bed and breakfast we've been told. The front porch has tall columns and wide wood planks. We approach the substantial, white oak door and can see into the foyer through the thick glass in the large window light. There's an antebellum feel to the place and it seems ripe for a movie set in one of those "back home to discover yourself" films.

Patricia comes to the door and invites us in. On the left is a room with high ceilings and a massive fireplace, a parlor decorated with antique furniture and lamp shades with tassels hanging. Claude and I are guided to a long couch with exposed feet which have animal paws engraved in them. Patricia excuses herself to retrieve her son, we assume. In a minute she returns with Jonathan Foster, the attorney we met earlier.

"Gentlemen," Foster begins, "I would like to suggest some ground rules before we bring Kenny in."

I think it's interesting that a lawyer uses the term "suggest". He obviously plans to be in charge of the meeting. Claude and I both nod approval as if we had a choice. I feel like I'm about to sit down for a deposition.

"I've asked Jonathan to be here in order to make Kenny more comfortable," Patricia says.

My instincts tell me that there's a relationship
and legal assistant which goes beyond the office.
wearing a wedding ring.

"Whatever makes your son more at ease," (

Standing across the room from us Foster says, "One thing
would like for us to agree upon is that Kenny will not be forced to
answer any question which implies that he did something wrong that
evening,"

"We're not here to blame your son, Mrs. Edwards," I say.

"Good," Foster replies. "The boy has had a difficult experience
and does not need to undergo any undue pressure. We also don't
want you to ask him anything about his father. Kyle is very sick, likely
to not survive this latest round of chemotherapy. Kenny and his dad
have remained close since the divorce."

Claude and I both assure them that we do not wish to force the
young man to speak of family matters.

Patricia leaves the room and comes back in with a tall, lean
young man. He walks with a shuffle; his Nike's squeak on the polished, dark wood floor. Kenny Edwards sits on the raised hearth of
the stone fireplace and looks to his mother as to what to do. He's
wearing a sweatshirt with his school logo and cargo pants with bulg-
ing pockets, filled with communication devices, I assume.

"Kenny's on the school basketball team and has just finished
his season. They lost in the regional finals," his mother says.

"What position do you play?" I ask the gangly youngster.

With a deep mumble he answers, "I'm the starting shooting
guard."

Jonathan Foster picks up, "Kenny averaged almost sixteen
points a game. He led the team in scoring. He knows that you two
are Mrs. Brewer's husband and father."

"I wait for the obligatory "sorry" from the young man but none
comes. Instead he hangs his head so we can't see his eyes.

"Let us begin by telling you that Kenny was in the car that evening," Foster says. "Your wife, Reverend Brewer, offered to take him
home. He had gotten a ride to the hospital in Greenville by a friend
and planned to come home with her, a girl in his high school class

was there visiting her sister. He and Mrs. Brewer were talking ¿nen his friend was ready to leave and your wife asked him to stay a few minutes longer, promising to take him home."

Kenny raises his head and looks straight at me. I can see that he's very uncomfortable as he begins to speak. "We were talking about my dad, and she asked me to stay longer, so I told Shelley that I had a ride. She was nice and was telling me about my dad when he was in college, before he met my mom."

"Kyle and I met his senior year in college and got married as soon as he graduated. Kenny was born the same year," Patricia adds. "Kyle never mentioned your wife until a few weeks ago when she came to see him in the hospital."

"Kenny, you were in the car when it wrecked?" Claude asks.

He looks at his mom again, and she signals for him to answer the question. Kenny starts slowly, "It was dark, and we were talking about my school and all. Then this old man just walks right out into the road. I saw him first and warned her. There just wasn't much time. She swerved to keep from hitting the guy, and then I saw the stop sign. It all happened so quickly. We were out in the other highway; she turned hard. I looked down the road to see if anything was coming, and when I turned back we flew over the ditch and there was the tree. I yelled something, but it was too late."

The boy sits upright on the hearth as he finishes the story, his hands on his knees. He looks at Claude and me with eyes wide open now, waiting, I suppose, for our response. Both the lawyer and his mother sit on blue fabric chairs across the room, neither showing any signs of speaking up. I'm frozen by the account of the accident; my mind trying hard to figure out a way she could have avoided the collision, knowing it's a useless exercise now.

Finally, Claude speaks, "Kenny, what happened after the vehicle hit the tree?"

Kenny Edwards takes a deep breath and reaches down placing his hands on the top of his sneakers. He remains in this position for ten or fifteen seconds then straightens again. "The air bags filled the car. I couldn't see, and then they went down. I opened my door and got out of the car. I raised my arms to see if I could move. They worked fine; then I felt my head. It hurt right above my right eye, but I didn't feel any blood. Then I walked around the car to the other side. The engine had cut off, and the front end on the driver's side was messed up. Her head was against the side window. It looked like she was hurt bad; she wasn't moving. I tried to open the door; it was jammed. I remembered from my driver's ed class that you shouldn't move people after a wreck if they were like her. I just stood there and looked at her. The windshield was broken; and I knew she hit the tree on her side pretty hard."

"Tell them what you did next," Foster says. "It's important that they know this."

Kenny looks at his mom and continues the story, "I got my phone out of my pocket and dialed 911. It was a man who answered, and I told him there had been a car accident and a woman was injured. I knew we were at some church but didn't know what it was called. I told him to wait until I could go see the sign. I read it to the man. I told him she had hit a tree and I didn't see any other cars around. He never asked me if I was hurt or if I was in the car. I guess he assumed I had just come along after. Then I saw headlights coming so I went over to the side of the church and closed my phone. This guy gets out of his truck and goes over to the wreck. He looks in the window like I just did and pulls out his phone. He never saw me."

Patricia Edwards then picks up the account. "Kenny stayed there, behind the church as other cars came along. He sat down on the ground in the shadows and waited to see what would happen. Soon the rescue squad came. You have to realize, Reverend Brewer, that he was afraid."

"Thank you, Kenny," I say. "You did the right thing in calling for help, and I know it was an awful experience." The highway patrol never told me there were two 911 calls that evening. I wonder if they even knew that.

"You were not hurt at all?" Claude asks.

"No, sir. The bump on my head was not that bad. I don't know how it was that I didn't get injured. The other side of the car was all torn up."

"How long did you stay there?" I ask.

Jonathan Foster answers. "He remained behind the church for over an hour until everyone left. The ambulance took your wife to New Bern. After a long time a wrecker came to tow away the SUV. The last patrolman finally drove away, and the church yard was empty."

"I was out that night late and thought Kenny had been brought home by a friend," Patricia says. "He had called me from the hospital at nine and told me that was the plan. I got home about 12:30 and realized he wasn't in his room. I tried to call his cell, but it was turned off."

"I didn't want it to make any noise while all of those people were there," Kenny adds. "I thought the patrolmen would take me to jail or something when I tried to explain why I was with her. It was after one when I called my mom. It was pretty cold while I waited there for her to come get me."

"Patricia did not tell me what had happened until after you two came by the office the other day," Foster says. "If she had, I would have called the authorities."

"Kenny begged me to not tell anyone," Patricia says. "I didn't see how his coming forward would change anything."

"The only thing it changes," I say, "is that I now know what happened that night. Thank you, Kenny, for sharing all of this."

"She was really nice," Kenny says. "She told me she had a son younger than me. She asked all about my life. She listened good. She cried when we talked about my dad. I couldn't understand why she was so upset since she knew him so long ago."

Again I thank Kenny.

"Reverend Brewer, there is one more thing you should know," Patricia Edwards says. "Kenny, tell them what happened at McDonalds."

The boy looks at his mother and then at the lawyer. They both nod encouragement. He then faces me with a pained expression on his face. "She stopped in Greenville at a McDonalds to get coffee and bought a coke for me. We sat in a booth. I put my ball cap on the table. She picked it up and started to cry again. I didn't know what to say. After some time she handed the cap over to me and said, 'You could have been my son.' It freaked me out. I guess she meant if she and my dad had married back then. She just looked so sad."

"I thought you might want to know that," Patricia says.

I don't know what to say. Claude recognizes that it's time for us to go and stands up. "We want to thank you, Kenny, for helping us learn more about that night. It must have been a terribly difficult time for you."

"One more thing," I say. "They found a receipt from a Bojangles in New Bern in her car. Do you know anything about that, Kenny?"

The boy looks puzzled and up at the ceiling. "Shelley and I stopped at Bojangles that day before we went to Greenville and got drinks. I got a tea. I guess it may have fallen out of my pocket."

"Yes, that must be the case. Thank you again," I say.

Claude and I leave the Edwards house and head back to the beach. For the first few minutes neither if us wants to talk. We're both trying to let all of what we learned sink in.

Claude finally says, "I'm so thankful the boy wasn't hurt. All I can think of is that any one minute delay in the timing that night could have meant Katherine would still be here. If she had left any seconds earlier or later, if the old man had only strayed into the road a few feet different in any direction, or if the impact would have been a foot to either side she would not have died. I've spent my whole life as an engineer working with probabilities. I know well the odds of variables being modified. The odds of that sequence of events being adjusted some way must be extremely high."

"My guess is," I say, "almost all traffic accidents occur because certain alternate scenarios did not happen."

"I suppose you're right."

Neither of us brings up what the boy told us at the end about Katherine saying he could have been her son. There is nothing to be said. Katherine was dealing with her past that evening. I can't help but wonder what her future would have been like if not for the accident.

chapter thirty nine

THERE WAS AN evening about a year ago when I came home and told Katherine that I was burned out from trying to minister.. The week had been horrendous, the pressures too much. In the span of six days: I counseled a young man who talked of suicide, had a run in with one of the deacons over church finances, and had dealt with two deaths in the church family. The young man's situation absorbed almost an entire day before we found him a psychiatric hospital situation. The deacon had pushed some of my buttons in what he said to me, and I responded with accusatory words toward him. One of the funerals was that of a man I was very close to in the church. There were the usual pressures as well: several church members in the hospital, a sermon to prepare, and a Bible study to lead.

Katherine was my sounding board. "There is just too much expected of me," I told her.

She sat beside me on the couch in our living room. "You're too sensitive for your own good," she said.

"I'm just not cut out for this. I'm not sure anyone is."

"You're a gifted minister. One week is not the measure of your work."

"I don't feel very gifted this evening," I said. "To be honest, I was at a loss as to how to help someone with suicidal tendencies. I never should have lost my temper with Hal over the expenditure of a few thousand dollars on his pet project."

Katherine rubbed the back of my neck and whispered in my ear, "I don't want anyone else to hear this, even God, but you're the best pastor I know."

That certainly ended my complaints for the moment.

That evening Katherine helped me calm down. She listened to my grumblings and doubts. She reassured me that I was a capable minister. I now realize that she was the secondary victim of my stress. Like many pastors, I had the tendency to come home and dump all of my insecurities in her lap. Add that to her normal pressures as wife and mother—it was too much. She did not complain nor give me any hint that she also wondered about her role that night.

***

Peter Gomes of Harvard once quoted an English writer who noted, "There is little good in filling churches with people who go out exactly the same way they came in." Gomes recalls this in a message on Paul's letter to the Corinthians where the Apostle writes, "Therefore if any man be in Christ, he is a new creature: old things have passed away; behold all things become new." I think a great deal about change now. I would not say that I'm a new person since my wife's death, but I'm a different person. I don't think I'm any wiser, just more experienced.

Of course, Paul in the New Testament is talking about a new faith. I don't think I am more faithful, just more aware of how much I need God. I'm also aware of how much I need other people. When you lose someone close to you there's a new sense of dependency. Our suffering allows us to speak with other people like we never have before, to be honest with them. I'm now closer to Claude and Diane than I ever was before. We've traveled down a road together we never would have traveled if we had not lost Katherine. Yes, we lost Katherine, not just I. Luke and Grace lost her as well. I'm now not as self absorbed, I think. If only Katherine were here to see that.

I'm not coming out of my grief the same way I went in. I am changed in that I'm more aware of my family responsibilities. It's my hope that I stay this way for the sake of my children.

Today is Luke's first baseball game. The Broad Creek team hosts a team from Craven County. Claude, Diane, Grace, and I are in the stands. Sitting beside me is Alan Johnson, a church member whose son is also on the team. It's a warm, early spring day. Grace has talked Diane into a visit to the concession stand to buy popcorn. They return with candy bars also. I'm surprised at Diane's willingness to indulge her granddaughter this way.

Luke's in the outfield, Alan's son is the first baseman. Alan is not a mild mannered fan and likes to slap me on the shoulder when our team makes a good play or scores a run. We're ahead six to three so my shoulder is beginning to get sore. Claude's on the other side of me and is a little annoyed by Alan's boisterous behavior. Claude's the epitome of civility.

"Say, Paul," Alan says, "I heard that some old man caused your wife's accident."

I look at Alan and shake my head to signify he's right. I would rather not get into that discussion here.

"I have a friend who's in the sheriff's department over in Craven County who tells me that the old guy has altimers. It was a crying shame they let him out at night."

We have tried to keep any talk of the accident from Grace's ears, but Alan is loud, and I see my daughter look our way. Claude gets up and asks Grace to come with him. He takes her over to the left field fence where they can see Luke better. In a minute Diane gets up to join them.

Alan gets the hint. "Say, man, I'm sorry. I guess this kind of talk is not good for your kids."

"We're trying to not discuss the details of that night in front of Grace," I say.

"Look, I apologize. My wife and I have both said this must be hard for you, now having to raise Luke and Grace by yourself. I don't think I could handle it."

"We're working on it," I say.

A deep fly ball is launched by the Craven team right in Luke's direction. I stand up and grit my teeth, hoping my son makes the play. It seems the ball stays in the air for five minutes. Luke's under it and it ends up securely in the webbing of his glove. This is the third out. He looks over at his grandfather with a big smile. My often stiff father-in-law pumps his fist in the air. Everyone in my family is handling the pressure pretty well. Katherine would be proud of us, I think.

***

The call comes around dinner time. Kyle Edwards passed away about four this afternoon. It was Patricia Edwards who called. She thought I might want to know. I've never met the man, only watched him sleep in the hospital bed. For some reason I get a lump in my throat. It's as though this is the end of the story of Katherine's depression.

This evening I read through her journal again. Her last entry is the one I hold onto.

March 12

I told Paul tonight I hated him. That came from my anger at his insensitivity to my feelings. I do hate his unwillingness to understand what I need. How do I get him to grasp that I am not happy with my life? How do I help him notice that I am suffering? My suffering absorbs every part of me. It changes who I am. I've found I can live with the pain inside, but I cannot live in the same way I have before. Something needs to happen. There must be some dramatic relief from the aching I feel within me. I pray that tomorrow I will have the courage to do something bold.

***

The paper mill rises from the woods like a luminous monster, smoke billowing from its nostrils. The thousands of lights almost negate the pitch dark night. The only sound is the steady rumble of the tires on the blacktop as the Honda's headlights reveal the lone center line separating the north/south lanes. The glow of the Weyerhauser plant fades as we cross the bridge over the silent Neuse River. Soon we make a right and it comes to me where I am.

The country road is a narrow tunnel through the trees. Their branches hang low so as the roof of our vehicle parts them like the strands of soft tentacles in a car wash. I duck to keep them from hitting me in the face, but the windshield deflects them off to each side. Our headlights are not strong enough to overcome the thick fog, so I can barely see the next white dash which divides the road. We're moving too fast. We need to slow down. My foot can't find the brake. My hands can't find the steering wheel. I'm on the wrong side. I'm in the passenger seat, not in control. I need to be in control.

Finally we begin to slow, and then another turn, and then another. Again we are on a back country road, this time with houses appearing and disappearing in rapid succession. Some are small cabins; others are castles, then a high rise tower juts up out of a cow pasture followed by a mobile home with antennas on the roof taller than a cell tower. The fog is now gone and the moon is as bright as a bank of stadium lights in a minor league ballpark, so bright that I can hardly see and have to shield my eyes. I can't stand my lack of command over our speed and direction.

I'm afraid to look to my left. I don't want to see the face of the driver. A force turns my head as though hands have grabbed my neck and twisted it counter clockwise. She's looking straight ahead. Her long hair hides her face. I struggle to turn my head away, but the grip of the hands on my neck is too powerful. Looking out of my right eye I see the figure. It's a shadow moving down the center of the road, then clearly a deer with ten points. No, it's now an old woman with a child beside her; it quickly morphs into an old man, the child no longer there. He stops in the middle of the road; the lights show only his face, then a finger rises and points straight at me.

I try to make a sound, a warning. The driver accelerates, the old man still points. At the very last second we swerve sharply to the left. My head snaps to the right, the grip of the hands released. I see the old man out the passenger window, his finger still pointing as it barely brushes the glass as we speed by. Again the hands grab my neck and force me to take in the scene out the windshield. Trees are looming, close and tall. The car now pointed straight at the thick forest. Again I try to yell; the only sound is a muffled moan as I calculate the impending impact. SUV meets tree; my head is tossed back like a balloon on a rubber band. Something covers my face, suffocates me; I can't breathe. Everything stops. The engine sputters; my face is finally clear.

Again a force pulls my head up and to the left. Her head leans on the driver side window; the windshield is shattered; air from the outside penetrates my lungs. She looks at me with wide eyes, blood trickles down her face. Her mouth opens just enough for the lips to form whispered words. I can't make them out; all I know she begins with "I" – "hate you" or "love you", which one?

I open my eyes and take in the dark room. No car, no bloody face; no, shattered glass, only a quiet bedroom surrounds me. I return from the nightmare tired, confused, and alone. Even in the dream I could not save her, promise her life would be different. Was there anything I could have done to save her, to save us?

chapter forty

IT'S BEEN TWO months now since the accident. Claude and Diane have gone back home. Luke, Grace, and I are a small family, learning to cope. Three of the ladies in the church take turns picking Grace up after school and caring for her until I get home, except on my day off. Luke is doing very well in baseball; his batting average is climbing. It's not easy being all the places I need to be, but I'm managing.

The summer's almost here and the children will be out of school. I've been working on a schedule. I'm a schedule person, a planner. It saves my sanity. Grace will spend two weeks with her grandparents in Raleigh, mostly with Claude and Diane, a few days with my mom. Claude and Diane are going to come here for two weeks in July. I have Grace enrolled in a day camp for two weeks as well.

Luke has ball through June. Jesse Miller, a teenager in our church, will be Luke's chauffer. His parents volunteered him, but I will pay him to see that Luke gets where he needs to be. I can't believe how mature my son is. Last week he asked me at breakfast if I thought I would ever get married again.

"That's something I've not considered," I answered.

"Mom would want you to," he said.

"What makes you think that?" I asked.

"She told me that's what she wanted."

"When did she tell you that?"

"One day last year when we were talking about why Nana never remarried after granddad Charles died. I asked her if something happened to you would she want to find another husband. She told me that was not a subject she liked to think about. I didn't stop asking questions. You know me. So, I asked her if she would want you to remarry. She said yes but that I should not worry about something happening to either of you.

"Luke, I will tell you the same thing your mother did. I don't want to think about that now."

"Okay, but I have a suggestion if you ever want to think about it. I think Susan would make a fine wife for you."

"Luke, let's not go there."

"I certainly wouldn't mind."

"Listen, son, let's just not talk about this anymore."

"Okay, Dad, I know it's too soon."

"Yes, it is."

***

I have to go back to Greenville today to visit Jeff Whitaker who's back in the hospital for some follow up tests on his bypass surgery. He's doing well and hopes to get back to work soon. The last time I made a visit to this hospital I saw Beverly, the nurse who cared for Kyle Edwards, and spoke with her briefly. She told me that Kyle passed quietly in his sleep.

It's two in the afternoon and I'm approaching the little church. There's a pull to this place, perhaps some morbid fascination. Plastic flowers and a small white cross have been placed by the tree where the accident occurred, signifying this is a location where a life was ended. I assume church members have done this. I had not planned to stop, but the flowers beckon me to again stand on that spot where Katherine lost her life, where I lost a big part of my life. The temperature on this May day is approaching eighty, and the sky is a pale blue. The tall pines stretch high into the natural canopy above.

Vehicles pass, eyes turn towards me, but they continue on their way. A truck stops at the sign across at the place where Katherine was startled that evening by Omar Salley's nighttime excursion to who knows where. The pine straw has long covered the few traces that a Honda SUV once bolted into these trees and came to rest here in this quiet mini forest. The scar in the bark is the only natural memorial to the collision that night. I look over to the place behind the church where Kenny hid after the accident.

John Williams comes walking over. I turn to face the senior pastor.

"I hope you don't mind if our church members mark this place with this small memorial," the resident pastor says.

"No, it's a nice idea," I say. "I like the thought that other people are keeping her memory alive. Hispanics call these memorials, 'descansos'. It means resting places. It goes back many years to when travelers would stop and rest on sad journeys and place a monument to mark the location."

"I always wonder when I'm driving down a highway and see one of these roadside displays what were the circumstances of the accident," John says. He and I have talked on the phone on two occasions, so I feel I know him to some degree. "This one I do not have to wonder about," he adds.

I walk over and shake his hand. We stand beside each other, our backs to the church, facing in the direction of the small grouping of pines. John walks over and adjusts the cross so that it stands more upright. He remains there for a moment, his hand on the makeshift monument.

"I put flowers on my wife's grave this week." John says. "She always liked carnations, so I put some there every month."

"My wife preferred roses. Her parents put red ones on her grave regularly. I'm going to take the children up to Raleigh next week and visit the cemetery."

"Have you put a stone on her grave yet?" he asks.

"We've picked one out. It has not been placed as of now."

"My wife designed her own. One day while she was in the hospital, she took pen and paper and drew what she wanted it to look like. It was the most unusual idea I'd ever seen. At first I thought it was the medication but found her to be quite aware of what she was doing."

"What did she draw?"

"There were these two hands together as if locked ready to arm wrestle. The two thumbs formed a distinct letter X and the two index fingers pointed up. Above them were these words, 'Always hand in hand, always seeking heaven.' Then there was the typical birth and death dates below."

"Did you have it made the way she designed it?" I ask.

"What, not do it the way she wanted and risk her sending some angel down to scold me like she used to herself fuss at me when I did something contrary to her earthly wishes. The woman was so opinionated."

"Sounds like you had no choice. My wife had her ways as well. She always liked to have the last word. When she thought she had made her final point, she would put a finger over her lips and wave me off with her other hand."

"I'd give anything to be scolded by my wife today," Reverend Williams says. "Funny, how you miss even the things you once didn't like about the one who has passed."

"Yes, strange isn't it?"

As I leave Reverend Williams I think—this churchyard will be a place I visit as often as the cemetery in Raleigh. It was here she was last alive. As I go to my car I take one last look at the pine. It soars high into the blue sky, a living monument to my Katherine.